CS Yelle
NORTHERN LIGHTS CODED TO KILL

Author: CS Yelle
Cover Photograph: Viv Mueller Rosand of Aurora, MN

http://csyelle.com

CS Yelle
NORTHERN LIGHTS CODED TO KILL

Northern Lights Coded To Kill

CS Yelle

CS Yelle
NORTHERN LIGHTS CODED TO KILL

Chapter 1

Cali lay in bed staring at the wall filled with her artwork: etchings, paintings, and photographs from a life she felt lost to her. The sunlight moved across the vibrant colors and deep shapes, animating them. She groaned as her alarm went off, signaling another dreaded day at the horrible school in this archaic town her mother insisted on dragging her too.

How could her mother grow up here in the middle of nowhere? And now she expected Cali to do the same? That was so wrong in so many ways. It had to be some kind of child abuse, or neglect, or something.

Cali needed to talk with her dad. She 'd convince him to let her move to New Delhi with him when he came for a visit. She couldn't take White Water, Minnesota. Only two weeks and she wanted to scream.

Budget cuts did away with the photography department at school, and the art programs were too elementary. No Barnes and Nobles, only the local library with a dreadful sampling of books or the school library filled with more reference material than anything else. No museums, no art galleries, nothing like New Richmond, Pennsylvania. She now knew the meaning of culture shock.

Slipping out of bed, she put her feet on the cold hardwood flooring and scampered to the shower with a shiver. And they said it would get colder? She asked her mom, grandpa, and grandma how much colder, they laughed. "Really?" she moaned. They laughed even harder, grandpa doubling over as if he had gut cramps or something.

She grimaced at the possibility as steam surrounded her in the shower, caressing her in warmth and comfort. Taking a long hot shower was her only escape and she didn't want it to end, but she shut the shower off and begrudgingly stepped out as she pulled her long black hair back from her face. The warmth wafted away with the steam, leaving her cold, and shivering again.

Cali trudged down the stairs into the kitchen after fixing her hair and putting on her makeup, as much as she could get past her mother's inspection. I'm going to be sixteen, she thought frowning. I should be able to wear it the way I like it. Cali set her chin in defiance, but that argument hadn't swayed her mother, Sandy.

"You're not going to look like a tramp," Sandy told her on her first day of school, shaking a finger at Cali, emphasizing each word.

Her mother sat at the island in the kitchen, drinking her cup of coffee in her light blue terry-cloth robe and reading the morning paper, her hair a brown, matted mess around her pale face.

"Morning, dear," Sandy greeted.

"Humph," Cali grunted, pulling the cereal off the top of the refrigerator, opening the fridge door, gathering the milk, and setting both on the island across from Sandy.

"Come on," Sandy urged. "How's the day going to treat you if you don't start off with a positive attitude?"

"It's going to stick it to me no matter what," Cali said, her back to her mother as she grabbed a bowl from the cupboard and a spoon from the drawer.

"Cali," Sandy sighed.

"I've tried everything for the last two weeks, and still, no one sits with me at lunch." Cali looked up at her mother as she

2

poured her cereal and then her milk, spilling some milk onto the counter when it deflected off a random frosted flake.

"You should try sitting with them at *their* table," Sandy suggested.

"Tried that last week." Cali said, looking at her, the girl's green eyes filled with pain. "They all got up and moved. I draw less attention when I sit by myself."

"They're not used to someone like you. It takes people up here a while to warm up, that's all."

"Yeah, I'm sure you're right. Hopefully, someone will talk to me by graduation. Is that long enough to warm up? Three years." Cali rolled her eyes. "It is kind of hard to blend in up here when I look like this," she motioned to her entire body.

"They will get used to it and realized that just because you look different on the outside, doesn't mean you are different on the inside."

"I don't feel it is as much racism as it is me being new and an outsider."

"They will come around," Sandy shrugged, turning back to the paper.

Cali finished her breakfast, placing her bowl and spoon in the sink and putting the milk and cereal away before she went upstairs to brush her teeth and run a brush through her silky hair. Looking in the mirror, she surveyed herself one more time, assuring her nothing would draw undo ridicule.

After checking her dark green shirt and faded jeans for any signs of complaint, she pulled on her soft green sweatshirt and zipped it part way. She tugged on her tennis shoes, swung her backpack over her shoulder and headed downstairs.

Sandy waited, her cheek extended.

Cali kissed her as she passed, rolling her eyes.

"It's not that bad," Sandy protested.

"That isn't, but having to walk to school is." They had been over it numerous times, each argument ending the same. They couldn't afford another car right now.

"It's only a few blocks and it's good for you to get some fresh air," Sandy gave her the worn-out line, as much as you can wear out a line in two weeks.

"I'm not a dog, Mom," Cali moaned. "I don't need fresh air, or to be taken for a walk."

"Have a good day, honey." Sandy smiled as Cali walked out the door.

"Easy for you to say," Cali said, the door closing behind her.

She paused on the porch – surveying the enemy's territory. Every back-woods hick at White Water High School thought her an undocumented immigrant at best, a terrorist at worst. She felt it. Illegal? Big deal. But terrorist? That hurt. She wanted to stand on the lunch table and scream, "I'm an American," but no one cared.

She shuffled to school as she did every day since arriving. Only 118 weeks until graduation, she sighed, hefting the backpack further onto her shoulder.

But today felt different. Goose bumps raised on her arms. She had a strange sensation someone watched her, studied her. She stopped, turning slowly, scanning for anything out of the ordinary. She completed her appraisal, beginning to start off again with a nod of satisfaction when she saw it, a black SUV, not something completely out of place up here where the winters are cold and the snow deep. *Not* owning an SUV would be considered out of place.

But this one sat there, somewhat odd even in the slow pace of White Water. The windows, tinted black, prevented her from discerning how many people were inside. It sat about half a block back on a side street, its front end pulled forward, giving the occupants a clear view of her.

She looked a moment longer and the vehicle turned away, accelerating down the street. Cali stared after it. It could be a pervert, up here in the middle of nowhere, looking for a girl to kidnap and disappear into the surrounding wilderness.

She shuddered, starting off again, turning her attention to another day of being ostracized by her fellow students, the SUV lingering in the back of her mind.

Buses passed by and other students walked to school, even from her neighborhood, but not a single one acknowledged her. She thought one girl wanted to talk to her, but then she tucked her head and went on without a word.

Cali glanced at the house a few blocks away, set on a hill overlooking a lake, the only bright spot in town, the old Victorian. She planned to stop by this weekend and take some pictures of the structure to add to her architectural photo collection. It needed some work, but the bones were there, just like the homes she photographed all over New Richmond.

Cali walked up the sidewalk to the large brick school. The new bricks and straight lines betrayed the lack of architecture Cali loathed. She loved the old buildings in her town, some as old as the revolution or older. This school gave her a sterile, institutional feeling, sucking the creative, artistic juices from her body. She needed to find inspiration in this wilderness. But where? The bronze deer on the lawn in front of the school, the only artwork. White Water White Tails, Cali rolled her eyes. How lame.

As she approached the school, the same SUV sat on the street. She paused, looking at it, and it drove off in the opposite direction once more. Creepy.

Cali walked through the halls, people bumping into her without a word or a glance. She ditched her extra books in her locker and then dropped her backpack at her first class, heading for the commons area to grab a diet coke. The machine stayed plugged in until the first bell. After that, your caffeine addiction had to wait until the end of school. She raced to the machine, having no doubt her history teacher would mark her tardy if she were a second late, just as he warned her every day this past week when she began her routine.

She needed her diet coke in the morning, the only slice of comfort she could glean from this oppressive, bland place.

Cali put her dollar into the machine, pressing the red-and-white button. She heard the familiar sound of the bottle dropping into the shoot and then it suddenly stopped. Her heart sank. No, this couldn't be happening. She had minutes to make it to class. She didn't have time to go to the office and get them to open the machine to get her coke. She hit the machine on the side, hoping to dislodge the bottle. Nothing, she hit it again. Still nothing, she began to hit and kick the machine over and over again, taking out her frustrations on this mechanical monstrosity, denying her the last piece of sanity she had.

The noise echoed through the empty commons area as the first bell sounded, giving her two minutes before class. Cali panicked. Winding up, she unleashed a final, desperation blow. It never made contact. A person stepped between her and the machine taking her punch in between the shoulders; Cali stumbled back. The stranger struck the machine smoothly, the bottle slipping down through the flapped door and clunking into the tray.

Cali turned to the person in shock, grabbed her coke, and raced for class.

Chapter 2

Josh Taylor leaned against the porch railing of the large, old Victorian they now called home, watching some neighborhood kids walking to school. He shivered, lifting his shoulders as a breeze lifted his long hair from his neck. He came out here early this morning, trying to steel himself for the next step in his life as his teeth chattered. He missed the California fall, the sun warming everything to a bearable temperature.

He longed to be there, heading to school and amped with anticipation as he and his friends rushed to the beach afterward, getting a few hours of surfing before sunset. The wind rose up again forcing him into motion. Taking a deep breath, he ran a hand through his sun-lightened hair and frowned. Pine and grass, not the smell he hoped for. Not the scent of the salt on a moist ocean breeze he loved and missed so much.

Why did he have to do this now? Why did he want to start today? His dad gave him the choice. Hell, he already missed two weeks and if he put it off for another day or two...shit, he wouldn't want to go, ever. He refused to be a frube. He'd rather chance a rail bang than not man up and start. He took the few steps to the sidewalk, turned back towards the house leaping back onto the porch.

His heart wasn't into it, that's all. His heart wasn't into much of anything.

He and his dad, Kevin, did something neither of them thought they would be doing a week before Josh's sixteenth birthday. Bury Josh's mom, Kathy. Breast cancer started their ordeal, but in the end, pancreatic cancer took her. Josh didn't care. The pain stayed no matter what took her.

Josh grabbed one of the porch chairs, throwing it onto the front lawn as his emotions flared, again. They did that a lot lately, bursting from him out of control, his rage, his anger surging to the surface. A passing group of students glared at him as the chair bounced a few feet from the sidewalk.

"Sorry," Josh mumbled, none of them indicating they heard his apology. "Shit. Nice first impression, dude."

He slunk out, retrieved the abused chair, and placed it back in the pile of dilapidated seating next to the broken-down table. He paused, staring down the road towards the cemetery, just making out the hill with a dark brown patch on it. Seeing it pulled his loneliness to the surface again and tears filled his eyes.

His mother supported moving to White Water, MN on the Iron Range. This had been the plan, to return to Dad's hometown at the start of Josh's sophomore year of high school.

His mom, a West Coaster through and through, agreed with Kevin, to Josh's dismay. Kathy instilled a love of the ocean and outdoors in Josh as she had experienced it all her life. Why would she want to come here, where the ocean and all she loved, were so distant?

She insisted Kevin and Josh move, taking her with them, as she lay dying a few weeks earlier. They postponed the move until after she passed, then all three came to White Water.

He urged himself into motion, walking down the steps, taking one last glance back at his home that felt nothing like home as the Victorian loomed over him. He doubted anything would feel like home again. He pushed through the thought, heading down the cobblestone walk and stepping onto the white sidewalk, now nearly deserted of students. He could just make out people walking in the distance.

He didn't quicken his pace; he would get there when he got there, late or not. School waited this long, it could wait a while longer.

A black Suburban with dark, tinted windows, oversized tires, shiny chrome rims, and dual straight pipe exhaust pulled up to a stop sign as Josh crossed the street in front of it. Josh glanced up at it and plodded on.

The vehicle pulled onto the street behind Josh; he expected it to pass by any second. It didn't. It rode along, idling just out of his peripheral vision. He thought to turn and look, but decided to ignore them, hoping they'd turn off.

A good idea, but Josh had no such luck. "Damn," Josh cursed as he could make out the soft rumbling of the vehicle's pipes. What did they want? He sped up as the school entrance came into view. He stole a quick glance over his shoulder, the vehicle nowhere in sight.

Josh stopped, looking around in disbelief. He sighed, grinning at his paranoia, turning back towards the school's entrance. There it sat, parked along the far street on the other side of the school, the black windows reflecting the leaves and clouds around it, the exhaust puffing out white whisps from the tailpipes.

Josh eased closer to the large high school, giving one last glance to the SUV, turning his attention away with a shrug. Probably someone wondering about the new kid, that's all, he thought, pushing it back in his mind, but not out.

The school felt smaller than the one in Monterey as he stepped inside, but still big enough to make him feel nervous. He smirked as he realized the large statue, he had just passed on the front lawn was of a white tail deer. Right, the White Water White Tails, he thought with a chuckle. Give me a break.

He entered the main doors, which opened to a commons area with tables set up spaced a couple of feet apart. A hard pounding sound echoed off the walls of the vacant room. He looked around in surprise to find a girl in torn jeans and a baggy green sweatshirt kicking the crap out of the coke machine. Her long black hair shone in the sunlight, swinging around her face as she abused the dispenser.

Josh shrugged, walked over, and stepping in front of the girl gave the machine a sharp slap in the same spot he needed to hit the coke machine at Del Monte Beach every day after school and was rewarded with a hard punch in the middle of his back from the girl. A diet coke slid out the flap door and clumped into the tray.

The girl turned, her green eyes filled with surprise, stepping back. Without a word, she snatched the bottle, hurrying down the hall and around the corner out of sight.

Josh stared as she disappeared. Looking up at the clock overhead, he nodded, late for class, he mused. He then continued to the office on one side of the commons to check in. The first period had started, and a secretary escorted him to his classroom after he told her who he was, and she gave him a big smile and a "Welcome to White Water High." He met his history teacher in the hall for a moment, glancing into the room filled with students. His stomach turned, letting out a soft gurgle.

Inside, his teacher pointed to a seat in the back. He eased between the desks, keeping his eyes down, sliding into his seat. The teacher walked up, setting a textbook before him.

There he sat: a new school and a stranger amongst strangers, feeling as if everyone stared at the new kid. Of course, he felt self-conscious, paranoid, totally uncomfortable, but he couldn't shake the feeling of being watched. Not just watched, but more like… analyzed. Hair stood up on the back of his neck, a slight tingle running through him.

He turned to see "coke" girl staring at him. Her inquisitive face wore a slight smile. Their eyes met and she turned away. Josh looked around the room at the other students. They were all shapes and sizes, but most of them were like him, Caucasian with a spattering of different nationalities. The lack of diversity of this small town didn't surprise him.

There were some good jobs from time to time, with the power plant, the paper mill, and the taconite mines in the area attracting all kinds of people up to this isolated place, but the majority would be born and raised here.

A tone came over the intercom announcing the end of the period, and Josh looked at the schedule and map the secretary gave him. He didn't have time to find his locker, so he concentrated on finding his classes.

He made it through the morning with only a few glitches, like when he asked for directions from someone who turned out to be a senior, sending him down to the boiler room for laughs.

Josh picked out a chicken burger, fries, and milk for lunch and wandered around the noisy lunchroom in search of a seat. He walked around for a few moments, ready to squeeze in between two exceptionally large guys in football jerseys, when he spotted "coke" girl sitting at a table by herself.

He smiled, walked over, and sat down across from her.

She glanced up from her book, for a moment, and then turned back to it.

He sat eating, looking over at her from time to time, then just turned and stared.

She finally noticed, looking at him flatly. "What?"

"Why ya sitting alone?" he asked.

"I'm not," she said, looking over her book.

"I mean before," Josh said.

"I know what you meant," she rolled her eyes. "They don't like new kids much, at least new kids who remind them of terrorists."

"Hah, you, a terrorist, right. What's with their aggro?"

"Where you from?" she asked.

"Monterey, California."

"What is aggro?"

"Bad rap, bad attitude."

"I would suspect you've seen people like me before?"

"I got some friends from Indonesia and others whose parents are originally from Egypt," Josh said.

"My father's from India. I guess they've never seen someone like me before. I can't really blame them, but it sucks being treated like a part of 911." Her eyes glistened with moisture.

"I'm Josh," he said, extending his hand.

"Cali," she grinned, clasping his hand, and shaking it.

"How long you been in White Water?" Josh asked.

"First year, started two weeks ago."

"So this is what I can look forward to in the next two weeks? Sitting by myself and reading a book at lunch? Bummer."

"I've done it and have to say it sucks." Cali smiled.

"I suggest the new kids stick together, during lunch at least," Josh grinned, taking an exaggerated bite of a fry. "What ya reading?"

"Nothing much," Cali said, holding the book up so Josh could see the cover.

"*Minnesota Photography* sounds gripping." Josh smirked.

Cali shrugged. "I'm trying to find inspiration, so I'm not stuck taking pictures of wildlife up here."

"You into that stuff, huh. I guess that's cool. At least you brought your hobby with you. Can't surf without the ocean."

"I loved the old buildings and architecture in Pennsylvania, not many buildings up here to rave about, except for the Victorian down the street."

"Really? Cool. That's my house."

"You're kidding. You're so lucky. I live in the cookie-cutter neighborhood in a cookie-cutter house." Cali sighed.

"At least it's not log." Josh smirked.

"Good point." Cali laughed.

"Seems we both have a problem then, we need to find different hobbies."

"Or learn to adapt," Cali offered.

Loud laughter interrupted from behind them, and Josh turned. A group of guys in football jerseys at one table tossed fries at the table next to them.

Students dressed in black filled the table, most with their hair dyed black, several having streaks of bright colors running through it. Some wore long trench coats, and a few had black platform boots on. All had very pale skin and wore black eyeliner, some with black lipstick as well, drawing out the white of their skin even more. Many had multiple piercings and a few even had nose or lip rings.

The teens ignored the fries being thrown by the football players and continued eating their lunch in silence, not looking their way, except for one larger kid. He glared at the jocks. He began to get to his feet, but a girl firmly took hold of his arm, pulling him back down. Taking his chin in her hand, she turned his purple-streaked head her way.

Josh observed as the antagonists soon lost interest and left the lunchroom, leaving their trays and garbage scattered around.

A teacher approached the table of black-clad students. He pointed at the mess on the floor. The teens stared at the teacher and then turned back to their eating. This only infuriated the teacher. The word detention wafted across the commons and the teacher stormed away.

Josh turned back to Cali, who stared at him, a puzzled look on her face.

"What?"

"Why does that bother you?" she asked.

"It doesn't," Josh said, going back to his food.

"Yes, it does. You tensed up when the jocks threw food at the Goths, and then again when the teacher gave them detention for making the mess."

"Yeah, so?" Josh shrugged.

"Why does that bother you? You must have seen that in California."

"Just because I've seen it, doesn't make it less bogus."

"Hasn't anyone told you life *is* bogus? Just because we're in the middle of nowhere, doesn't mean it's going to be *less* bogus."

"I know, but I hate it. Like the way they dump on you."

Cali stared in disbelief, her face turning red. "Is that why you came to sit with me, out of sympathy or self-righteousness?"

"No, I, I, I would never do that, Cali," Josh stammered. Cali stood up abruptly.

"Don't do me any favors. At least they're honest about not trusting me because of the way I look. You're accepting me only because of the way I look. They might be prejudice, but you're a hypocrite." She stormed away.

Josh looked down at his lunch, shaking his head. How could he mess up trying to do the right thing? He glanced at his watch, nearly fifteen minutes to sit there alone.

He noticed movement off to one side as a girl stepped to the table and sat down. He looked over and she smiled, causing him to smile back.

"Hey, my name's Sydney," she said, her deep-brown eyes shining at him as her bright smile sparkled. Her light brown skin glistened in the light.

"Josh," he grinned.

"Yeah, I know," she chuckled. "You going to sit with the new girl and piss her off every day, or is this a first-day-only event?"

"Dude, you saw that?" Josh rolled his eyes.

"The other kids haven't been too nice and welcoming to her, but I think she's okay. It's nice you sat with her."

"No big deal. I'm the new, new kid now," he shrugged.

"You fit in more than some of us, but they eventually get used to you. They may not accept you, but they tolerate you and leave you alone."

"What do you mean, fit in?"

"Me, Cali, Tal," she motioned to the large Goth student at the other table. "We don't look like the rest of them, and they don't take to new things easily. Tal and I've been here most of our lives. He is part Korean, and it took a while for them to warm to him, but they've learned to accept us, kind of—more like, put up with us—but it's a slow process for newcomers. Especially Cali since there's so much anger about the war and everything."

"So how do you deal?"

"Music," Sydney grinned.

"Music?"

"I let myself disappear in my music." Sydney blushed.

"What kind of music?"

"I write and sing pop music, but I really love traditional Mexican music. It helps me stay in touch with where I'm from.

15

The rhythm and beat speak to me, pulls at my soul, allowing me to escape the judgmental eyes following me around every day." She looked over at Josh, her face beaming.

The tone sounded the end of lunch break, and they stood to leave.

"Thanks, Sydney," Josh said, "catch ya later."

She glanced back over her shoulder as she walked away. "See you tomorrow. Don't tick Cali off before I get here. I want a chance to meet her too."

Josh laughed as he walked to his next class. He would be himself, he decided, accepted or not.

Chapter 3

Josh soon retraced his steps home as the rest of the day flew by. Fluffy, white clouds dotted the brilliant blue sky, and a cool wind blew. If he didn't know any better, he would swear the sky hung over a crystal blue ocean. He listened, half expecting to hear the surf break on the shore and the gulls cry overhead.

He stopped, looking back at the green grass turning slightly brown in places. Josh slipped on his jacket, zipping it up as far as it went. He picked up his new backpack, stuffed to capacity with tons of homework, and swung it heavily over one shoulder.

Josh came to a corner, hesitated for a moment, and then turned off his path of that morning. He walked up a gradual hill, onto a gravel road leading between two rock pillars and a metal arch. He moved through the manicured grass and fresh flowers scattered with small American flags, stopping in front of an area of fresh dirt and a black granite marker.

Kathy Taylor, loving daughter, wife, and mother. We miss your joy. He sat crossed legged on the ground, letting his backpack drop beside him, and stared emptily at the marker. He closed his eyes, picturing his mother, not as he last saw her, but as he remembered her, on the ocean, board between her legs, waiting for the next wave, full of happiness and life. He put his head in his hands as tears crept down his cheeks.

He wiped them with the backs of his hands, sitting up straighter as someone sat down beside him. He turned, expecting to see his father, shocked to see Cali sitting there.

Compassion spilled out of her watery eyes.

"What are you doing here?" he asked, wiping the last remnants of tears from his cheek.

"I live over there," she motioned with her head to a group of homes on the other side of the cemetery. "I thought I'd see if you're alright. I saw you turn in."

"Fine," he said, staring at the grave.

"I'm sorry for being hard on you at lunch. It's been really difficult here."

"No sweat. I wasn't there out of sympathy."

"I know. The more I thought about it, the more I realized you weren't like that. With all the suspicions in this town, leave it to me to be mean to someone who doesn't feel like that."

"It must've been hard." Josh looked at her.

"This must be harder," she said, looking at the headstone.

"It really bites," he admitted.

"How'd it happen?" She then put her hand up stopping his response. "You don't have to tell me. We just met, if it's too soon, I understand."

"No, it's cool." Josh took a deep breath, exhaling slowly. "She died of cancer two weeks ago. It took us until last week to get her here and have the funeral." He paused, turning from Cali back to the headstone. "They say when you die from cancer, you lost your battle. I have a hard time feeling mom lost. She lived life loud, dropping into every wave she could. If that's losing, what's winning? We all have to kick sometime."

He fought back tears pushing to the surface.

Cali took his hand.

He glanced down at their intertwined fingers, at her neatly manicured nails with red polish, and then up at her. Tears rolled down her face.

Josh turned back, gazing at the writing once more. They sat holding hands for a long time until Josh shook his head, clearing his thoughts. They looked to each other and reluctantly let go of each other's hand.

Cali stood, and he came to his feet stiffly. Their eyes met as awkwardness hung between them, unable to think of anything to say.

Cali started to leave, but Josh reached out, taking hold of her upper arm, and she turned back. He leaned in, their lips brushing softly, never really kissing, but feeling the other's breath on their skin, standing motionless, caught up in the emotions surging through them. He looked down at Cali, her eyes closed, face so soft, so content, so at peace.

She opened her eyes, peering up at him.

"Thank you for understanding, Cali," he whispered.

She nodded, turned slowly, and walked away without a word.

Cali kept walking, her mind racing over what just happened, or almost happened. Had she *wanted* him to kiss her? She brought her fingers to her lips, wondering at the soft brush of his lips upon hers. She tingled at the memory. She just met him. Did she actually have feelings for someone she just met?

She felt something she hadn't felt in a long time. She nearly didn't recognize it, happiness.

****

Josh watched her walk away, hoping she'd turn back. She kept going without the slightest glance, disappearing over the hill before he moved. He hurried home, the sun already setting, certain his father would be worried.

He walked through the front door of an empty house. He went into the kitchen, finding a note on the counter. "Josh, I had to work late at the plant tonight. Sorry, will be home after nine, Love, Dad."

Josh went up to his room in one of the two high turrets rising above the rest of the house. He picked the room giving him a view out over a large lake and field, as opposed to the heavily wooded side of the house.

He tossed his backpack down and flopped onto his bed, staring out the window.

"What a way to spend your birthday," he said. He never guessed he'd be in Minnesota instead of Del Monte Beach on his birthday tomorrow. He stared longingly at his surfboard hanging on his wall as a decoration, instead of waxed and ready to use.

He felt destined to be a Shubie with no sign of a wave on the lake outside. He shivered at the thought of the cold water even as he tried convincing himself he would take his board and give it a shot on a warm day. Did they have warm days up here?

He contemplated going down and getting something to eat, but he didn't have much of an appetite lately. He stood, pulling off his shirt as he walked in front of a full-length mirror. He stopped and stared. He squeezed the excess skin and some fat around his waist. He wished he could get rid of this. He jiggled it with a frowned. He flexed his arms and grimaced, too much below his arm instead of above. He reached over and grabbed the lax skin with his opposite hand. He needed to hit the weights. He walked into the bathroom and got ready for bed.

He lay in bed staring at the dark ceiling, wondering when the pain would start to subside.

He heard a car pull up and he waited for the garage door to open as his father pulled in. The sound never came. He hopped from his bed, running to the front bedroom facing the driveway.

Sitting on the street in the shadows of the large oaks bordering the boulevard sat the black SUV. He would know those rims anywhere. He looked for the occupants, but none were visible.

His breathing stopped. Through the still house came the discernable squeak of the front door. Terror planted him in place even though every ounce of his mind screamed to run, to hide.

The top step in the hallway creaked—just paces from where he stood. He gasped. He covered his mouth, but the sound had already escaped. He took two strides towards the room's attached bath, but a figure burst in. Dressed in black.

He turned to the hallway, but a larger figure barred his exit. He spun towards the large bank of windows, the moonlight shining in. The two circled him.

He opened his mouth to shout. The larger figure jumped him, driving him to the floor as he struggled. A vice-like grip clamped down on his arms, holding them firmly to his sides as Josh lay pinned under him.

The other figure held something delicately in one hand as the first pulled the sleeve of his t-shirt out of the way. The hand with the object lowered. The moonlight glinted off the needle and realization came to Josh as it pierced his skin, and he let out a cry of surprise.

Piercing pain erupted. Burning with every inch, pushing deeper into his organs. He lay on the floor, writhing as shapes hovered over him, watching him, but not helping.

Is this the way he was going to die? Is this what death felt like?

Thoughts burst as the pain gripped his head. He screamed. He held his hands to his face, trying to keep his brain from bursting through his skull. His surroundings blurred; dread filled him. He was dead. Why? Why me? Who? His thoughts trailed off, the possible answers with them.

Chapter 4

Cali skipped in the front door of their modified split entry two story in the middle of a subdivision. Identical to the house next to it, and to the house across the street. The lack of uniqueness, the sterility of it all, made her think sadly about their old house in Pennsylvania.

Their home had been an1810 Colonial. When you walked in, the centuries flowed through you. From the heart pine flooring to the gray Pennsylvania stone walls, it made Cali feel a part of something greater, bigger than her. The craftsmanship shown in every detail gave Cali a sense of balance in her life. That balance, strikingly missing in this modern dwelling.

That life lay far behind. Her mother and she were all alone after her father went back to India. With the move already planned her dad announced he his intention of returning to India. Cali's life changed completely.

Sandy stood in the kitchen when Cali walked in, reading something on the counter, brown hair hanging down, obscuring her face.

Cali approached. Sandy's shoulders shook and tears dropped onto the letter sitting on the counter, leaving blotches of watery ink where neat handwriting had been.

Cali looked at the letter from her father.

Sandy and Cali, I want you to know how much I miss both of you and how hard this decision has been for me. I feel it is best if Cali stays in America and does not come to visit me here in New Delhi. If I can get back to the States, I will come and visit, but it seems unlikely with my new position in the company. I'm truly

*sorry it has come to this, but I wish you both the best and send
my love, Malik.*

Cali saw the edge of divorce papers jutting from under the
tear-soaked letter.

She stood glassy-eyed, staring at the papers, putting her
arms around her mother, biting her lip, trying to maintain
control.

Sandy turned, crying on Cali's shoulder, shaking
uncontrollably.

Cali stared out the window to the cemetery.

What hurt more, she thought, losing your mother, knowing
you will never see her again, or knowing your father is choosing
to never see you again? In some ways she felt Josh would accept
the finality of his mother's death much better than she could
accept her father's conscious decision not to see her.

She stood there, strong for her mother until the tears
stopped. Sandy leaned back, wiping her red eyes, and forcing a
smile. "How was school?" she said, turning away and dropping
to a knee, cleaning up the remnants of a glass and its contents
from the floor.

Cali cleared her throat, "Okay, I guess."

"Anything new and exciting?" Sandy picked up broken shards
of glass and ice cubes off the floor.

Cali hadn't even noticed the mess until now. "Met a new kid
today, he seems okay."

Sandy stopped cleaning, looking up from a crouched position.
"He must've made an impression. Is he cute?"

"I guess," Cali shrugged. "Haven't decided." She touched her
lips.

"Why don't you leave that, and we can run out to eat?" Cali
said pulling her mom up by her arm. "I feel like tacos."

NORTHERN LIGHTS CODED TO KILL

"You do, do you?" Sandy chuckled. "You always feel like tacos." They walked to the entry, grabbed their coats, and headed out the door. Sandy paused, glancing at the family picture hanging on the entry wall, and then closed the door behind her.

Cali cleaned up the mess in the kitchen when they returned, amidst Sandy's objections, and insisted her mom go upstairs and relax.

Sandy finally gave in and went upstairs to watch some TV in her room.

Cali wiped up the floor and switched off the light, walking upstairs, checking to see her mom sleeping in her bed with the TV on. Cali eased the door shut and then walked into her room, flipping on the light, and dropping her backpack to the floor next to her desk. She glanced at the clock, a load of homework and already eight. She sat down at her computer, moving the mouse to bring the screen back up. She clicked her mailbox, ten emails waited for her. She pulled the phone out of her pocket and stared. She forgot to charge it the night before. No wonder none of her friends texted her today. She reached over and plugged it in as she opened her first email. Cali became homesick for New Richmond as she read. All her friends emailed every day.

She quickly read and answered every email and then turned to her homework, iPod plugs fitted in her ears. She crawled into bed after 1:00am and turned off her light. She thought of Josh, feeling nervous, but excited, about seeing him again. She smiled, closed her eyes, and drifted off to sleep.

She sat at the kitchen island eating breakfast when her mother came down in her bathrobe the next morning.

"Good morning, Cali." She yawned, wiping the sleep from her eyes.

"Morning, Mom," Cali said with a mouthful of cereal.
"What do you want to do for your birthday tomorrow?"
"Haven't given it much thought," Cali said, as cereal and milk spilt down her chin. She quickly caught it with the back of her hand. "We can go out to eat."
"Your grandparents want to come if that's okay?" Sandy said about her parents.
"Sure."
"Good, I'll tell them to come over around six and we can go wherever you want. Have any ideas?"
"No, I'll let you know after school. Got to go," she said, putting her bowl in the sink, grabbing her backpack, and hefting it onto her shoulder as she headed out the door.
"Bye honey, love you," Sandy called after her.
"Bye, love you too," Cali said over her shoulder.
She hopped down the steps and headed towards school, definitely not through the cemetery, but down the sidewalk, the way she usually went. She glanced over to the hill where Josh's mother lay. Butterflies filled her stomach. She felt odd a cemetery made her smile, but what happened there stuck securely in her mind. She shook her head at herself, grinned, and quickened her pace, looking forward to the day ahead. She never thought she would feel this way about going to school here.

Chapter 5

Josh sat up with a start as the alarm went off. He thrashed at his unseen assailants, looking around the room, his room. He expected to see the two figures standing over him, examining him. They weren't.

A bad dream, yeah, that's it. A dream, that's all. He started to laugh, reaching over to scratch an itch on his right arm.

"Owe." He lifted his t-shirt up and looked at his arm. A large bruise with a red dot in the middle covered his bicep. He jumped out of bed, racing to the front room.

The room and its contents appeared undisturbed. He rushed to the window, looking for the SUV. Not there.

Rubbing his arm, he returned to his room and stood before the mirror, examining the mark.

He studied the injury and turned away, pulling off his shirt. He furrowed his brow and cocked his head. His extra skin and fat, gone. Hard muscle and taunt flesh now in its place. He stared.

What the ...? He swore his muscles were getting larger.

What did they inject him with? He raised his arms, flexing his muscles, a broad smile splitting his face in two.

"Morning, son," Kevin said, standing in the doorway.

"Dad!" Josh raced over to him.

"Josh, what is it?" Kevin said, standing with his hands behind his back.

"There were two people here last night and they injected me with something," Josh blurted out.

Kevin looked calmly at Josh, listening, and shaking his head slowly.

"You don't seem surprised," Josh said, stepping back from his father.

"I think you may have had a bad dream, that's all," Kevin replied.

"Did I get this from a dream?" Josh asked, pointing to his arm.

"You got that at birth, Josh, your arm?" Kevin said.

"Not my arm, dude, the bruise with the red needle mark in the middle," Josh said pointing to his arm again.

"Are you on drugs?"

"No, I'm not on drugs," Josh exclaimed and looked down at his arm. His eyes shot wide as the bruise, the needle mark, nowhere in sight, nothing but pristine flesh. Josh stared as he ran his hand up and down his arm.

"It was there a minute ago," Josh pleaded.

"You've had too much emotional trauma these past few weeks, son. Maybe we should concentrate on what today is, instead."

Kevin held out a wrapped package.

"But it happened, really," Josh said, looking at the package, remembering his birthday.

"I believe you, and I'll contact the police to see about anything suspicious going on last night in the neighborhood. Do you want this or not." He tossed it to Josh.

Josh caught the gift, tearing it open and staring at a set of car keys.

"No way, dude," he cried as his dad beamed.

"Yes way," Kevin grinned.

Josh raced down the stairs in nothing but his boxers. He threw open the door leading to the garage and let out another scream. "No way, dude."

There it sat, sleek, shiny, and black, gleaming in the dull sunlight filtering through the windows in the garage door. A brand-new Challenger SRT. He slipped into the driver's seat, pausing to stare at the consul, and gripped the leather steering column, a giddy smile on his face. He touched the garage opener button on his visor and the door rose slowly as the sunlight reflected off the shiny paint of the hood.

Kevin reached the doorway, smiling. "I think you might want to get some clothes on before you go for a drive."

Josh looked down and blushed. He reluctantly pressed the door opener again and sat watching the door close on his birthday gift once more.

Kevin came to the open driver's door. "Did you check in the glove box?"

Josh shot his dad a look, eyebrows rising. He leaned across the passenger seat, flipping open the glove box. An envelope dropped out. He picked it off the floor and turned it over slowly. His mother's handwriting scrawled out his name on the front.

He looked up at Kevin, their eyes filling with tears. Kevin nodded and Josh ripped open the envelope to find a birthday card.

"Sorry I missed your birthday," Josh read. He showed the front of the card, the smiley face, his mother's tradition, to his father.

Opening the card, tears began to roll down his face as he read out loud. "I so wished I could have been here when you saw your gift this year. Every year after as well, come to think of it." Josh stopped, choking up at his mother's sometimes-misplaced sense of humor. "Your father and I tried to raise you well, and this is something we feel you deserve at this point in your life. I hope you enjoy it as much as we enjoyed picking it out for you. Just remember, you can handle anything this world throws at you, because you're a Taylor, and Taylor's are fighters."

Josh looked up at Kevin, who now cried openly.

Josh continued reading. "I love you son, always. And come to think of it, I'm sure I *did* see your face when you got your present. Keep me in your thoughts, Mom."

Josh leaned on the steering wheel and sobbed; Kevin placed a comforting hand on his shoulder. Josh turned and they embraced, sharing their loss for the first time since the funeral. They straightened, wiping their tears.

Kevin glanced down at his watch and gave a start. "I'm going to be late. I'll take you for your driving test after school today," he said, jumping into his car next to Josh's, pulling away as the garage door closed.

Josh got out of his car and headed upstairs to get ready for school.

He dried off after the shower and put on his favorite navy Billabong t-shirt. It slid on tighter than before but fit nicely. So, his muscles were bigger, and his extra skin and fat disappeared overnight.

Josh grabbed a foil pouch of Pop Tarts from the kitchen and headed for the door. Pulling his jacket on, he swung his backpack onto his shoulder. He caught sight of a picture of his mother on the table in the entry. As he ripped open the packet and began to eat breakfast, he took the picture in his hand and stared.

The reality of his life being, 'new firsts,' hit hard, this, his first birthday without her. He wanted to swing by and visit her before school but didn't have time. He needed to get going or be late.

He set the picture down and turned quickly. His backpack hit the picture. He spun back, crouched down. He caught the frame just before it reached the floor.

He looked at the object in his hand with shock.

Setting the frame down once more, he carefully turned and went out the door, trying to figure it out.

He looked for Cali all the way to school and after arriving but didn't see her. Dropping his coat off at his locker, he went straight to his first class. He spotted her sitting at her desk next to his with her diet coke when he entered the room. She looked away when he turned to her, but she stole glances as he maneuvered around the other students in the isle between the desks.

Sitting down, he pulled his book from his backpack and looked over at her, leaning forward.

Cali made eye contact with him and began to blush.

"Hey," he said.

"Hi," she smiled.

"How's it going?"

"Okay. You?"

"Awesome," he paused. "About yesterday," he began.

"Yeah, about yesterday," she said, looking down at her desk and then back at him. She gave Josh a look, making *him* blush.

"I wanted to apologize about…"

"You don't need to apologize," she interrupted. "Nothing happened."

"So, we're cool?"

"Think so." She shrugged.

"I don't want you to think I'm some kind of jerk, but I like you." He stared at her as she held his gaze. Her eyes sparkled as he spoke, and his heart soared.

"So, you're going to sit with me at lunch?" She grinned.

"If that's cool?" He smirked back.

She gave him a quick nod before being interrupted by the teacher beginning class.

The morning dragged on as Josh waited for lunch. The break finally came, and he slid into a seat next to Cali at the same table as the day before. Only a few moments passed when Sydney came up and sat on the other side of Josh.

"Hey, Syd, how's it going?" Josh asked.

"Okay," she said. "Is it okay to sit with you?"

"It's cool," Josh answered, but realized she looked at Cali.

"Sure," Cali said. "My name's Cali."

"Sydney." She smiled.

The girls nodded to each other, and they ate for a moment in silence.

Sydney started to speak several times but hesitated and went silent. Finally, she got up the nerve and leaned forward, speaking around Josh to Cali, "I wanted to come over and sit with you the last two weeks, but felt too nervous about what you would say."

"I would say, what took you so long," Cali grinned. "I saw you staring at me sitting over there." She motioned at an empty table not far away. "I don't bite, Sydney. I'm as uncertain about new things and new people as you are," she paused, glancing at Josh, and smirked.

"You two seem to be getting along better," Sydney commented.

"We just had to come to an understanding." Cali chuckled, brushing his leg with her hand.

Josh took hold of her hand. "I'm kinda psyched." He grinned.

"Wow," Sydney laughed.

"What?" Josh turned to her.

"The two of you are together," Sydney told him.

"Why do you think we're together?" Cali questioned.

"You'd have to be blind. It's kind of steamy." Sydney smirked.

Cali and Josh didn't have a chance to respond as some guys in letter jackets walked over, stopping in front of them on the other side of the table.

Josh glanced up, raising an eyebrow.

"So, the new guy likes 'dark meat,'" one of them said as the others laughed.

Josh started to come to his feet; Cali and Sydney pulled at his arms, but he didn't notice. He focused on the blond haired 'ass' in front of him.

"Better sit down like your harem wants, pretty boy, before you get hurt." The guys around him laughed and heckled.

Josh stepped over the bench and shook off Cali and Sydney.

He stood as tall as or maybe a little taller than his antagonist. He glared back into the student's eyes with steeled determination. His muscles flexed, and his fists opened and closed at his sides as he struggled to keep them down.

"Dude, that's not cool. You need to leave," he said in a flat, threatening tone. Fury raged in him, waiting for an excuse to be released. He fought it, confused as to its origin.

"Or what, you going to take all five of us, pretty boy," the teen sneered, but then a boy next to him tugged on his arm. He motioned to Josh.

"If you're going to be snaking like that, then, yeah," Josh said.

The first boy stared at Josh, his confidence siphoning away as fear spread across his face.

"Sorry, man," the boy stammered. "We didn't mean anything by it."

The group backed away, glancing over their shoulders as they retreated.

Josh watched them scurry, amazed at the change of course. He felt certain the kid would be a Barnie.

He turned back to the girls; they looked at him with a mix of surprise and shock.

"What?" Josh asked, raising his arms from his side. Then he realized. He held a fork in one hand and a knife in the other. More accurately, the remnants of the fork and knife. The twisted metal bore no resemblance to the original utensils. He squeezed them into hunks of unidentifiable metal.

Josh sat down between the girls, dropped the mangled silverware, and picked up his chicken sandwich to take a bite. He looked over at Cali, who stared in disbelief, and then to Sydney who mirrored Cali's expression.

"What?" Josh shrugged.

"What? Is that all you have to say after you squeezed those into submission?" Cali whispered, gesturing at the twisted metal.

"How'd you do that?" asked Sydney.

"Beats me," Josh admitted.

"What do you mean, beats me?" Cali pressed.

"Something weird happened to me last night, it's a long story," Josh said, hesitantly. It sounded crazy to *him*. He didn't need to scare Cali and Sydney off.

The tone announcing the end of lunch pulled Josh from his dilemma. He stood with a shrug. "Catch ya after school."

He strode off, feeling both girls' eyes on his back as he went.

Josh avoided eye contact with the other students of White Water High the rest of the day. When he did look, their eyes were filled with questions he didn't want to answer. Not that he could.

He dropped his stuff at his locker and found Cali waiting.

"Amped *that* day's over." Josh smiled.

"Me too." Cali laughed. "Going to walk me home?"

"Cool, and this time without walking through the cemetery," he said. "Besides, it's been the longest birthday ever."

"Today's your birthday?" Cali stopped. "It's my birthday tomorrow. Why didn't you tell me?"

"You can't just blurt it out." He grinned sheepishly.

She reached over, taking his hand, and they strolled into her subdivision, taking turns looking over at each other and smiling.

They exchanged cell numbers on her steps, and she gave him a kiss on the cheek goodbye. Josh gave her one last squeeze as he turned and walked down the sidewalk, a new lightness in his step.

Cali watched after him until he rounded the corner and was out of sight.

"Who's that?" A voice made her jump.

She turned to see her mother leaning on a rake in the yard.

"His name is Josh, he's a friend," she stammered.

"Seems more like a boyfriend, when are you going to introduce us?" Sandy smirked.

"It's his birthday today. Maybe he could come with us to dinner tomorrow. He's new in town and his mother died a few weeks ago. It's just him and his dad. They moved into the old Victorian down the street."

"Kevin Taylor's boy?" Sandy asked.

Cali spun around. "How'd you know that?"

"I went to school with Kevin, and your grandmother told me he's back in town and his wife died from cancer before the move."

"So, it's okay he comes, if he wants?" Cali pressed her lips together.

"Invite your friend and tell him his father is welcome too. They probably could use some friends right about now," Sandy said, laughing as Cali jumped up and down with excitement.

"I'll call him right now," she said, dialing his number.

"The poor boy won't even be home yet and you're already calling him," Sandy laughed.

"Josh, this is Cali. Would you and your father like to go with my mother, my grandparents and me to dinner tomorrow for my birthday?" She paused, listening. "Okay, let me know after you talk to him. Bye."

"He said he'd let me know at school. Are you sure grandma and grandpa won't mind?"

"I'm sure they'll be excited we know someone other than them in town," Sandy assured her, walking over and putting an arm around Cali's shoulders. "Let's get some dinner." She said as they walked into the house.

Chapter 6

Josh ran the rest of the way home after Cali's phone call. He covered the last block so quickly it surprised him. He skipped up the front steps onto the porch as his dad backed his new car out of the garage.

"You ready?" he asked as Josh raced to jump into the driver's seat. Kevin hurried out of the way, avoiding being run over, and hopped into the passenger seat as Josh revved the engine with delight.

"Let's go, time to get you a license," Kevin grinned.

A victorious Josh and proud Kevin pulled into the drive a little later. They stopped for supper to celebrate, and now Joshed eased his ride into the driveway. Kevin got out as the garage door opened when Josh spotted it.

The black SUV cruising by, slowing a bit as it passed. Josh's head swiveled, following the vehicle. The decision came in a split second, and he slammed the car into reverse, squealing the tires as he screeched onto the street behind the SUV.

"Hey," Kevin shouted, but Josh sped after the SUV as it accelerated away.

Josh lost it after a few blocks. He decided to drive around and see if he could spot it again.

Josh drove around for over an hour and still hadn't seen the SUV. He glanced at the dash clock, nearly midnight. Kevin called on the cell again, but Josh ignored it; his father wouldn't understand, since Josh didn't understand.

Conceding his failure, Josh decided to cruise past Cali's before heading home. As he turned onto her block, a chill ran down his spine. There sat the SUV, outside Cali's house. He cut

36

his lights and pulled up behind it. He killed the engine and got out, pushing his door shut, just until it latched. He crept closer, peering into the dark windows, but could see nothing.

Backing away from the house, he looked up.

He spotted the two figures he would recognize anywhere slipping into an upstairs window from the roof of Cali's house. Adrenaline raced through him as he ran to the front door. He thought to knock and alert Cali and her mom but realized it could put them in more danger if the intruders were startled into acting. He leapt for the eave from the step, overshooting his mark and landing on the roof. He looked around in shock.

Josh pushed his amazement aside, scurrying towards the window the intruders entered.

He peered in and saw a reenactment of last night's attack, but with Cali. He leapt through the window and chaos erupted.

****

Cali went to bed early that night, giving her mom a soft kiss on the forehead as she lay sleeping in her bed with the TV on.

She slept until she heard something strange, out of place, waking her. She opened her eyes, unable to focus as something dark hovered over her. She let out a feeble cry, but a gloved hand smothered it. Her vision began to clear as she struggled against someone holding her to her bed.

Movement to her side alerted her to a dark figure. The figure raised an arm, holding something in its hand.

A cry came from the window, and whoever held her down flew from her bed, slamming into the far wall, just as something sharp stuck her arm. She jerked her head as he withdrew.

Pain gripped her, curling her into a fetal position, engulfing her in agony. With each pump of her heart, the pain spread first to her organs, and then to her extremities. It finally reached her brain, and she thought her head would explode as the pain pounded loudly in her ears with each labored breath and excruciating beat of her heart.

She vaguely comprehended the struggle going on in her room as she succumbed to the pain. Mom?

****

Josh burst into the room, catapulting the larger figure against the wall. He heard the air forced from the intruder's lungs as he crumbled to the floor. Josh turned to the bed where the other intruder withdrew the syringe from Cali's arm and turned his attention to Josh.

Josh started to advance but froze as the moonlight reflected off the barrel of a gun. He dove to the side as the gun's silencer sounded and something impacted the wall where he once stood.

Josh rolled to his feet; the leg of the smaller figure disappeared through the open window. The larger intruder was already gone. Josh raced to the window, grabbing the sill to jump through when Cali moaned. He looked over at her, helpless, and then at the SUV speeding down the street.

He wanted to pursue them but turned back to Cali with a frustrated grunt.

He sat beside her as her body went rigid and limp over and over again. This is what he must have gone through, he thought.

He considered finding Cali's mom, only, how could he explain his presence? Would she believe him more than his own father did? He doubted it. He moved over to the door, opening it enough to see Cali's mom snoring away in her room at the end of the hall, the glow and flash of the television lighting up her face.

He closed the door and sat down beside Cali. He took her hand, holding it tightly as her body struggled against the changes the drugs induced.

****

Cali opened her eyes, fearful of what she might discover after the last images she recalled. Instead of dark, predatory figures, Josh sat beside her, propped up against the headboard, her head resting on his chest and her hand in his.

She began to sit up and Josh jolted awake.

"Oh, hey, you, okay?" he stammered, looking around.

"Fine, I think. What are you doing here?"

"It's kinda hard to explain without sounding bogus," he said, lowering his eyes from her gaze.

"Try me, after last night, I might believe you," she said, putting a hand to her arm and cringing when she touched the injection point.

"What happened to you last night, happened to me the night before," he blurted out.

"Huh?" she said, sitting up straighter.

"Two people broke into my house the night before last and injected me with something," he said.

Cali's mind clouded over as she looked at him.

"No, dude, really, they injected me too and I changed. When I scoped the black SUV in front of your house, I stopped. I saw two people sneak into your window and I tried to stop them."

"Black SUV?" The memory of being followed the other day coming to her.

"Yeah, but I didn't reach you in time. They injected you and bailed out the window."

"Oh my god, we have to call the police, we need to catch those guys," Cali said, reaching for her phone.

"What do we tell them?" Josh said, gently pushing the phone down to her lap.

"We show them what they did to us and tell them we were assaulted, violated," Cali shouted.

"There's nothing to show, dude. My marks are gone, and I bet yours are too." Josh shook his head.

Cali pulled the sleeve of her shirt up and the urgency drained from her. There were no marks at all. She pursed her lips and let out a heavy sigh.

"I told you, even though we changed, we don't have any proof anyone caused it or that anyone was ... here," he slowed his thought and looked over at the far wall. "Wait," he said holding up a finger as he climbed out of bed. He walked over to the wall, scanning it as he moved closer.

He leaned in, pulling something from the plaster.

He walked back to Cali, holding the object between his thumb and finger at eye level. He sat down on the bed as Cali looked at a dart.

"They didn't want to kill me, why would they, they just created me. This looks like a tranquilizer."

"You said you changed. How?" she asked, rolling what Josh told her over and over in her head. Nothing made any sense.

"Yeah, I got stronger, faster, chiseled." He emphasized his statement by pulling his shirt off.

A noise came from the hall and Cali panicked. "Josh, my mom, you have to get out of here."

"Chill, I'm going," Josh grinned, putting his shirt on. "We'll sort this out after school. Catch ya later, and happy birthday." He gave her a peck on the lips and disappeared out the window.

Cali got up and looked at herself in the mirror. Unbelievable. Rock hard muscles and smooth skin covered every inch of her body. But at what price?

She discovered soon enough as she walked into her mother's room to find the TV on, but no Sandy. She checked the bathroom, the kitchen, even the damp basement, but no Sandy.

She gave up when she saw an envelope on her mother's pillow she missed the first time. She lifted it from the pillow and read her name scrolled across it.

She tore it open. Cali's eyes grew wide as the message registered. She raced to her room to get dressed, dialing Josh as she went. Did he have a license? She didn't and she needed a ride. Now.

Chapter 7

Josh pulled into his driveway, hitting the opener button as the door moved slowly upward. His father's car sat in the garage, and he prepared for the confrontation that would ensue. After ignoring his father's calls and not coming home last night, he knew his father's reaction.

He strode into the kitchen, expecting to see Kevin at the table eating breakfast, but the kitchen sat empty. A sick feeling formed in the pit of his stomach as he spun and climbed the stairs.

"Dad, I'm home," he called, prepared for his father to rush out of his bedroom and give him a piece of his mind.

"Dad?" he said, opening his father's bedroom door.

The sick feeling grew to the size of a bowling ball. An envelope sat on his father's pillow. He picked it up and read his name on it.

"We have your father," it read. "Meet us at the old air base on the north side of town ASAP. Don't contact the police or authorities."

No signature.

Terror seized him as he ran down the stairs, racing for his car. He couldn't let anything happen to his father, all he had left. He burned out of the garage and onto the street, skidding to a stop and tromping on the gas as he laid a strip of rubber nearly a block long, the smoke rising behind him.

Coming to a crossroad, he hesitated for a moment, and then took a right, skidding around the corner noisily. He had a hunch, and he went with it.

He pulled up in front of Cali's house just when his cell rang, Cali's name on his display. He answered as Cali ran out of the house, frantic, a sheet of paper in her hand, phone to her ear. He rolled down his window as she ran up. "You too?"

She nodded.

"Get in."

They sped north.

"Who would do this?" Cali screamed.

"I don't know," Josh admitted. "Maybe the same people who attacked us."

"I can't believe this is happening," she cried.

They followed old, dilapidated signs still pointing the way to the old base. They pulled through open gates. Numerous buildings painted a dull yellow and green, mixed with gray primer and red rust, lined short avenues. They drove into the heart of the base until they spotted the SUV.

"Look," Cali pointed.

"How come I'm not surprised," Josh said.

They parked a few buildings away, leaving the car concealed behind a yellow hanger.

Creeping along the side of the hanger, they came to the corner and surveyed the area around the SUV. The place looked deserted, no sign of activity or anyone.

They approached the suburban cautiously, crouching behind it as Cali placed a hand over her eyes, trying to peer inside through the tinted windows. She crouched back down, shaking her head, no one inside.

Josh reached over and placed a hand on the hood. "Still warm," he whispered.

Josh paused at the back of the SUV, looking around, and then hurried to the building as he flattened himself against it, avoiding the window in a white door. Cali did the same and they carefully approached the window, Josh leaning slightly forward to glimpse inside.

He held up a finger and then pointed to himself. Cali nodded her understanding, one man inside.

Josh started to circle around and look for another way in.

The door swung inward, a large man stood looking at them without expression.

The man with a gray crew cut motioned them forward as he held the door open. Josh and Cali, resigned to the fact they were found out, went inside, following him across a large hanger into a small conference room. A slender blonde woman in a dark business suit stood at the head of the table, patiently waiting for them.

"I would like to thank you for coming. I'm Ms. Swanson and this is Mr. Grayson," she said. "We are here to complete a transaction begun over sixteen years ago that is now due. Come in and take a seat." She smiled, motioning for them to sit at the conference table.

Josh spun on the man as he entered the room, grabbing him by the neck, lifting him off his feet and slamming him violently into the wall.

The clicking of a bullet being loaded into a barrel stopped Josh as he ignored the struggling man and looked to the woman who held a gun to Cali's head, the girl staring into the barrel.

"I would advise against any more outbursts unless you want this to end badly," the woman cautioned.

Josh let the man drop heavily as he walked away, his hands held up, palms exposed. "No problems."

The man stood, looking back at the crumbling sheetrock where Josh thrust him, rubbing his neck, rage burning in his eyes, but a warning look from the woman sent him over in front of the door, out of Josh's reach.

"Very good." The woman removed the gun and clicked the safety.

Cali and Josh looked at each other, confused.

"You injected us, didn't you?" Josh spoke up.

"Very perceptive, Josh," Ms. Swanson said.

"Why?" Cali said.

"We've waited sixteen years to activate you," Grayson stated.

"Activate us?" Josh's brow furrowed.

"Let's catch you up quickly so we can deal with the here and now, shall we?" Ms. Swanson interrupted. "You are two of four subjects the CIA designed to aid in our fight against domestic terrorism."

"Designed?" Cali asked.

"You and your friend are genetically engineered to be perfect covert operatives to fight terroristic plots against your country," Grayson said.

"So, the shot?" Josh raised an eyebrow.

"We needed to wait until you reached sixteen to inject you with a serum to remove the remnants of a time-release genetic inhibitor and expose your true genetic abilities," Swanson explained.

"Why wait for sixteen, why not twelve or thirteen?" Cali questioned.

"Your bodies had to mature enough to handle the physical changes once we removed the gene inhibitor. The change could have killed you," Swanson went on. "We needed to make certain you could handle it."

Grayson grinned. "You will be joined by two others and function as a top-notch covert ops team specializing in infiltrating and eliminating potential plots before they unfold."

"We were hoping to activate all of you and brief you together, but Josh became too suspicious, putting our plan in jeopardy. We needed to get the two of you on board and collect the others without your interference," Swanson explained.

"What do you mean by eliminating plots?" Cali questioned, a hint of horror in her voice.

"When there are plans to do our nation or their interests harm, you will be deployed to stop those plans from happening, by whatever means possible," Grayson stated.

"Whatever means?" Josh questioned.

"Whatever is necessary to stop the plot," Swanson said with a curt nod.

"Nope, won't do it. Not what I planned for my life," Cali said, her hands crossed over her chest. "Sorry, but you need to find someone who actually likes what the United States is doing in the Middle East and elsewhere in the world. I, for one, do not."

"Yeah, I'm with her. You're a Grom if you think I'll drop in on a wave like that, dude." Josh nodded as he folded his arms as well.

"We are so sad to hear that, as I feel your mother and your father will be. You can discuss it during your afternoon exercise time at Guantanamo Bay detention facility," Mr. Grayson said, giving Ms. Swanson a nod. The woman pressed a lever, opening a wall behind her to expose a window. Through the window Sandy and Kevin sat in the next room, oblivious to their presence on the other side of the glass.

"Mom." Cali rushed to the window with Josh right beside her.

"Dad," Josh whispered, peering through the glass.

"Why are you doing this?" Cali pleaded, tears running down her cheeks.

"Your parents agreed to this in order to conceive you. You became official CIA property on your sixteenth birthdays. All the paperwork is legal, in a top secret sense, at least," Grayson gloated. "If you fail to cooperate with us, you and your parents will be considered enemy combatants and sent to Guantanamo Bay."

"For how long?" Josh asked, still looking at his father through the glass.

"Until you cooperate, or the CIA deems you have served your time, but I wouldn't hold out much hope for a short stay," Swanson explained.

Josh stared in shock at his father. Kevin made this decision, and Josh would be paying for it the rest of his life. His mother must have known as well. She went to her grave with the secret, and the guilt.

Cali looked at her mother, the reason her father left became clearer. She turned to Swanson—Grayson seemed to be enjoying this too much.

"What about my father?" she asked.

"Malik will be sent to Gitmo when we are able to secure him if you don't cooperate. He is never out of the CIA's reach, no matter what he believes," Swanson assured.

"So, what do we do now?" Josh asked.

"You will do as you're ordered," Grayson grinned. "Your parents will be allowed to return home tonight if you agree to cooperate. If you complete your mission and agree to continue your involvement with the team, they will be allowed to remain free and financially taken care of."

"And if we choose after that first mission, we won't do it anymore?" Cali asked, still looking at her mother through the window.

"Like your father, your mother can never stay out of our reach forever. She remains free as long as you cooperate. The minute you choose otherwise, club Gitmo," Grayson chuckled.

Sadistic bastard, he enjoyed watching them squirm with nowhere to turn, like a worm on a hook, being plunged into the water as bait.

"I'll do it," Josh spoke up. "But I want to talk to him first."

"Fine." Swanson said.

"I'll cooperate," Cali sighed. "Can I speak with her?"

"Of course," Swanson smiled.

Cali felt like throwing up as they followed Grayson to the next room. He opened the door as the teens entered and closed it behind them.

The bank of mirror on the one wall created a theatrical atmosphere in the small room and caused Cali to smile disdainfully. A theatre, she thought. They were performing for Swanson and Grayson in the room behind the mirrors.

"Cali," Sandy cried, running to her, and taking the girl in her arms.

"Josh," Kevin said, as the boy walked into his open embrace.

The four stood hugging for a moment, the teens well aware of their audience.

"Sit down dad, we need to talk to you," Josh told his father as they slid the chairs from around the small table and began to sit.

"You too mom," Cali motioned to Sandy. They also sat down across from the Taylors.

"I'm so glad you both are alright," Kevin started, but Josh stopped him with a raised hand. Kevin looked at him, dumbfounded.

"They told us everything, well, at least everything about how we were "designed," and you and mom were in on it," Josh said, glaring at him.

"It didn't happen like that, Josh," Kevin said.

"That's right, there's more to it," Sandy joined in.

"Don't you start," Cali warned. "You all knew exactly what you had done. You knew results when we reached sixteen, but you never thought to tell us, to warn us about it."

"We knew we couldn't have children without help, and we had exhausted all the normal channels. "We were desperate," Sandy defended.

"The CIA didn't enter into the equation until you were born. They explained we agreed to an experimental program to create genetically engineered children," Kevin said.

"That may be, but you never thought in all those years to tell us?" Josh jumped in.

"We were told not to give you any information," Kevin argued.

"So, you knew they were going to break in and assault us?" Cali accused.

Sandy and Kevin fell silent, looking at each other, the guilt on their faces answering Cali's question.

"That is wacked," Josh cried, coming to his feet. "You knew what they were going to do, and you acted like nothing happened," Josh shouted, pounding his fist on the table, leaving knuckle imprints.

"Josh, take it easy," Cali tried to calm him, her anger rising making it exceedingly difficult to stay in control herself.

"No, I won't take it easy," Josh turned away from her, staring into the mirrors, picturing Swanson and Grayson looking on. "This is shit and you know it. We should let them put all of us in prison."

Sandy and Kevin hung their heads, the only sound in the room, Sandy's sobs.

"So, you going to have them put us all in prison?" Kevin spoke up after a long silence.

"We should," Cali answered him, Kevin looking up at her as she stood over them, the guilt heavy in his eyes.

"We agreed to cooperate," Josh said, not turning from the mirrors as he answered. "For now."

"I guess that's all we can ask," Kevin said, putting a hand over his mouth as soon as the words came out, Josh spinning on him.

"No, it's not, obviously, because you have asked too much of Cali and me already, from birth. Don't you realize that with your actions, you've imprisoned us for the rest of our lives?" Josh screamed, his face turning crimson, his veins on his neck and head bulging. "You've taken away any future we might have hoped for, dreamed of." Josh turned back to the mirror, flipping off Grayson and Swanson in the other room.

"Josh," Cali said as she put a comforting arm around him, leaning in close, placing her head on his shoulder. "If we have to do this, we need to stay in control of our feelings. They will use it against us otherwise. At least we're in this together," she managed a slight smile.

Josh looked down at her as she gazed up from his shoulder. "I guess we have that," he admitted. "No one else I'd rather be a slave with than you," he reached around and gave her a squeeze.

He turned back to Sandy and Kevin, staring at them from the table. "I'll get them to let us out of here," he said and walked to the door.

Grayson opened the door as he knocked and escorted Josh back to the conference room and Ms. Swanson. She looked at him as he entered.

"Can we go now?" Josh asked, forcing himself to look at her.

"Of course, but you and Cali need to return on Saturday after we have activated the others."

"Who is that?" Josh questioned.

"Well, I suppose it doesn't matter if you know or not," Swanson hesitated slightly. "Sydney Espinoza is the next one. I prefer not to mention the last member quite yet."

The name hit Josh between the eyes and his head snapped up. Sydney, Sydney who sat with them at lunch?

"Do you know her?" Swanson questioned.

"Don't think so," Josh said.

"Little Mexican girl, wears her hair in a ponytail a lot, seems to like music?" Swanson pressed.

"I've only been here two days, haven't met anyone except Cali," Josh lied.

"We're hoping to go in with you and Cali and explain the process and maybe it will be less traumatic on her." Swanson said.

"That would be a good thing." Josh replied.

"Grayson will show you out."

Josh nodded and walked out, his mind racing with how he could warn Sydney, and she could avoid the mess they were in. He came up to Grayson who stood, cross-armed, outside the door to the room where Cali, her mom, and his dad waited.

Josh stopped in front of him. When he didn't move, Josh raised an eyebrow in question.

"I want you to understand something, right off," he leaned down to stick his face right in the face of the shorter boy. "If you ever touch me again, I won't be as forgiving, understand?"

Josh nodded, he didn't want to antagonize the man in charge of your training.

"Good," Grayson sneered, stepping aside, and opening the door.

Cali, Sandy, and Kevin looked up expectantly as Josh entered the room, Grayson hovering behind him.

"We can go," he told them.

Questions crossed their faces, but Josh gave a curt shake of his head, and their faces wiped clear. Josh turned as the others approached and followed Grayson out the way they had entered.

Reaching the outer door, Grayson held it open and eyed each as they walked through, giving them one last look before he closed the door behind them, the lock clicking.

Fog rose from the pavement as the morning sun burned off the remnants of a crisp morning. They looked to each other, at a loss. Josh took the initiative to wrap an arm around Cali's shoulders and walk with her to his car, Sandy and Kevin followed behind.

Josh opened the passenger door for Cali and Sandy to slide into the back seat. Kevin paused as Josh stood in the doorway. The guilt weighing heavily on his features, Kevin looked at Josh.

"No, Dude, not now," Josh shook his head, walking to the driver's side. He paused, looking over the roof of the car as his dad tried to speak.

"No, wait," Josh urged again, looking around cautiously then slipping behind the wheel.

Kevin climbed in, shutting the door as Josh started the car and squealed out of the parking space and raced off the base. They were down the road a mile or so when Josh finally turned to his dad.

"They're going to 'activate' Sydney tonight," he said, turning over his shoulder to Cali.

"Oh my god," she cried. "We have to do something, warn her it's coming."

"What are we supposed to do?" Josh raised his hand in distress. They want us to go with them so it will be less of a shock on her."

"Like I'm going to be ok with that?" Cali protested.

"What choice do we have? I'm sure her parents are as clueless as ours were," Josh gave Kevin a glance.

"Hey," Kevin complained.

"Well, you kind of were," Josh pointed out.

"How were we supposed to know?" Sandy chided in.

"Mom, really? Some strange people come and tell you they will help you have children and do something no one else has been able to do, and you don't wonder just a little?" Cali rolled her eyes.

"You have to tell Sydney," Sandy pushed. "You both understand how scary this is; at least you can help her understand it's not that bad."

"It isn't?" Cali shot her a look. "I think being forced into doing 'whatever it takes' which I interpret as killing people, no matter how good the cause, is pretty bad."

"Your mom's right though," Josh said and received a dirty look from Cali. "No, really," he said looking nervously over his shoulder at her. "We need to explain to Sydney before it all goes down and maybe she won't freak out like we did."

Cali still glared at him, but her look softened as she considered it. She nodded with a resigned look on her face. "I guess it would have helped if we didn't have to be attacked and all that. We can talk to her after school today," she agreed.

They pulled up to the Taylor's house where Josh dropped his father off and then proceeded to the Abdullah's house where Sandy jumped out while Cali slid into the front seat and motioned for her to go inside. Cali watched her mother disappear inside the house before she turned back to Josh.

"That was one choka ride," Josh smirked.

"Do you just make words up?" Cali laughed.

"No, it means bitchin, epic," Josh explained.

"That's one way to put it. I'd say this is the worst day of my miserable life," she said as a tear ran down her cheek.

"Listen, things could be worse," Josh assured her.

"How?"

"We could have turned green and ugly," he pointed out.

"There is that" she did a combination laugh and cry.

He reached over and took her hand. "I know you don't agree with this, but our parents put us in this and we're the only ones who can get us out. I guess I feel as if I can do some good and keep my dad and myself out of prison. That's the best option I could hope for now." He leaned forward, taking her chin in his hand and gently turned her face up to look at him. "I understand that you hate violence and the thought of killing someone horrifies you but think about all those innocent people we may be able to save from a terrorist's attack."

Cali's look softened, but only slightly. She gave a little nod and then leaned forward and kissed him. She held her lips to his for the longest time, savoring the sensation. His lips parted and his tongue touched her lips and then pressed on to her tongue as she let it happen.

The innocent kiss turned animal as they wrapped their arms around each other and let their emotions take control. Cali leaned over on Josh's lap before they pulled apart, gasping for air. Cali's heart raced and a warm feeling spread throughout her body as she looked into his light blue eyes.

She smiled sheepishly and he blushed.

"Wow," he whispered.

"Yeah, wow," she sighed.

"I better get going. I'll pick you up on my way to school."

Cali nodded and gave him one more pressing kiss before she jumped out and headed into the house, watching him drive off, the passion still boiling inside.

She walked into the kitchen where her mother stood waiting for her. This wasn't going to be pretty, she thought as she stopped to stare at the woman who gave her a life sentence.

Chapter 8

Josh pulled into the garage and hurried through the garage door leading into the entry. He rushed in and found his father sitting on the steps leading upstairs.

"We really need to talk," Kevin started.

"I've got to get ready for school," Josh said, walking past Kevin as he stood up.

"We didn't mean to put you in this situation."

"Then why did you?" Josh shot back.

"We had no other choice," Kevin argued. "If we didn't, you wouldn't be here, and we wouldn't have had sixteen wonderful years with you. Don't you think this weighed on our minds your entire life?"

"But you didn't feel compelled to tell me anything until today?"

"I didn't have a choice," Kevin protested.

"That seems to be your standard answer now. We didn't have a choice. Everyone has a choice, dad. You taught me that. Just consider yourself lucky I'm choosing to do this to keep us out of prison, at least for now."

"What do you mean by that?" Kevin shouted.

"I mean I haven't decided how far I'm going to go with this. I'm going to play it by ear." Josh turned and went up the stairs leaving his father standing with his mouth open, staring after him.

■■■

"What in the hell were you thinking?" she shouted.

"Now, Cali, watch your mouth," Sandy warned.

"Watch my mouth? Is that all you have to say?"

"What do you want me to say?"

"Why'd you do it? You could maybe start with that, and I'll let you know where we can go from there." Cali said with her hands on her hips.

"Like I'm sure they explained," Sandy began.

"Don't quote those two government puppets," Cali cried. "You tell me why you did it. Your reasons, not some canned response you were told to tell me."

Sandy walked over to the table, pulled a chair out, and motioned for her to sit down.

Cali glared, but Sandy motioned again. Cali sighed, walking over, and dropping heavily into the chair.

Sandy pulled a chair out on the other side of the table and sat down.

"First, I want you to understand we are not the enemy here. We're on your side. I understand this is hard for you to take in, but I'm here to support you and help you make the adjustment to these circumstances."

Cali rolled her eyes, turning her body away from her, and looked back towards the kitchen appliances to her left.

"Obviously dad knows about this," she said still facing away.

"Of course, he's known from day one. I suspect that's one of the reasons he decided to leave us. He couldn't accept what he had been a part of and doesn't want to face the consequences with it all coming to a head."

"So, you didn't feel you had any other choice than this path to have children?" Cali said, her shoulders dropping slightly as she began to calm.

"It's true, we were told we could never have children, so we had given up hope and contacted an adoption agency to see about finding a child. Then Mr. Grayson and Ms. Swanson showed up at our door. They told us we had a slight chance to have a child of our own."

"A Frankenstein child of your own, you mean." Cali said, not looking at her.

"They never told us what they meant to do," Sandy explained. "We had no idea you were to be genetically altered. They assured us they were going to use my egg and your father's sperm. You would be our biological child."

"But you and dad knew before today," Cali pointed out. "When did you know?"

"After I became pregnant, they showed up at one of the ultrasounds and pointed out the conditions in the papers we had signed, giving them access to you once we conceived. We tried to argue, but they spelled it out plain enough. We thought they would want access in order to study how the procedure went, but then they said when you turned sixteen; you would become property of the United States of America. We could still have contact with you if we cooperated, but the decisions about your life after sixteen were up to them.

"We didn't have anyone to turn to," Sandy pleaded, reaching across the table, and putting her hand on Cali's arm.

Cali looked down at her mother's hand on her arm and then back at her mother without emotion. Sandy pulled back.

"We had to decide if we were going to let this destroy our marriage and family or strive to take what time we had and make the most of it. We feel we made the best choice for all of us, keeping it a secret and letting you live like a normal girl."

"Until dad decided he couldn't face this final step he helped lay out for my life," Cali said, disgust heavy in her voice.

"But why here? Why did they come to this dinky town in Minnesota?" Cali asked, looking at her mother.

"I have always wondered that," Sandy admitted. "It could be the old air base gave them a place to operate."

"How could there be four couples at the same point in their lives at the same time?" Cali questioned. "I don't have that answer, honey," Sandy said. "That might be something you can ask Mr. Grayson or Ms. Swanson tonight."

"I have to get ready," Cali said standing.

"Are you going to tell this Sydney what she is?"

Cali stopped, she hadn't thought about that. Josh and she intended to tell someone that they are freaks. A freak with no options, besides. She and Josh should maybe rethink this. "I guess we were going to," she said uncertainly.

Sandy stood and began to give her a hug, but Cali put her hands in front of her, keeping her mother away. "I'm not to that point yet. We still have more to sort out. Until we do, I think you should give me some space."

Sandy nodded her understanding as the pain and dejection showed across her face and she dropped her eyes.

"Don't forget, I love you and always will," Sandy told her.

Cali turned, heading upstairs to get ready for school.

Chapter 9

Josh picked Cali up and they drove to school. The responsibility of warning Sydney of what would befall her tonight weighed heavily on their minds. Sadness filled the car as they pulled into the parking lot, the reality of breaking someone's dreams bitter in their mouth.

"How are we going to do this? Cali asked as the car pulled into a parking spot.

"It's already after lunch, we missed our chance to tell her then," Josh shrugged.

"Right, so she could freak out in front of everyone, good thinking," she rolled her eyes.

"Chill, it's only a thought. Let's worry about finding her first," he sighed.

They went inside, the commons area sat empty, and they slipped past the office into the building.

"Where would she be now?" Josh turned to Cali in the hallway.

"She likes music, where are the music rooms?"

Joshed pulled his tattered map out of his jeans pocket and unfolded it. "We're right here," he said pointing to a spot on the map. "So, the music department should be down here," he pointed to an adjoining hallway.

They hurried down the corridor and were soon in a hallway of doors spaced six to eight feet apart. Listening, they could hear various instruments playing and some people singing as well.

"These must be practice rooms," Cali said. "She could be in one of them."

Josh shrugged and started down the row on one side, placing an ear to the door and then moved on to the next. "Syd said she sings and plays pop music, but she likes the Mexican flair. Go down the row until you hear someone singing and listen for the style."

"Why don't we just open each up and see?" Cali suggested.

"We don't want to draw attention to us, which would give us away." Josh put his ear to the next door. "Trumpet," he said, pulling away and going to the next.

Cali did the same. "Sax," she said and moved on.

About midway down, Cali stopped and listened for a long time as Josh continued.

"Guy singing," he moved to the next. "Piano, boring stuff." He looked back at Cali as she stood listening, her ear to the door.

"I think I got her," she motioned for him.

Josh placed his ear to the door next to her head and listened. The piano trilled out a Latin beat and then a smooth, confident voice came in and brought it all together perfectly. He placed a hand on Cali's shoulder and moved her back as he pulled the door open.

Sitting at the piano as it faced the doorway, Sydney sang, her eyes closed and a smile on her face as her fingers lightly flew up and down the keys.

They stepped inside and pulled the door closed behind them as Sydney was still concentrated on her music. She built to a crescendo, pounding on the keys as her voice built to the final note and she bowed her head as the cord hung in the air, reverberating through their chests.

Sydney opened her eyes and gave a start. "What are you doing here?"

"That was bitchin," Josh smiled.

"Very awesome," Cali agreed.

"Thanks, but what are you doing here?"

"Can we talk privately here?" Cali asked as Josh opened the door and glanced into the hall, assuring no one lurked outside.

"Yeah, but why are you acting so strange?" Sydney asked her face filled with trepidation.

"You remember yesterday when Josh crushed his fork and knife at lunch?" Cali began.

"Yeah," Sydney nodded, looking to Josh.

"There's a story behind it that I didn't know about until today," he told her.

"And last night, I had the same experience as he did," Cali added.

"Ok, you are really creeping me out. What is going on and what does that have to do with me?" Sydney pressed.

Josh pulled a folding chair against the wall, and spun as he sat down, leaning on the back of the chair and staring eye-to-eye with her. Cali stepped in behind him, placing a supportive hand on his shoulder.

"You see Syd, you, Cali, and I are all caught up in something that started before we were born. It is really hard to explain." He stopped and looked over his should at Cali for help.

"What Josh is trying to tell you, is the three of us were made the same way," she said, searching for the right words.

"I kinda know about how it all works, so why don't you just come out and tell me?" Sydney sighed.

"We're genetically engineered to be covert special operatives for the CIA." Josh blurted out, his face turning red after he spilled it.

"What?" Sydney whispered.

"I know it sounds crazy, but you need to listen to us and let it all sink in," Cali said, slapping Josh on the back of his head for blurting it out.

"You're kidding me, right? You're trying to make me feel better for being treated different up here by making up a story that makes me really different, right?" Sydney looked back and forth between them.

"I know it sounds wacked, but you need to believe us," Josh assured her. He recounted everything that happened to him and then Cali the last two nights, from the attacks to the meeting with Grayson and Swanson. He finished with the orders they were to return to the base on Saturday after all the activation had taken place.

"We're supposed to meet at the base on Saturday. They plan on 'activating' you tonight." Josh concluded, emphasizing statement by pointing at Sydney.

"Oh, my, god," Sydney stared at them. "This is real?"

Cali and Josh nodded.

"I don't know if I can believe you guys," Sydney said staring at them.

"I know what you mean," Cali assured her. "I'm in the middle of it and it doesn't seem real to me."

"Maybe we need to show you," Josh suggested as a tone came across the intercom ending the period. "What period is it?"

"The last," Sydney said.

"Let's go to the weight room," Josh suggested.

"The weight room, what for?" Cali protested.

"I haven't seen what this new body can do and that may help convince Syd that we aren't just psyching her."

The three walked out of the music practice room and down the hall to the weight room. Once inside, Sydney dropped her

63

backpack and followed Cali and Josh over to the free weights to one side of the room in front of a wall of mirrors.

"Do you want to go first?" Josh asked Cali.

"I've never lifted before, maybe you should go first. Have you lifted?"

"Not too much. They don't want you to lift too heavy until you're at least fourteen. I did a little out in California."

"Let's start with 150 pounds and see how that goes." He started adding the weights and Cali did the same on the other side of the barbell, looking to be sure she matched the plates.

He slid his six foot frame onto the bench and ran his hands along the bar to get a grip. He easily picked it up and benched it over and over, finally placing the barbell back onto the holder.

"That was cake." He told Cali.

Cali slid her slim, toned body on the bench and positioned her hands. She easily benched the weight over and over. Placing the weights back on the rack with a heavy clank, she stared at them with amazement.

"Awesome. I've never lifted in my life, but it felt like picking up my backpack," she grinned.

"What now?" asked Sydney.

"We need to kick it," Josh reasoned. "Let's add another hundred pounds and see."

He added fifty pounds on each side and then looked down at Cali still lying there on the bench. Her green eyes shone up at him, stirring something inside. Pushing the feeling aside, he gave her a nod as he stepped back a bit to spot her.

Cali tentatively pushed the bar up and then laughed as she benched it with ease. After several reps, she slammed the bar back in the holder.

"That's incredible," she said sitting up.

"Do you want more?" Josh urged.

"I think we should," she said with excitement.

"Don't you want to try?" Sydney asked Josh.

"If I can lift it, I'm sure Josh can. Let me see how much I can lift and then see if he can lift more," Cali explained.

Josh added more weight to the bar.

Cali lie back down and set her hands. With a slight grunt, she lifted the weight and pressed it several times, exhaling as she pushed it away from her body. She slammed it back on the rack and sat up.

"How much was it?" she asked.

Josh grinned, looking at Sydney who stared back with her mouth open.

"Three hundred fifty pounds," Sydney said in disbelief.

"Was it hard?" Josh inquired.

"I had to work at it, but I think I can do more." Cali giggled.

"What's the point, we know you're really strong." Josh pointed out. "Let me try."

Cali and Josh switched positions, and he put his hands on the bar.

"Hold on," Cali said reaching for more weight. "You might as well see if you can lift more since you're doing it." She put more weight on each side and stepped in over his head to spot him. Looking down at his deep brown eyes made her want to lean over and kiss him right there, but she gave him a nod and he pushed the weight off the rack and began to rep it.

He did several reps without much effort and banged the weights down on the support rack. He sat up, looking at the weight on each side.

"How much was that?" He asked.

"Four hundred fifty pounds, I can't believe it." Cali said with a grin.

"That is crazy," Sydney said her eyes wide.

"Hey, what are you doing in here?" A large man with a blond crew cut wearing black t-shirt and sweatpants came walking in, glaring at them with accusing blue eyes. "You can't be in here without supervision."

"Sorry," Josh said as the three gathered their things and rushed out the door.

The teacher walked over to the bench press, scratching his head, and looking at the door after them in disbelief.

Once outside, they stopped to talk.

"I can't believe this is actually happening," Sydney said.

"We're going to be come over tonight, so try and chill," Josh told her.

"Try not to worry too much," Cali rolled her eyes at Josh. "Of course, you're going to worry, what else are you going to do?"

"You know what I meant," Josh sighed.

"I know," Sydney said. "Thanks for being here for me guys."

"We're in this together," Cali assured.

They walked out to Josh's car and climbed in, Sydney in the back.

"Who do you think the last one will be?" Sydney asked, leaning forward between the front bucket seats.

"Don't know," Josh shrugged, "but they said the person has a birthday the day after yours."

"Tal's birthday is the day after mine," Sydney told them.

Cali and Josh looked to each other, could he be the last one? A Goth kid? He hardly fit the image, but what kind of image was there, really? A surfer, an artist/photographer, and a singer. Why wouldn't a Goth fit right into their strange menagerie?

"It kinda makes sense," Sydney read their mind. "We're a diverse group. Josh is European descent, Cali is Indian, I'm Mexican, and Tal is Korean. The different heritages must have something to do with it."

"We need to tell him," Cali said.

"Tell him what?" Josh argued. "Hey dude, we don't know for sure, but you may be a genetically engineered special covert operative, and you can either join us or go to prison with your dad. Or maybe you're not." He looked to the girls with skepticism.

"He's right," Sydney agreed. "We can't tell anyone unless we know for certain."

"Maybe they'll tell us tonight who the last member is when we confront them at your house," Cali nodded.

They pulled up to Sydney's house and she climbed out as Cali opened the door and leaned forward. Sydney turned back and leaned on the door as she looked in the open window.

"What should I do about my parents?" She looked for advice.

"Wait until we get here tonight, and it may be easier," Cali suggested.

"Give us your cell number and we can give you ours," Cali said pulling her cell phone out of her pocket. All three gathered around and exchanged numbers and saved them. "Calls us if something comes up or you just want to talk."

"Thanks, I'm kind of nervous for tomorrow," Sydney admitted.

"Don't worry. You don't feel any different except all your muscles become honed and all your fat and flab disappear. Not that you have any," Josh added seeing the hurt look.

"I know what you mean," Sydney grinned. "Thanks guys, I guess there isn't anyone I'd rather be a government experiment with." Sydney gave a resigned smile, nodding as she stepped away from the car, giving them a somber wave as Josh pulled away.

Josh looked at her in his rearview mirror, head hanging down as she shuffled to her house.

"She's going to be alright, isn't she?" Cali asked.

"We all are," Josh nodded confidently, "as long as we stick together."

As they rounded the corner and pulled into Cali's neighborhood, she turned and looked at him.

"What?" he glanced over at her.

"You do realize they expect us to kill people sometimes," she frowned up at him.

"I suppose if the need arises. For the safety of innocent people," he assured her.

"I don't know if I can do that. I'm a pacifist and abhor war and violence. I don't even agree with striking another human being. What's going to happen if I can't do what they want me to do?" She leaned her head against his shoulder.

"We'll have to figure that out together, all of us. This is a team now and we need to work as a team to solve all kinds of problems. Sydney's already on board, it's just a matter of time before Tal, hopefully, comes around. You'll see," he reassured her as she looked over uncertain.

"Josh, he's *Goth*."

"Yeah, I know."

"Goth's don't traditionally like authority or control. Do you really think Tal will go along with all of this?"

"I don't know, but the dude has to see there isn't much choice, unless you think he would go to prison along with his folks?"

"I don't think Tal will agree to everything; maybe not anything Grayson wants us to do," Cali sighed.

"And you, how do you feel about it?"

"I feel for the people of the region whose lives are nothing but a nightmare. My father is from India and went back to try and help in some way. I know my father's side of the family doesn't believe the war is going to solve this decades-long problem in the region."

"So, you and your mom are alone?" Josh asked.

"Mom got divorce papers along with a letter telling us he doesn't even want me to come and visit him. He's aware of all of this and wanted nothing to do with me after the change." She stopped, sitting up in her seat again. She stared at him, her face filled with an epiphany.

"What is it? It looks like you've seen a ghost." Josh asked walking back to her.

"That's why he left and asked for a divorce," she whispered. "He couldn't face the reality of what I was going to become. My father has raised me to hate war and violence. My becoming a covert operative was more than he could take. I've turned into the very thing he fervently disagreed with all these years."

"It's not your fault," Josh comforted.

"I know," she shot him a look, sending chills down his spine. "Grayson, Swanson and the government did this and one day they'll pay for ruining mine and my mother's life."

He put his arm across her shoulders, pulling her against him. Hugging her tightly, he whispered in her ear, "When the four of us are done with them, they'll wish they never had guinea pigs like us."

They sat outside Cali's house for a long time without saying a word. He kissed her lightly on the lips, gave her a squeeze, and then drove home through the cemetery.

Standing at the foot of his mother's grave, he thought how she had escaped all this. She must have lamented over this time arriving and would have felt guilty for leaving Kevin to face it alone. He saw his father in a different light. Not as an accomplice to this, but a victim like himself. Grayson and Swanson took advantage of their parents in their time of weakness. Grayson, Swanson, and the government were to blame, not the parents.

Saying goodnight to his mother, he climbed into his birthday present and drove home with a sense of enlightenment and clear conscience. He burst through the door and into the kitchen where Kevin waited for him at the table.

"Sandy Abdullah called this afternoon. She asked if you and I would like to join her and Cali for a birthday dinner with Cali's grandparents."

"I completely forgot. What'd you tell her?" Josh raised an eyebrow above his reddened eyes.

"I told her I would speak to you and get back to her. So now I'm speaking to you. What do you think?"

"Can grandma and grandpa come with since we didn't get to see them on my birthday?" Josh suggested.

"I was thinking the same thing. We can all celebrate yours and Cali's birthday." Kevin tilted his head waiting for an answer.

"Choka." Josh forced a smile.

"Great, I'll give Sandy a call to confirm it," Kevin stood reaching for the phone and then stopped turning back to Josh. "How has the change affected you and Cali?"

"Both of us are really strong," he grinned. "We stopped by the weight room and checked it out."

Kevin waited patiently for him to continue, "And..."

"Cali could lift 350 pounds pretty easily and I did 450 pounds before a teacher came in and we had to leave."

"You need to be careful. You can't let anyone discover your abilities. If they do, it will put you in peril," Kevin pointed out.

"Don't worry, we'll be careful. It's what we were designed for anyway."

Kevin's head dropped and his eyes looked away from Josh.

Josh walked over in front of him, placing a hand on his father's shoulder. "I know you and mom didn't intend for this to happen. I can't imagine the stress you two were under as this time grew closer."

Kevin looked up with tears in his eyes.

"I forgive you for the decision you and mom made sixteen years ago. I'll try and make the best of it for the both of us." Josh nodded as he finished.

Kevin reached up and gave his son a hug. Josh stood stiff for a moment and then put his arms around his father, hugging him back.

"I'd better get ready," Josh said breaking the embrace and heading for the stairs.

"About Cali," Kevin said, spinning Josh in his tracks.

"What about Cali?" Josh asked.

"You have feelings for her?"

"Yeah, I guess I do," Josh said looking up as he thought for a second, then giving a nod.

"Was this before or after you two realized how closely linked your lives were going to be?"

"The day before my birthday, we met at school and then she followed me to the cemetery when I was visiting mom. She gets me and I get her," Josh said with a little defiance.

"No, no, it's ok. I'm just curious," Kevin said holding his hands up in front of him, palms up. "I'm glad you have someone you care about."

"Who knows, Dad, Cali's mom remembers you from high school. Maybe you two can find something in common besides your mutant children."

"Isn't she married?" Kevin raised an eyebrow.

"Cali's dad went back to India. Guess he couldn't take the big changes that were going to take place, so he bailed. They're getting a divorce."

An awkward moment of silence hung in the air and then Josh shrugged. "Better get ready," he said, running up the stairs two at a time.

Chapter 10

Josh and his dad pulled into the parking lot of The Harbor after swinging by the local drug store, the only store open this late, to get a card and some flowers for Cali. It appeared upscale. Upscale for White Water that is. The circular drive leading to the door and the overhang that sheltered passengers from the elements stood unmanned by a valet but merely provided a convenience for the customers.

Entering the lobby, they were greeted by the host in a white blouse and black skirt.

"Good evening. Welcome to the Harbor, two tonight?"

"We're meeting some people here and they might already be here, the Abdullah's" Kevin told her.

"The Abdullah party is in the west room, please follow me." She led them around the corner and down a narrow hallway that opened into a larger room with about fifteen tables set up with white table clothes and nautical themes around the room and on the walls.

"Thank you," Kevin said as he saw his parents sitting visiting with another elderly couple.

Cali came rushing over to greet them, leaving Sydney and her parents.

"Hey Josh," she smiled. Her green eyes were even a deeper green if that were possible. Her light green Minnie skirt looked incredible, causing Josh to stand staring as he handed her the flowers and the card.

"Happy Birthday Cali," Kevin said looking over at Josh in disbelief. "It was nice of you and your mother to invite us."

"Nice of you to come, Mr. Taylor," Cali smirked looking at Josh still staring at her.

"Kevin," he corrected. "Mr. Taylor is Josh's grandfather," he laughed.

"Kevin," she grinned motioning to her mother who walked up to them. "You remember my mom, Sandy."

"Nice to see you again, Sandy," Kevin said taking Sandy's extended hand and shaking it.

"You too Kevin, at least it's under better circumstances" she beamed. "Your folks were getting caught up with my parents. You know they belong to the same lodge up here?"

They all walked over and made introductions with the grandparents and greeted the Espinoza family.

They were soon eating and drinking, having an enjoyable evening. Josh said very little caught up in gazing at Cali. He didn't know why, but she glowed tonight.

Sydney sat visiting with Cali, pausing every so often to see if Josh wanted to add anything. He seemed content observing tonight. The three teens sat at one end of the table while the adults visited about the old times and when Sandy and Kevin were in school. The Espinoza's shared how much things had changed over the years since they had moved to White Water six years ago.

The night ended with a huge birthday cake with Happy Birthday, Josh, Cali, and Sydney on it.

"I sure hope the final person isn't Tal," Sydney told Josh and Cali.

"Why is that?" Cali asked.

"Tal will never go for it," Sydney said.

"Then he and his parents can spend some vacation time at Gitmo," Josh said.

"You don't get it," Sydney turned on him, fire in her eyes. "He's not an only child like us. His parents had four more after him. He would never do that to his siblings, even if he wanted to do it to his parents. He'll do as he is told, but not of his own choice."

"I'm not sure I'm going to do this by choice either," Cali admitted. "I'm doing it for mom, not them."

"Choice or not, things are changing for all of us," Josh looked between them. "I'm going to use this as an opportunity to do some good. Plus, this may have some perks," he grinned lifting his right arm up and flexing his bicep.

The girls laughed at him and took the cake and ice cream Sandy handed them.

The night ended and everyone said goodnight. Josh gave Cali a light kiss goodnight before she slipped into their car and headed home. He hopped into their car and rode home with a satisfied smile on his face.

Kevin and Josh pulled into their drive and the black suburban sat parked to one side. As they pulled by, Grayson and Swanson stepped out, watching the Taylors pull into their garage.

Josh and Kevin got out and walked to the back of the vehicle, waiting for the two visitors to come up to them.

"I thought you didn't need him until Saturday," Kevin said.

"Something's come up and we need to get Josh up to speed quicker," Grayson said.

"We'll pick Cali up on the way," Swanson added.

"Where're we going?" Josh asked.

"You're going to have to get used to the idea of doing what you're told without question, son," Grayson said.

"I doubt that will happen," Josh muttered as he looked back at his dad with a nod and followed the pair to the suburban.

Getting in the back seat, he sat quietly as they pulled into Cali's drive.

Ms. Swanson got out and went up on the porch and rang the doorbell while Mr. Grayson waited with Josh.

"Are you going to tell us where we're going?" Josh pressed.

"We'll fill you both in when she gets here," Grayson said pointing to Cali joining Swanson on the porch and heading over to the car.

Cali slid into the back seat with Josh, giving him a worried look and forcing smile.

Josh reached over, taking her cold, clammy hand. She squeezed it back and sat looking at Ms. Swanson, who turned to address them while Mr. Grayson drove.

"Something has come to our attention that we need to begin preparing for immediately. We have to hope your genetic makeup will allow us to accelerate your training to unheard of levels."

"What about Sydney and the last member of the team?" Cali asked.

"We'll get them up to speed as they change, but we need to get you on the path first to assure we have a response in place to the threat in time." Grayson said over his shoulder.

They pulled up in front of Sydney's house and Ms. Swanson started to get out when Cali put a hand on her shoulder from the back seat. The woman turned to her with a questioning look.

"Can Josh and I go in with you, it may help?" Cali asked.

Ms. Swanson exchanged a glance with Grayson, and he gave a curt nod.

"Alright," Ms. Swanson said and all four got out.

"You let us do the talking. I don't want this to turn into some kind of fiasco." Grayson instructed. The two teens nodded their agreement.

Swanson rang the doorbell and Sydney's father answered. Recognition crossed his face and it turned to resignation. He nodded, backing inward, allowing them entrance. He looked curiously at Cali and Josh as they came in behind.

"Who was at the door?" Sydney's mom came around the corner from the kitchen. "Josh, Cali, did we forget something at the restaurant?" She saw Grayson and Swanson and her smile vanished.

"It's time," Ms. Swanson said.

Sydney's mother nodded her understanding, giving one last glance back at Cali and Josh before climbing the stairs.

They waited there, awkwardly, until Sydney came down with her mother. The girl looked physically ill as her face turned pale. She gave a scared look to Cali, who nodded and then Josh who gave her an unconvincing thumbs up. She turned to Grayson and Swanson, her fear causing her body to shake.

"Why don't we sit down," Ms. Swanson motioned to the kitchen table. "Josh, you and Cali can wait here," she said, nodding at the couch.

Cali sat with Josh beside her as the others walked around the corner, out of their sight, into the kitchen. Both her and Josh leaned forward straining to hear the conversation. Surprise spread across their face as they realized they heard every word clearly as Swanson explained their current situation and then Grayson pointed out what would happen if they didn't cooperate.

They reached the point in the conversation where she needed to get the injection. Cali stood, walking to the kitchen with Josh scrambling to follow after.

"You two can go back and sit down," Grayson instructed.

"I want them to stay," Sydney said. Her brown eyes were red from crying, and she still had remnants of the tears on her cheeks.

Sydney's mother and father sat zombie-like, staring at their daughter, tears running down their faces, the horror of this day finally catching up to them.

Grayson bristled, but a calming hand on his arm from Swanson and an assuring look relaxed his tension. He gave a sharp nod without looking back at the teens.

Swanson pulled out a syringe with a long needle. It looked a lot bigger here in the light than it had to either Josh or Cali. Sydney tensed at the sight of it and Cali walked over to stand beside her, a comforting hand on Sydney's shoulder. Josh walked over and place his hand on Sydney's other shoulder and turned to Ms. Swanson.

"Are you ready?" Swanson asked the girl.

Sydney looked up at Josh and Cali, their silent resolve and support flowing into her. She set her jaw, looked at Ms. Swanson and gave a nod.

Ms. Swanson lifted Sydney's t-shirt sleeve and looked one more time assuring that the girl was ready. Sydney gave another slight nod, and the woman plunged the needle into Sydney's arm.

Sydney cried out in pain, her body shaking nervously as Swanson pressed the plunger, sending the drug into her system, 'activating' another member of the team.

Swanson withdrew the needle along with the empty tube and sat back to observe.

Josh then realized Swanson and Grayson may not have witnessed the change in either him or Cali since they needed to leave before being discovered. This time, they watched attentively, studying the effect of the drug.

Sydney's body went rigid as Josh and Cali supported her, lowering her gently to the floor. They knelt on either side of her, holding her hands as her body began to convulse, her screams of pain bringing tears to her parents eyes as they watched their child endure pain they could do nothing to prevent.

Sydney lost consciousness suddenly, causing everyone to lean in. Concerned she had succumbed to the pain. A deep gasp escaped her lungs causing everyone to jump and breathe a sigh of relief. Sydney lay unconscious on the kitchen floor, the 'activation' complete.

"She will sleep until morning," Ms. Swanson said.

Josh scooped Sydney up from the floor in his arms, looking to Sydney's mother. "Where is her room?"

"Oh, yes, this way," the woman said, coming back from her personal nightmare.

Cali followed after, tucking Sydney in and checking on her one more time. Mrs. Espinoza sat on the edge of the bed, tears running down her cheeks.

Cali and Josh turned to leave.

"You will take care of her?" Sydney's mother asked, causing Josh and Cali to stop in the doorway and turn back to her.

"Of course we will," Cali assured.

"You know we never meant this for you, none of us," she told them.

"We know," Josh said. "Do you know who the last one is?"

"The Vang boy," Mrs. Espinoza said. "He won't be as agreeable as you three, not that you're all that agreeable," she added seeing Cali's face turn crimson.

"We are doing this for our family," Cali told her.

"I hope you see there is good to be done here as well," she said, looking back at Sydney sleeping peacefully.

"I can," Josh said, but Cali remained silent.

"Good night Mrs. Espinoza," Cali said and walked out.

Josh gave the woman an awkward nod and followed behind.

Chapter 11

The teens followed Grayson and Swanson to the vehicle as Mr. Espinoza watched them get into the vehicle before he closed the door.

They were soon driving north, to the decommissioned air base. The gate opened in a jerking motion, not being serviced for many years. They followed the main road entering a large hanger, driving into the dark, cavernous building.

"This is a perfect location to headquarter our team without drawing suspicion from the community. There has been training here, on and off, over the years and a little activity won't draw unwanted attention. The only thing you need to be diligent about is to never let anyone see you enter. They must never associate any of you with this base. If you come here, do it in the night or in a vehicle able to conceal your identity, such as the tinted windows in this suburban." Ms. Swanson stared at each of them until they nodded their understanding.

The vehicle came to a stop, and everyone got out. They walked to the center of the structure following Grayson with a flashlight leading the way. He reached a point and paused, bending down to open a small control panel in the floor. He punched a code into a keypad as Cali and Josh both leaned over his shoulder just enough to see the code, but not be discovered. Only after turning to each other did they realize both had garnered the code and became aware of their great distance from Grayson. Neither had expected to be able to discern the code that easily at that distance. They looked surprised to each other but were pulled from their shared moment when an elevator lifted out of the floor in front of them.

They entered the waiting elevator, and the door slid closed. Cali and Josh turned to face the door only to see a reflection of them against the highly polished inside of the elevator. Fidgeting, they descended into the depths of the air base.

As the elevator came to a sudden stop, the doors opened to expose long concrete tunnels branching out in all directions. Grayson pushed his way between the two teens and headed straight ahead as Ms. Swanson squeezed through and followed.

Cali and Josh glanced to each other with raised eyebrows and Josh gave a hand gesture for Cali to go ahead. She smiled with a shrug and followed down the echoing corridor. They turned sharply into a doorway and entered what amounted to a classroom.

Grayson tossed his coat on the table in the front and motioned for Cali and Josh to take a seat. The two teens sat down and waited with questioning looks, as Swanson rifled through some papers in a satchel, and then nodded for Grayson to begin.

Grayson dimmed the lights with a remote as Swanson clicked on a light strapped to a head band she put on so she could see the papers in the dark room. A projector hummed to life and a picture of a large brown block building with many towers appeared on the whiteboard.

"The Chatterly Preparatory School is located in Virginia," Swanson began.

Grayson clicked the remote and the picture changed to numerous pictures of heads of state, congressperson, senators, and foreign ambassadors. He clicked again, changing the image to several images of teens ranging in age.

"These are the children of those dignitaries who go to Chatterly. Their presence requires the school to employ a high level of security, background checks for all students, and anyone who sets foot on the grounds." Swanson said, paging through her sheets.

A picture of a man, black suit, neatly trimmed hair, and beard, clicked up on the board. The professional looking man appeared to be of Middle Eastern origin.

"This is Jaffa Ahd Amed, an international terrorist vowing to make America and anyone who allies with America pay. He is demanding the release of several captives at Guantanamo. If we do not comply, he promises to "bring terror to the vile infidels and their spawn."

"So you want us to find Amed and kill him?" Josh asked.

"Not that easy, Junior," Grayson said.

Ms. Swanson gave Grayson a dirty look he ignored. "The problem with eliminating him, Josh, is these people never act alone and if we remove one leader, another will step up and take his place. No, we need to infiltrate the school, identify the people involved, and surgically remove them to neutralize the threat."

"You want us to go to school at Chatterly?" Cali asked, "For how long?"

"As long as it takes," Grayson said.

"We just got started here, how are we going to go to school here and at Chatterly?" Josh complained.

"We've made arrangements with your school to temporarily home school you when we decide to send you in," Ms. Swanson explained.

"We don't have time for your insecurities," Grayson grumped. "We need to see if the genes controlling learning and retention are able to escalate your ability to absorb procedures and Intel."

The lights came up in the room and a large, sealed packet now sat before each of them.

"You will be given thirty minutes to review the information on weaponry, operating procedures of equipment, military jump, boating, recon, and other essential survival tactics. We need to test you on your retention and see how quickly we can move forward." Ms. Swanson explained.

"Please begin," she said starting a stopwatch.

Cali and Josh exchanged momentary glances, tore open the packets and started to read. Josh read the first line, then the second and soon the words were entering his consciousness so quickly, he couldn't even identify individual sentences, but more like absorbed the information as a whole. He kept turning page after page and slammed the last sheet down on top of his finished pile as Cali did the same.

They shared a grin and looked up at Ms. Swanson who first stared in shock, and then, realizing the stopwatch still ran, quickly clicked it off. She gazed down at the watch as Grayson moved over to her side. She held the time piece out for him to read. His eyes shot wide, and his jaw dropped.

Grayson walked over to a shining stainless steel cabinet, unlatched a few fasteners, and swung it open on its wheels. Inside, black foam cut out in shapes accommodated its precious cargo. Grayson unfastened an assault rifle, walked over, and placed it in front of Josh.

Josh looked down at the weapon. M4A1 flashed across his mind. Carbine Delta Special Forces weapon of choice, this one known as a "shorty" due to its reduce muzzle length. Josh hesitated. How did he know all this? He looked up at Grayson.

"All right, soldier," Grayson barked, "Disassemble the weapon and reassemble the weapon." He pulled a stopwatch from his pocket. "Ready, begin."

A click of the watch sent Josh into motion without thinking about his actions. Remembering the information he absorbed, he let it flow through him into his hands and fingers. He considered closing his eyes, but didn't have time to do more than that as the weapon lay completely apart on the table in front of him.

He glanced up at Grayson who then clicked the watch again and he began to assemble the weapon once more. The reconstruction of the weapon seemed to go faster, and he put the last piece into place, setting the gun to his shoulder and pulled the trigger with an empty click, which Grayson followed with the stopwatch clicking off.

Grayson walked over to Swanson, showing her the times on the watch. She stared with disbelief and excitement at Grayson.

Swanson followed Grayson back to the cabinet and they each chose a new weapon and placed it in front of Cali and Josh. With stop watches in hand, they witnessed, with undeniable delight, as their students mastered the task before them.

After the weapons case sat empty and all the guns lay assembled on the table before the teens, Grayson and Swanson sat down with a sigh.

The Josh and Cali glanced at each other, proud of the accomplishments of the evening.

Cali slowly raised her hand and sat there until Grayson noticed.

"Yes Cali, what is it?"

"How did we do that?" She asked.

"Part of your genetic makeup," he said.

"You have genes allowing you to learn massive amounts of information and retain it for long periods of time," Ms. Swanson answered, giving Grayson an exacerbated look. "This is what we were hoping for when we..." she hesitated.

"Designed us?" Josh finished.

"It sounds so impersonal when you say it like that," Swanson said.

"But that's exactly what it is," Cali said.

"Fine, if you want to look at it like that," Grayson said standing, his arms flailing in the air. "We are the big bad government conspiracy taking over and ruining your precious lives. Is that what you want to hear?"

"Dude, tell us why we should see it differently," Josh countered.

"It *is* different, Josh, *very* different" Swanson reasoned.

"If we're supposed to be so smart now and can comprehend anything you put in front of us, then maybe you should explain why it's different," Cali suggested.

"Very well," Grayson said picking up the remote once more and dimming the lights. The white board lit up with images of the World Trade Center Towers. The footage surprised the teens. Instead of the now infamous coverage of the 911 bombings and subsequent collapse of the World Trade Center in 2000, they saw footage of people being evacuated from the basement of one of the buildings and then discovery film of the damage done in the lower parking garage.

The lights came up and Grayson looked at each of them.

"Josh," Grayson said. "You seem confused by what you just saw."

"I expected to see the towers collapse," Josh admitted.

"That's the problem with today's society," Grayson said, disgust in his voice, "memory is so short. It only goes back to the biggest events. Never mind the towers were bombed nearly seven years earlier for the first time. We knew after that first attack, this would be a long fought battle between terrorism and our homeland security. We were not prepared for that first bombing. We had information warning about it in November of

1992, but couldn't or didn't do anything to stop it when it actually took place in February of 1993."

"But we were born September 7, 1993. If the bombing happened in February 1993, that would only be seven months before our birth," Cali pointed out.

"That is correct," Grayson admitted.

"We had intelligence reports years before events escalated to this point" Swanson said. "We knew we had to do something, to try something, and increase our chances to be proactive instead of reactive. We began your program, and you were conceived in November, shortly after this plot first came to light."

"You have the unique opportunity to help make your country a safer place for generations to come," Grayson told them.

"Why wouldn't you get, like, real marine, or seals, or covert ops?" Josh asked.

"Because we couldn't be certain they would have the complete skill set we need to do this job," Swanson explained. "We're not just a covert operation or a special forces operation. What we want is a unit that can gather information, interpret that information, and react to either prevent the threat, or eliminate that threat. We are crossing boundaries currently separating the CIA, FBI, Special Forces, and Covert Operations. We will answer only to the President of the United States."

"You mean the President will be deciding every mission we take on?" Cali asked with distaste.

"No," Grayson turned to her. "He will be the only person we need to give any reason for our actions after we have taken them. He is the only one who knows of our existence except for those in the unit. I have briefed the President before contacting you yesterday and he is confident you will be up to the challenge."

The teens sat in silence, each deep in thought, staring straight ahead. Josh felt a sense of pride, but something else bubbled to the surface. It felt like that piece of corn stuck between your teeth after eating corn-on-the-cob, the butter dripping down your chin. He didn't like the feeling.

"What about our parents and friends?" Josh asked. All heads swiveled to him in unison.

"What do you mean, Josh?" Swanson asked frowning.

"Our parents obviously know about the unit, but do they know about our mission?"

"They only know you will be fighting domestic terrorism. That is all," Grayson said. "You're not allowed to tell them what you've been doing or where you've been or where you're going. They agreed to the level of secrecy required for this program."

"Our friends are going to wonder what's up, aren't they," Josh asked.

"That's one of the reasons you moved here from where you grew up," Swanson explained. "You and Cali have already removed the closeness of those friends with distance, and you will be able to keep them from wondering too much. Unfortunately, Sydney's and Tal's parents didn't abide by that request and now there will be questions from their group of friends. However, Sydney is somewhat of a loner and Tal is involved with his Goth friends who will allow him his secrecy."

"What about boyfriends or girlfriends," Cali asked.

"Of course we're not going to forbid that you date," Swanson told her. "It's normal at your age."

"But we highly discourage you getting into anything too intimate," Grayson interrupted. "The more you get involved with outsiders, the greater the risk of security breech."

A heavy silence hung over the room as Cali and Josh absorbed their new reality. They were in the service of their country now.

"What if we decide we don't want this?" Cali asked.

"We explained that" Grayson pointed out. "We cannot allow you to wander around with your new abilities and knowledge. If any of you choose not to participate, the contract your parents signed before your conception would be considered in default and they would be detained until you do decide to participate. You would be detained in a high security prison for military criminals until such time you choose to fulfill your part of your parent's agreement."

"Listen," Swanson said stepping up to the table with her hands held out before her in a calming motion, "We understand you are not robots. We need your abilities to think on your own and interpret situations with the human factor. Many of your missions will include interacting with others in order to gain their trust and gather information. We want you to be who you are, but we need you to be who we have created also. We have to work together in order to fulfill our missions to keep our country safe. With the wars, our military and intelligence community is stretched thin. We need to fill in some of the gaps that have been created."

"Why here?" Josh spoke up. "Why in nowhere Minnesota?"

"This is a very isolated base which gives us the secrecy we need," Grayson said. "It's also located in a very strategic location with respect to the Canadian border and our coastal boarders. We can get to the Canadian border, East or West coasts within hours, which is crucial. Fast response is crucial. We have many more military facilities in the southern United States covering the southern boarders.

"Enough discussion," he redirected. "We need to get some physical training underway now that we know you're up to the mental requirements. The locker rooms are down the hall. Grab the gear laid out and meet me topside in ten." He spun and left the room without another word.

"Let me know if you need to talk more about this," Ms. Swanson told them and then followed after Grayson.

"I guess we're stuck," Josh said getting to his feet and stretching his hands above his head.

****

Cali and Josh wandered down the hall, finding what Grayson referred to as locker rooms. Josh watched Cali go into hers, and he went to change in his.

They rode the elevator together to the main hanger and began their physical training procedures. The teen's extra-exceptional strength and extreme speed soon became apparent. Cali and Josh exceeded all previous recorded records for the drills while barely breaking a sweat. Neither pushed hard, letting the natural flow of their newfound strengths come naturally.

Swanson and Grayson beamed as they witnessed the times and weights each had achieved. The lack of fatigue proved the most noticeable commonality between the teens. They performed the physical training at the highest level, but never seemed winded, or tired.

Grayson called them over next to the suburban.

"Great work," a rare smile crossed his face. "We will continue with Seal training tomorrow and proceed with ranger, delta recon, and the rest until we finish up. Attend school as before but try not to make your relationships too obvious. Let some days go by before you associate with each other all the time.

We will meet in the classroom again tomorrow with Sydney and cover some of the CIA covert operations procedures."

They climbed into the suburban, proceeding off the base, and headed home.

Josh held Cali's hand in the concealing darkness of the back seat as they stared straight ahead. They pulled in front of Cali's home, Josh gave her hand one last squeeze, and she hopped out, looking back with a smile before shutting the door.

Josh, Grayson, and Swanson rode the short distance to the Taylor home in silence until Josh opened the door after the vehicle stopped in his driveway. As the interior lights blinked on, Grayson and Swanson turned to him in the back.

"Josh," Swanson began, "I hope you understand how a relationship between you and Cali will become very complicated for the unit and for the two of you."

Josh froze, staring at them dumbfounded.

"Did this begin after you found out about your special abilities?" Grayson questioned.

"No," Josh shook his head. "It happened the day before my birthday," he said.

"You should end it now if you can," Grayson cut him off, "before you get too attached."

Grayson's and Swanson's face showed concern mixed with fear.

Rage surged through Josh. His eyes narrowed to slits and his lips thinned as he fought back his initial outrage.

"What we are trying to say and not having much luck relaying it the way we would like," Swanson stumbled, "is the more you care for Cali, the harder it will be for you to concentrate on your missions. You'll worry about her safety, and it may influence your judgment in certain situations."

"That's bogus, we haven't had a mission yet," Josh said.

"We know, but we've seen this happen before, with other units," Grayson explained.

"You've never dealt with any unit like ours," Josh shot back. "Maybe you should let this run its course before you tell me to stop caring for the only person that matters since my mother died."

"Fair enough," Swanson nodded, giving Grayson a warning look.

Grayson hesitated, his mouth open to respond, and then snapped it shut.

"Good," Josh said as he slipped out the door and shut it behind him.

"We were in dangerous territory there," Swanson told Grayson as they watched Josh walk up the steps to the porch and into the house.

"He's just a kid," Grayson shrugged.

"Are you forgetting what that 'kid' did in training tonight?" Swanson reminded him.

"Oh," Grayson nodded, "Oh," he added as his eyes grew wide.

"That's right," she sighed. "He might've killed us, just for suggesting he shouldn't see Cali and we couldn't have done anything to stop him. Even armed, I doubt it would've helped."

"I think I could defend..., surely you could have...," Grayson started, but stopped, staring out the window at the Taylor house. Looking back at Swanson, she sat deathly white.

"We have to remember, they're weapons. If we cross them, it may be the last thing we do. We walk that fine line between guiding them and staying in control. If we lose either, we may lose the little influence we might have. I'd rather diffuse an IED." She turned away, looking out the passenger window as they backed out of the drive and drove back to the base.

Chapter 12

Josh stood next to Cali digging in her locker the next morning at school as Sydney came running up. She lifted Josh into the air, grinning from ear to ear and spinning around.

"Put me down, people might see," Josh whispered.

Sydney set him down, laughing as she turned and hugged Cali.

"So I assume you're excited it's your birthday?" Cali said raising an eyebrow.

"It's awesome," Sydney laughed. "I woke up this morning and looked in the mirror. Feel my six-pack," she said taking Cali's hand and placing on her stomach.

Cali nodded, feigning a shock and amazement.

"Ok, fine. I'm psyched, that's all," Sydney pushed Cali's hand away.

"I'll feel your six-pack, Sydney," Josh grinned, reaching for her stomach.

"Oh, no you don't," Cali took hold of his arm. "Sorry Sydney.

"That's ok," Sydney nodded.

"Hey, no its not," Josh shook his head until he saw the expression on Cali's face. "Yes it is," he nodded.

A boy passed in the hall, slowing to look at Sydney. Sydney looked over her shoulder as they smiled at each other. The boy walked into an open locker door, too busy staring at Sydney to notice he had veered into the lockers on the other side of the hall. He collided with a bang, but jumped quickly to his feet, looked back at Sydney as he blushed and hurried away.

"I've liked that boy for nearly a year, and this is the first time he even looked at me," Sydney giggled. "I can get used to this.

"Did they tell you who the last member of the team is?" Sydney asked.

Josh and Cali made eye contact and then turned back to her. "Tal," Cali said.

"I was afraid of that," Sydney sighed. "He isn't going to take this well."

"Do you think we should warn him?" Josh asked.

"He hangs out in the music rooms before first period," Sydney told them. "We can tell him there."

"He's into music?" Cali questioned.

"Not like that," Sydney laughed, realizing what she implied. "He listens to his music. They have an awesome sound system and Tal gets along with Mr. Hagen, the music teacher."

"Oh," Cali nodded.

"We better hurry, we don't want to be late for history," Josh informed them.

The three hurried down the hall to the music department and stopped next to a door with a small glass window. Josh peered inside and nodded, he saw Tal inside. He opened the door and Sydney stepped into the room, Cali and Josh close behind.

Tal sat with headphones on, his eyes closed, his black trench coat rapped around him, deep into the music playing from the stereo.

Once the door closed behind them, Sydney tapped Tal's shoulder and the boy jumped with a start.

"Holy shit," Tal exclaimed, a hand against his chest and the racing heart beneath.

"Sorry," Sydney shrugged.

"What are you doing here?" he asked turning the stereo off. "And what are they doing here?"

"Dude, we need to tell you something and hopefully you won't freak out," Josh began.

"Well, dude, I don't think you could freak me out, but give it a shot," Tal glared.

"Tal, really, we need to tell you something and you need to be serious here," Sydney said.

"Fine, little Syd, what's on your mind?" Tal leaned back and crossed his arms over his chest.

"What we are here to tell you will sound kind of...unbelievable," Cali began as the boy turned his dark brown eyes traced with eyeliner to her.

"Shoot, new girl," Tal pressed.

"Something is going to happen to you tonight that all of us have been through in the last three days," Cali continued.

"Dudes, how long are you going to take to tell him," Josh sighed and turned to Tal. "Dude, you, along with the three of us, are genetically engineered by the CIA to be super special ops and tonight they will inject you with a drug that let those traits come through." Josh blurted out.

Tal looked at Josh as if he had three heads and then began to laugh. "You had me going until the covert op thing, man," Tal laughed, tears rolling down his cheeks.

"No, it's true," Sydney tried.

"Who put you up to this?" Tal asked Sydney.

"No one, Tal," she argued. "I *am* one of them. I changed last night."

Tal laughed again, but his laughter slowed as he realized they weren't laughing. "You guys are serious?"

"Yeah, we are," Cali nodded, Sydney and Josh joining in.

"So when is this crap supposed to happen? Tonight?"

"Two CIA agents will come to you tonight and inject you with the drug to make the change," Cali explained.

"My folks aren't going to let that happen," Tal said.

"Dude, your folks are in on it. They signed us up for this," Josh explained.

"It's true," Sydney said when Tal turned to her. "All of our parents couldn't have children and nearly gave up when the CIA approached them to have an experimental procedure done to assure pregnancy. None of them knew until after we were born what we were. They never imagined what would be expected of us on our sixteenth birthday."

Josh and Cali stared at Sydney in shock.

"What? My mom and dad filled me in this morning," Sydney shrugged.

The three looked back at Tal as his head slunk down in his hands as his elbows rested on his knees.

"I can't do this," Tal said. "No way am I doing this."

"Then you and your folks are going to Gitmo," Josh informed him.

"Guantanamo Bay?" Tal looked incredulous.

"That's the one," Josh nodded.

The tone rang over the intercom announcing the first period's approach. All four looked at each other with a start.

"We will make them bring us with tonight, so you won't have to do this alone," Sydney comforted.

"Yeah, right," Tal said, getting to his feet. "I got to go." He walked out without looking at any of them.

"That went well," Cali sighed.

"It is hard on all of us, give him some time to absorb it," Josh suggested.

"I don't think time is going to change Tal's opinion on this," Sydney grimaced.

"We better go too," Cali said, and they headed to class.

Tal, Josh, and Cali shared the first period history class and Tal spent the entire time with his head down on his desk. He bolted for the door when the tone ending the period sounded and left Cali and Josh staring after him.

The next time they spotted him he leaned with his elbow on the table at lunch, his hand supporting his head, staring off into space.

Sydney joined Josh and Cali at the table and ate in silence as they stared over at the Goth table and Tal. Each could feel the anxiety coming from the soon to be newest member of their team and the lack of choice he had in the matter.

"Like I told you before," Sydney pointed out, "Tal has siblings, and he could never send his parents to prison by not going along with Grayson and Swanson. No matter how much he hates his parents for doing this to him, he couldn't do anything to hurt his brothers or sisters."

"I wonder when they're going to change him?" Cali said.

"Hard to tell, they are really anxious to get Sydney up to speed, it could be later tonight, after some training," Josh surmised.

Lunch ended far too soon and the three went to different classes.

"Meet out front after school," Josh told them. "There's something we need to do." He turned and headed for class.

Josh had two more classes with Tal, and he reacted to him in the same manner. Josh waited outside after school for Cali and Sydney, Tal walked right past him, even after Josh spoke to him, asking him to stop. Tal ignored him completely.

Josh watched as Tal walked down the sidewalk, anxiously looking back at the school entrance, waiting for Cali and Sydney to join him. Tal reached about a block away and Josh contemplated following him without the girls, but they came out the door and Josh rushed up to them.

"I think we should follow Tal to make sure he's ok," Josh told them and headed for his car. The girls hurried after, hopping into the car as they raced down the street after Tal.

"Why are you so worried about Tal?" asked Sydney. "You don't think he would do anything stupid?"

Josh only glanced back at her.

"You think he might try to kill himself?" Cali asked as she leaned slightly ahead so she could see his face. The look on his face scared her.

"He doesn't want to do this. His parents have other kids, so he won't let them go to prison, separating them from his brother and sisters. The only way he can get out of this and keep his parents from prison, is by removing himself from the equations, thus eliminating the danger his parents are in." Josh's voice sounded logical, non-accusing.

They saw Tal enter their modest home on the corner, painted a calm green with white shutters. The porch's white trimmed rails and posts, inviting to visitors.

Josh pulled up and they hurried out of the car and walked up the porch. Josh knocked on the door. They waited a moment and the door opened, Tal standing there, hands on his hips and disgust on his face.

"What are you doing here?" he asked.

"Can we talk to you?" Josh said.

Tal stepped onto the porch, closing the door behind him. "About what?" he said, striding over to lean against the white handrail of the porch.

Cali, Sydney, and Josh exchanged uncertain glances. Sydney took a step closer.

"We're worried about you. You haven't been yourself lately." She said touching one of his arms folded across his chest.

"We?" he said pulling away. "You're the only one who knows me at all. I'm ok." He shrugged.

"All three of us are concerned you might do something..." she hesitated, looking up at him, her eyes filled with empathy.

"Something what," Tal shot back, "something stupid?"

"Not stupid under the circumstances," Cali said, moving next to Sydney.

"You don't have to worry about me," Tal stood up straighter. "I'm not stupid."

"That isn't why we're concerned," Josh walked over. "We're afraid you figured out a way to avoid doing this. A way your mother and father won't have to go to prison leaving your brother and sisters alone."

Tal shot Josh a venomous look. "Don't worry your sun-bleached head about it California boy. It's my business and I'll handle it."

"But Tal," Sydney pleaded. "We're in this together. We can do this together. You're not alone in this."

"I got to go," he said pushing between them to the door. "Besides, someone is looking for their mutants." He gestured with a nod of his head and the others turned, looking at the road as the dark suburban pulled up. "Go be good little soldiers," he sneered and walked inside, slamming the door behind him.

Chapter 13

They exchanged nervous looks, walking down the porch steps and up to the vehicle. The window rolled down on the passenger side and Ms. Swanson smiled at them.

"How is everything? Did the change go ok, Sydney? What's up with Tal, you didn't tell him anything, did you?"

Cali, Josh, and Sydney looked back and forth to each other until Sydney turned to Swanson.

"Fine, everything went fine. I feel great and ready to go. Tal is a friend, we just dropped by for a visit." She lied.

"You'll have plenty of time together after tonight," Grayson said from the driver's seat. "Hop in and let's get going. We've a lot of training to get done tonight."

Josh opened the back door for the girls to slide in, pausing to look back at the house uncertainly, and then stepped in, closing the door behind him. The suburban sped away towards the air base and the next stage of their training.

The three teens went into the locker rooms, changed into their fatigues, and then rode the elevator back up to the hanger where a repelling wall and other obstacles were assembled.

Going through their paces without a hitch, they laughed and joked about how easy it seemed. They moved from one drill to another without a break and then waited for Grayson and Swanson to decide what they should do next, since they completed all the training planned for the night.

They took the elevator back down to the classrooms and read more intelligence material and allowed Sydney to catch up on the material they covered the night before. They briefed her on their mission and the need to speed up the training in order to infiltrate the elite private school of Chatterly.

A soft buzzing brought all eyes on Sydney as she read over classified documents. Blushing, she pulled her cell phone from a pocket of her fatigues.

Staring down at it for a moment, she flashed a worried look to Cali and Josh.

"You're not to have cell phones with you while you are here," Grayson reprimanded. "Hand it over," he said, approaching her with his hand out.

"We have to go," Josh said, stopping the man in his tracks.

"What?" Grayson said.

"We have to go," Josh stated again, adding, "Now," looking at Sydney's panicked expression.

"You leave when Ms. Swanson and I tell you, you can leave and not a moment before." Grayson stood in front of Josh, his hands folded across his chest.

"Sir," Josh said, looking up at him. "We need to leave right now; it's a matter of life and death."

Grayson began to argue as Josh came to his feet, motioning for the girls to follow.

Grayson stepped into his path as Josh came up to him, staring him down.

"Mr. Grayson," Ms. Swanson said, walking up beside him. "Let's not do something we will regret later," she touched his shoulder.

Grayson turned slightly, looking at her and the three teens slipped past them, heading out the door in an instant. Grayson and Swanson ran after them, but the elevator doors closed as they ran up. Slamming his fist against the door, Grayson spun on Swanson. "Why the hell did you do that? Now they think they can take off anytime they get a call. That is no way to breed respect for authority."

"We couldn't stop them," Ms. Swanson explained. "You still can't read body language very well, can you? They were going, no matter what. Would you rather have them throw you out of the way or walk around you? For me, the respect can still be maintained as long as we don't put them in the position to choose between doing what we want and what they feel is right."

"They are soldiers," Grayson argued. "They need to follow orders."

"They're sixteen years old and need to go to the aid of a friend," Swanson corrected.

"Friend? What friend?"

"Tal. They went to help Tal."

"How do you know that?" Grayson looked at her suspiciously.

She smiled devilishly, showing him the device in her hand she held at her side. "The text came in from Tal's cell phone," she showed him the display identifying the number and caller. "This intercepts any incoming or outgoing communications so I can be sure none of them were texting the outside world without our knowledge."

"They know that isn't allowed," Grayson threw up his arms in disgust.

"Don't you remember when you were sixteen? Just because it isn't allowed, doesn't mean they're not going to do it. They'll just try harder not to get caught." She shrugged.

The keys were in the suburban and Josh hopped behind the wheel as Cali climbed in the front seat and Sydney jumped into the back.

Josh grinned, starting the engine and gunned it, pushing the girl's heads back against their seats and squealing the tires. They rocketed out the hanger and through the gates, spinning out as they turned onto the main road, Josh turning the wheel to keep them going in a straight line.

"What did Tal's text say?" Cali asked turning to look at Sydney in the back seat.

"He's sorry, but he can't face this. It's better to end it before it begins." Tears welled up in Sydney's eyes. "Take a right here, its quicker," she pointed between the seats as Josh squealed around the corner.

The buzzing sound came from Sydney's phone again as she received another message. "It's Tal again. He took some pills and says goodbye."

"Many people saved after a suicide attempt claim they regretted doing it after wards." Cali said.

Josh and Sydney stared at her dumbfounded.

"What?" She shrugged. "I did a paper last year on it. He's probably regretting it and we need to be there to save him."

The black suburban screeched to a stop and the three teens raced into the house without stopping. Sydney led the way up to Tal's room where his mother pounded frantically on the door.

"He won't come out," she cried. "I called his father, but he's still ten minutes away." Sydney grabbed the handle, finding it locked, she took a step back and then shouldered the door open, racing inside. Tal lay half on the bed and the floor, his cell phone just out of reach of his hand on the bed. Pills and empty bottles were all around him.

Sydney slid to a stop on her knees next to Tal, taking him by the shoulders and shaking him. Tal's head lolled to one side as his eyes were rolled back and the whites of his eyes showed between his lids. "Tal, Tal, wake up. It's Sid, wake up." Her shaking didn't get any reaction from Tal as his head hung heavily on his neck, drooping forward and then backward.

"Stand him up," Josh motioned to the girls. "Hold him up between you and watch your feet," he added as they steadied Tal between them.

Mrs. Vang stood just inside the door sobbing.

Josh took a hold of Tal's chin, forcing his mouth open as he held Tal's head steady by his spiky hair. Josh reached down the boy's throat with a finger, pushing it all the way to his third knuckle. Tal's body lurched and Josh withdrew his finger, leaning Tal's head forward and stepping to the side.

Vomit erupted out of Tal, spraying everywhere as bile and pill remnants spewed across the room and floor. When he had stopped, Josh stepped in front once more; ignoring the disgusting mess he now stood in and forced his finger down Tal's throat again. Stepping aside, Tal blew chunks again as Josh held his head forward. Once more Tal stopped and once more Josh repeated the maneuver. Josh continued until nothing more came out of the teen and he dry-heaved two consecutive times.

Tal's breathed weakly and his face remained absent of color. The girls carefully laid him onto the bed, looking to Josh. It appeared they had arrived too late as Tal's rising and falling chest became shallower.

Cali and Sydney began to cry with Mrs. Vang as Josh's eyes watered as he realized he could do no more.

The screech of tires came from outside and footsteps rushed up the stairs. Swanson and Grayson burst into the room, Swanson holding the identifiable syringe in her right hand. Grayson shouldered past everyone to get to the bed and past their shocked expressions as Swanson deftly applied the drug into Tal's arm.

Tal arched his back coming off the bed and his mouth open in a silent scream. He thrashed back and forth several times and then went limp. His chest began to rise and fall steadily, and his coloring came back to his face.

"Outside," Grayson said to the teens. "Now!"

Josh, Cali, and Sydney exchanged grimaces as they braced for an angry exchange. They reluctantly walked down the stairs and out onto the porch where Mr. Grayson sat on the edge of the rail waiting.

As they exited the house, he motioned for them to sit on a bench against the house as Ms. Swanson came and stood next to him at the rail. The teens kept their eyes on the porch floor, not looking at the man before them.

"It's been quite the night," Grayson started, glancing over at Swanson. "We're a team here, and I hope you come to accept Ms. Swanson and myself as part of that team. We're not the enemy."

Josh, Cali, and Sydney glanced to one another with their heads still bowed so the adults couldn't see their faces.

"What you did for Tal tonight is commendable and exactly the behavior a team should take when one of their own is in peril," Swanson added.

"That's right," Grayson agreed. "If you told us, we would've been right beside you, but you need to trust we are going to look out for your wellbeing above all else."

The teen's heads came up in unison as they studied Grayson and Swanson. Josh stared long and hard before relaxing his flexed jaw. With a slight nod, Josh acknowledged Grayson's point.

"We don't like the fact we're being forced to be in this unit. Holding our parent's freedom hostage isn't a way to gaining our trust. Tal felt he had no other choice. Killing himself would free his family from your control."

"Until all of you see the good you'll be doing, not only for your country, but for innocent people who would otherwise have no one to defend them, it's the only way," Swanson said, sweeping her arms around as she spoke.

"Still," Cali spoke up, "we don't like being used as puppets and Tal took that feeling to the nth degree."

"We'll keep an eye on Tal, and have him speak to a professional on staff," Swanson told her. "Once you realize the magnitude of what is before you, it won't get any easier, so we have to keep moving forward until you all see the truth."

"And if we always think this is bogus?" Josh asked.

"We're sorry, but the work you need to do is far too important to push aside. This is your life now, best you accept it," Grayson said.

"Can we check on Tal?" asked Sydney.

"Be sure to bring him with when you come to the base right after school," Ms. Swanson said.

"And don't let anyone follow you," Grayson added, pushing off the porch rail and walking down the steps to the SUV, doors still standing open.

The teens raced back upstairs to find Mrs. Vang still crying over Tal as he lay on the bed.

Cali, Sydney, and Mrs. Vang pulled back the covers of his bed and slid Tal in, sitting on either side of him as Josh finished up the last bit of the cleanup by tossing the empty bottles into the garbage.

"Mrs. Vang, if you could get us something to drink, we'll stay with Tal until you come back," Sydney said ushering the woman from the room and closing the door behind her.

Tal began waking up and he yawned, reaching up to stretch his arms over his head, striking the headboard. He opened his eyes and the hint of a smile on his face disappeared as he saw Sydney, Cali and then Josh at the end his bed.

"What the hell are you doing here?" he said sitting up. Realization spread across his startled features, and he lay back down. "Right, I took some pills, but how?" He looked up at Sydney.

"You texted and we rushed here. We found your mother outside the door, terrified, and you passed out with a bunch of pill bottles around you. Josh saved your life by forcing you to vomit out the pills and then they injected you with the drug."

Tal looked to Josh, Cali and then back to Sydney. "Pretty stupid of me, but I can't be a part of this."

"Do you think any of us would choose to do this?" Cali asked. "The way the government handled relations with people of Middle Eastern descent disgusts me. But they're not leaving us any choice. Besides, do you know what our first mission is going to be?"

Tal looked up at her, ashamed, and shook his head.

"We're going to go undercover at a school where diplomats and dignitaries send their kids. There is an imminent threat against the school. We're going in to try and stop it before it happens."

Tal looked at Sydney, not certain he believed Cali.

"It's true," she nodded.

"Dude, we aren't saying everything is going to be agreeable, but if we can save the lives of innocent people, then I 'm all for it," Josh told him.

"But rich kids?" Tal grimaced.

"They can't choose their parents any more than we could," Cali pointed out.

"I can relate to that," Sydney frowned and then began to laugh.

They all joined in, and it died off as Tal looked to each of them. "I guess we can't choose our genetically engineered brothers or sisters either."

"Hey, I wouldn't have chosen you either, dude," Josh shot back.

Someone cleared their throat at the door, and they turned to see Mr. Grayson and Ms. Swanson standing there.

"We thought you left?" Cali questioned.

"We did, but then we forgot that Josh's dad stopped by and picked up his car," Grayson explained.

"We also needed to introduce ourselves to Tal," Ms. Swanson added.

"I know who you are," Tal said. "My parents filled me in."

"Good," Grayson nodded. "Now I need to fill you in. If you kill yourself or get yourself killed in a way we feel is intentional, your parents will still be going to prison. That goes for all of you. Do we understand each other?"

"Perfectly," Tal sneered as the others nodded helplessly.

"Now that we have that cleared up, shall we get you three home?" Grayson asked as he headed for the door as Swanson moved beside Tal and began to check his condition.

The teens gave a look to Tal and followed Grayson out to the suburban and climbed inside. They dropped off Sydney, Cali, and then pulled up in front of Josh's house.

As Josh began to get out of the front seat, Grayson reached over, taking a firm hold on his arm between the wrist and elbow. Josh stopped surprised, looking back at the man.

"Don't ever disrespect my authority in front of the others again," he warned. "We can have our discussions and disagreements, but never in front of the others."

They exchanged a look for a moment, and then Josh nodded he understood. Grayson released his arm. "Have a good night, Josh."

"Good night, Sir," Josh said, shutting the door.

Grayson sat in the drive watching as Josh walked up the steps onto the porch and then went inside. The boy paused inside the door, looking out, until finally the suburban pulled away. He turned to head upstairs but nearly jumped out of his skin as his father sat on the stairs watching him.

Josh stood catching his breath with his hand on his chest feeling his racing heart.

"Sorry, I didn't meant to frighten you," his dad said softly.

"Dude, you nearly scared me to death," Josh said with an airy voice.

"Is everything ok?"

"Yeah, fine." Josh began walking past his dad up the stairs.

"Josh," Kevin stood up, placing a hand on his shoulder. Josh turned as they stood the same height looking eye to eye.

"I still worry about you," Kevin began as Josh rolled his eyes. "I know you can take care of yourself, especially now, but I need to know you're ok and would like it if you confided in me those things that you can. Maybe I can help you cope with some of the pressure on you."

"Dad, I don't think..." Josh began, but Kevin interrupted.

"You still have sixteen year old emotions and feelings, son. Just because you're stronger, faster ..."

"Smarter, can read faster and retain more information and recall it instantly," Josh added.

Kevin's jaw dropped. "That too?"

Josh nodded with a shrug.

"Still, the emotional things haven't changed inside, and you may need to discuss your feelings about certain subjects."

"Grayson says they have a psychologist on staff for that," Josh told him.

"Still," Kevin said forcefully, "I'm here to help wherever or whenever I can. I don't want to lose the connection we can still have here." Tears filled his eyes as he fought to stay composed. "I love you son and want to be a part of your life. You're all I have left in this world."

Josh reached around and gave his father a tight hug. "I love you too, dad, and I'm going to make you and mom proud."

Josh leaned back, giving his dad a smile. "Goodnight dad," he said and walked up the stairs.

"Good night Josh," Kevin said. "We're always proud of you," he said softly, turning and walking into the kitchen.

Chapter 14

Josh drug himself out of bed, the alarm going off far too soon. He ran the events of the last few days through in his mind, shaking his head at the absurdity of this entire situation.

He gathered his backpack and drove over to Cali's house, waiting patiently as she came out.

Cali smiled upon seeing him and skipped up to give him a hug. They turned together and walked to the car, shining in the early morning sunlight. They drove down the street where Sydney waited at the corner for them. They greeted her as she hopped into the back seat past Cali. They rode without a word until they got closer to school.

A dark figure stood leaning against a large oak, black boots, a black trench coat topped off by long black hair highlighted with purple. Josh stopped when the car reached the tree.

"Morning Tal," Sydney greeted, leaning out the window.

Tal gave a nod and a smile as he stood pulled away from the tree and walked up to the car. Cali opened the door, slipping into the back seat with Sydney, leaving the front open for the larger boy. Tal stepped in and closed the door, giving Josh a nod. Josh put the car in gear and eased away from the curb. They rode silently, not wanting to disrupt the uneasy balance that existed, at least for that moment.

"You guys ready for the test today?" Tal finally spoke up. Cali and Josh only had one class with Tal, first period history.

Josh and Cali stared at Tal in shock.

"Oh my God," Cali exclaimed, looking wide eyed at Josh.

"I forgot all about it too," Josh cried out.

"What are you guys so worried about?" Sydney said, looking back and forth between them as Tal grinned. "Just read the material before class. You'll remember everything you read, just like in training."

Josh glanced over his shoulder at Cali who shared his sigh of relief. They forgot how their new abilities changed their everyday life. Smiling, Josh gunned the Challenger as it squealed down the road, into the school parking lot.

Once they were in the classroom, Josh and Cali raced through the material, sitting with relieved smiles on their faces, a few minutes to spare.

The teacher handed out the tests and Josh, Cali, and Tal handed them back in only ten minutes. The teacher looked at each of them, then at the clock and then at the tests. As he read the answers, his eyes went wide, and jaw dropped. He looked up suspiciously at the three. Tal's sat away from the other two, and the teacher frowned, deciding how they had all cheated and what to do next.

At this moment, Josh realized the need to pace. Otherwise they would soon draw a great deal of suspicion. He glanced to Cali and saw she had surmised the same thing.

She looked at him and shrugged.

Tal didn't have any of it, beaming like a peacock as he looked around at the other students. He gave Josh and Cali thumbs up when he saw them looking at him and continued gazing around the room.

The four classmates were riding home after school when the now familiar black suburban pulled up next to them. The window on the passenger side rolled down to reveal a smiling Ms. Swanson.

"Please follow us, we have things to do."

Josh did a U-turn and followed the suburban back to his house where it pulled up front along the street and he pulled his car into the garage.

They all climbed out and hurried out to the street and the waiting vehicle as the garage door closed behind them.

The teens climbed in, acknowledging Mr. Grayson with a nod as he stared over his shoulder. Cali and Sydney climbed into the third seat as the boys slid in the middle row of seating. As they buckled up, the suburban rocketed down the road, sending the passengers sliding across the leather seats.

"Hey, hey," Cali protested from the rear trying to find her seat belt latch.

"What's the hurry?" Josh asked, clicking his belt into place.

"We fear the timeline for the plot is being moved up and we need to get you up to speed now the unit is complete," Ms. Swanson explained, hanging onto the handle over her door with both hands and looking back at them.

"It's time to put up or shut up," Grayson added, whipping the wheel around as they skidded onto the deserted base and through the open gates. "We've notified your parent to inform the school you will be gone for an extended period due to possible H1N1 virus infection. That will give us a couple of weeks excuse for now."

The vehicle screeched to a halt in the large hanger and the two adults jumped out as the others struggled to unbuckle and extract from the suburban after the jostling stop.

Tal looked curiously around, taking in the facilities for the first time, but Ms. Swanson took him by the arm and guided him to the elevator now rising above the hanger floor. Tal stared, mouth agape as the shining silver doors opened to admit them. The others walked right in, turning to see the boy frozen there.

"Come on, Tal," Sydney urged.

"You might not have heard me correctly," Grayson said. "We need to prepare you for this mission quickly. We ship out in the morning. Now, get in the elevator."

"What about our parents?" Sydney said what everyone thought. "Can't we even say goodbye?"

"We're sorry about that," Swanson said looking straight ahead as the doors closed. "Time is of the essence and every minute we delay could mean more casualties near the end."

"Get used to it," Grayson told them. "This will happen a lot and all of you need to come to terms with it, period."

Josh exchanged helpless looks with the other teens as they rode the elevator down in stunned silence.

"Get into your fatigues and meet in the classroom," Grayson ordered. "Taylor, show Tal the way." He stepped out of the elevator and strode off down the hallway without another look.

Swanson shrugged apologetically as she paused and then strode after him.

They looked at each other, hesitating, before Josh and Cali stepped out of the elevator, requiring Sydney and Tal to hurry in order to stay with them. Cali and Sydney turned into the first locker room while Josh led Tal into the next. The enormous locker room freaked Josh out as the automatic lighting came on in waves all the way to the back where the showers were located. He stopped by the first set of lockers where his name marked one locker and Tal's name marked another.

Josh motioned with his hand to the locker, "This is it." He smiled uneasily. "The gear will be a perfect fit and I'll wait for you to go to the classroom." Josh turned and began changing into the army issue, light brown fatigues.

Tal hesitated for a moment; his brow furrowed over his brooding brown eyes and then began to change. He shook his head as he pulled his clothing off.

114

Josh paused to look at him.

Tal glanced up, noticing Josh's curious stare. "I never thought this is where I would be on my sixteenth birthday, that's all," Tal sighed.

"All of us have been through what you're going through. None of us would have chosen this, but we've learned to accept this on our own terms, and you will as well." Josh pulled his pants down and then sat to draw them off over his feet.

"I'll do it, for my parents, but I didn't say I'd like it."

"I understand," Josh smirked as he stood, hung his pants in the locker, and took the brown pants, sliding them on.

"So, how are we going to be ready to leave by morning?" Tal asked, pulling the shirt over his head, and sliding his arms into the sleeves.

"You'll see," Josh grinned.

"Come on," Tal protested.

"We learn and remember things very quickly. Cali and I are slightly ahead of you and Sydney, but you'll be able to catch up tonight if we go all night like Grayson suggests."

Tal stared at him, incredulously.

"No, I'm not shitting you. We'll be ready to go if the information is available for us to learn."

Tal shook his head as he pulled his shoes on and then followed Josh out of the locker room. They walked down the hall and through an open doorway where Cali and Sydney sat waiting with Swanson and Grayson at the front.

"Bout time," Grayson griped. "You girls done gossiping so we can get rolling?"

"Hey," Sydney complained.

"We were here on time," Cali added.

"Sorry ladies," Grayson nodded. "Old habits."

Josh sat next to Cali as Tal slid over by Sydney. They looked to Grayson, and he began to fill them in on their mission.

"Word came in today. Within the next week, the terrorist plot to take a school hostage demanding the release of prisoners at Guantanamo will become a reality. We need to get you up to speed and into that school in order to find those involved in the plot and eliminate them or have you in the school when the plot unfolds in order to diffuse the situation from the inside."

He walked over to a file cabinet, took a remote control off the top and clicked a button. The projector came on as a building with old stone architecture and deep brown spire roofs surrounded by lush gardens and huge, majestic trees appeared before them.

"Chatterly Preparatory School is one of the most prestigious schools in the country," Swanson explained. "It's the home to a renowned teaching staff and school for some of the wealthiest and politically influential families in the world. The students attending Chatterly are children of the super-rich, or the politically powerful. Heads of industry and state send their children here. Ambassadors, emissaries, foreign diplomats, all send their children to Chatterly while living in the United States. Many corporate CEOs send their children to Chatterly."

"We get it," Tal spoke up. "Any spoiled rich kid who's anybody, attends Chatterly. So how do we fit in, as kitchen help?"

"We can arrange that," Grayson warned.

"No, Tal," Swanson interrupted giving Grayson a look. "You'll become a student and search for any students with an agenda putting innocent people in danger."

"And how do you propose to make me 'fit in'?" Tal questioned.

"Your covers have been chosen. You will be the son of a South Korean diplomat working in Washington. Josh is the son of a Russian Diplomat. Sydney is the daughter of the Spanish foreign minister, and Cali is the daughter of an Indian diplomat." Tal began to laugh, as the others turned to him, wondering if he had lost his mind. "I can't speak Korean. Its likely students who can, will figure out I'm a fraud."

"You'll be able to speak Korean before you leave here tonight, fluently." Swanson assured him. "As Sydney will be fluent in Spanish, Josh will know Russian, and Cali will be fluent in many dialects of Hindu," she said.

"Why can't some of us be American? Didn't you say some students at Chatterly were Americans?" Josh questioned.

"That's true," Grayson explained, "but conspirators won't trust any American, eliminating the possibility of gaining their confidence and reducing our effectiveness." He gave Swanson a nod.

"You will notice your iPhones in front of you. I know you were told we would go over their special programs tonight, but we first must get the learning as far along as possible. Each iPhone has been programmed with an accelerated language program corresponding with your identity for the mission. Take the time to play it through and then we will continue on with the next lesson. This should take you about thirty minutes. When you are done, wait here and dinner will be brought into you." She nodded for them to begin as Grayson turned and walked from the room with her close behind.

Cali, Josh, Tal, and Sydney looked at each other questioningly. Josh gave them a shrug and they slipped the ear buds in and started the program.

Josh listened to the instructions as he looked to the members in his unit. Tal stared at the ceiling, slouched down so his head rested on the back of his chair. Cali put her head on her arms folded on the table before her, eyes closed. Sydney folded her arms across her chest and listened intently with her eyes shut. Josh grinned to himself as the words in his ears went from something foreign to second nature. He leaned his elbow on the table resting his chin on his palm as he closed his eyes. By the end of the lesson, he couldn't tell if the words; 'The End' were spoken in English or Russian. At that point it didn't matter. He now understood both without effort.

Before he opened his eyes, the smell of food wafted to his nose. He glanced up from his concentration to see a tray of hamburgers, French fries and shakes wheeled into the room on a cart by a young woman in military fatigues similar to theirs. She glanced at him, smiling as she moved past, placing the food by the front desk where Swanson and Grayson sat. She exited the room, giving Josh one last look. Her blue eyes shone as she whipped her long blonde hair around her head, smiling seductively.

She wasn't military, Josh surmised by her hair style. He blushed, keeping his head steady, but moving his eyes to see if anyone witnessed their brief exchange.

Josh pulled his headphones from his ears, cleared his throat, and glanced over at Cali and the others to his right. Cali looked over to him beaming, knowledge of her ancestral language filling her with pride. He glanced at Sydney as Cali turned to the girl as well, her eyes closed, a contented look on her face. They turned to Tal as he sat in his chair, head leaning back, eyes closed and no expression on his face.

As Cali and Josh observed the other two, they slowly opened their eyes and looked around, Tal stretching his arms and leaning to get a crick out of his back. Sydney smiled as she took the headset from her ears.

"That smells great," she grinned. "I'm starving."

"Then get up here and dig in," Swanson told her.

They didn't need to be told twice as Cali, Sydney and Josh moved up to the tray and began to place burgers and fries onto the plates provided. Tal joined them and soon everyone sat eating quietly. Even Swanson and Grayson ate and sipped malts through a straw.

When they had eaten their fill, Grayson wiped the grease from his mouth, looking to the teens. "Time to get some technical training under our belts, background on the history of Chatterly, and their current teaching staff," he stated, tossing the soiled napkin into the garbage.

"You don't suspect the staff would have anything to do with a plan to take hostages at Chatterly?" Cali asked.

"We can't rule anything out. We have to suspect everyone until the players become known," Swanson told her.

"That's why Ms. Swanson is going undercover at Chatterly as well, as a teacher," Grayson told them.

The teens spun to Swanson who shrugged her shoulders.

"Someone has to work inside with you on your first assignment. Who would believe Grayson is an English professor?" she chuckled, turning to Grayson with a hand up, "no offense."

"None taken," Grayson continued. "I will be heading the command center with Kelli, who brought the food in. We will monitor all communications in and out of the school, keeping each of you informed. Speaking of that, please take your iPhones and touch the symbol on the screen that shows an antenna."

The teens did as they were instructed, and a map of the world appeared.

"Now put one earbud in and touch the area that is White Water," he waited tapping his foot until they did as he instructed and looked back up to him. "Now press the scan button," he waited a moment. "Those sounds you hear are any transmission being sent falling under the communications category. You can monitor police, emergency, military, or private transmissions with this program. It will allow you to do so undetected and if you press the find function, it will act as a homing beacon to pinpoint where the transmission is originating from or being received by. This will also patch into any mobile phone transmission allowing you to surveillance a suspect in close proximity. Kelli and I will be responsible for monitoring the entire area with larger, stronger equipment, but this is just another tool for you to use."

He began to turn away, but paused, turning back to them with his right hand raised, his index finger extended. The teens looked up from their iPhones expectantly as he searched for the right words. "If you ever need help," he looked at Swanson, including her in his message, "press the red button on the back of the iPhone and backup will come." He made eye contact with each of them to assure that they understood. The students nodded as he looked to them.

"What kind of backup?" Tal asked as Grayson looked away from them.

"I, Kelli, and Private Brandon who you haven't met yet," Grayson told him. "As we explained, only the president and those in the immediate unit know of our existence. Even the Joint Chiefs, CIA, and FBI don't have knowledge of our unit. We need to keep it that way. That's why we only have each other," he finished by pointing to Ms. Swanson and himself.

"That doesn't give me much confidence," Tal sighed as he slouched down in his seat.

"You haven't seen what we can do Tal," Cali told him. "Josh and I have been learning the entire time we were waiting for you and Sydney to be activated. Sydney didn't get much training last night," she hesitated, not wanting to mention Tal's attempt at suicide. "Tonight you both will get a real feel what we all can do."

"That's correct," Grayson agreed. "Ms. Swanson, would you please hand out the briefing packets so we can get through them and head upstairs. We have combat, hand-to-hand, and covert training to learn before midnight. Then we'll get into marksmanship with small firearms and knife combat in close quarters."

"Sounds like a busy night," Josh chuckled as he opened his packet. He read the first sentence and his mindset changed as the words 'Chatterly Hostage Situation' drove home the enormity of their mission. These were kids, just like them. Ok, not just like them, but just like they used to be before they changed into super soldiers. No, that wasn't the case either, since these students at Chatterly were the elite and privileged children from America and around the world. He closed his eyes, pushing the doubts from his mind. They needed to do this for their nation's security and these kids, no matter how privileged, were still just kids, with their entire lives ahead of them. No one deserved to be taken hostage and possibly killed in a game of political chess.

He glanced down the row and saw Cali, Sydney and Tal engrossed in the material as he turned back to it and started absorbing the information at an incredible rate. Soon, they were all waiting on him as he turned the last page and placed it down on top of the pile of pages before him.

He sat there a moment with a frown on his face, pondering.

"What is it, Josh," Ms. Swanson asked, reading his face.

"If there are students at Chatterly from powerful families, both monetarily and politically, then wouldn't there be some sort of security detail at the school?"

The other teens turned to him, shaking their heads in agreement, and then looking to Ms. Swanson for her response.

"You are quite correct. There is a highly trained security force at Chatterly, there to prevent a direct assault on the school, not to eliminate a plot before it can be implemented. They search for security breaches, bombs and risks that may harm the students, but as we found from 911, security measures sometimes miss the forest for the trees."

"What Ms. Swanson is saying, is we are going to be there to search and remove any possibility of a threat to the students of Chatterly. We cannot show direct force and must keep our presence and our results secret. If people knew how close they are to disaster every day, they would be frozen with fear and wouldn't be able to function normally."

"We have to find the terrorists and stop them, all while not being discovered ourselves?" Cali asked.

"That's right," Grayson nodded. "That's what 'covert' is all about." He smiled, rubbing his palms together. "We now need to educate you on the defensive and offensive tactics you will need to perform those missions. Put your headphones on and press the button labeled monitor. We will watch a training film on combat Aikido and all it entails, along with various Navy Seal, Marine, and Army Ranger training. When the film is finished, we'll go over what you've seen."

He nodded to Ms. Swanson, and she started the film as the teens put their headsets on and pressed the appropriate button on their iPhones.

The films ran one after another. Two hours later, the lights came up as they squinted and stretched.

"Is that the way it's really going to be?" Cali asked raising her hand.

"How do you mean?" Grayson asked.

"In the Aikido portion, they emphasize there will be times where we will not use controlled force, but only deadly force, striking pressure points for the certain kill."

"That is correct," Grayson nodded.

"I'm not sure I'm ok with that," Tal added.

"Me either," Sydney agreed.

Josh sat quietly as the others spoke up, watching intently, gauging each of their reactions in silence.

"I don't think I could ever intentionally kill someone," Cali continued.

"It's easy to say that now, as we sit in the classroom," Ms. Swanson said standing and walking in front of their tables. "But it's never clear how we will react when the time comes for us to decide."

"I'm with Cali," Sydney motioned to Cali. "I can't kill anyone."

"Sure you can," Josh said, breaking his silence and drawing incredulous looks from the others.

"What?" Sydney said her face mixed with disbelief and outrage.

"I know I'll be able to kill, for the right reason, at the right time," Josh said leaning back in his chair and crossing his arms across his chest.

"Josh," Cali leaned towards him. "How can you say that?"

"Easy," he came forward, putting his hands down forcefully on the table. "There I am, standing in a room with a man about to detonate a bomb that will kill innocent people. He only needs to press down on a little button he holds in his hand and even if I injure him badly, and then take him into custody, he still might be able to press that button. I would use one of the maneuvers

NORTHERN LIGHTS CODED TO KILL

we just saw, to kill him instantly. Never giving him the opportunity to press the button and kill those people."

The others stared at him, mouths open, still as statues.

Tal finally spoke up. "I don't care what you say. I would try and take the trigger from him and then capture him."

"Ok," Josh nodded. "How about those people in danger include your family?"

Tal stared at him, long and hard. He finally shrugged his shoulders and nodded his understanding.

"You too?" Cali cried.

Tal shrugged.

"I'll always try to resolve the situation without killing," Cali insisted.

"I agree, but Josh does make a valid point," Sydney said, gesturing with her hands. "We can't say for certain, we won't ever take a life in impossible situations. If we did, we wouldn't be truthful. I'll try to avoid taking a life, but if I there is no other way, to save lives, I will."

Cali glared at Sydney with her eyes wide and her eyebrows raised, wrinkling the skin on her forehead.

"I'm sorry," Sydney shook her head.

The teens digested the epiphany they just encountered in silence.

"Enough education, we need to get you trained physically for the mission, everyone top side."

Chapter 15

They stood and followed Grayson and Swanson to the elevator and soon stood in the hanger, mats spread out on the concrete floor in one corner with a light hanging lower than the rest of the lights in the building, giving an eerie spot-light effect. A man in identical fatigues stood patiently at attention, waiting for his orders. His brown eyes stared straight ahead, not contacting anyone, and a single bead of sweat ran down the side of his clean shaven face from his short brown hair.

"Sergeant," Grayson addressed, and the soldier snapped even stiffer, if that were possible. "Show these students what it means to be a master in martial arts."

The man began a flourish of moves, flowing seamlessly from one to another. Some hand gestures and footwork along with a sudden kick thrown in here and there.

Josh tried to identify each maneuver with their style of martial arts he had seen in the videos, finding the man used a combination of all of the martial arts they had learned.

The Sergeant finally came to a halt, bowed to them, and moving back to attention.

"Thank you Sergeant," Grayson said as he stepped in front of the teens. "Now what was so unique about the Sergeant's demonstration?"

"It was a combination of all the special forces martial arts along with combat aikido," Josh said.

The others nodded their agreement as they looked over at him.

"That's correct," Grayson nodded. "You think you could repeat the Sergeant's demonstration?"

Josh glanced at the others, giving them a nod as all four teens sprung into motion, simultaneously going through the patterns the soldier had performed. They glided across the mats effortlessly, finishing the demonstration with a sweeping kick, just as the Sergeant had. They came to attention, smiling, as they waited for Grayson and the Sergeant to snap out of their shocked stare.

Ms. Swanson stood just off the mats in the shadows, but now stepped into the spotlight as the men did not move. "Very good, now we need you to work with the Sergeant to assure you can perform the skills to defend yourselves. Josh if you please," she motioned Josh to step forward.

Josh hesitated for a moment, exchanging a quick glance with Cali before stepping before the larger man.

Without warning, the Sergeant lunged for Josh, striking at his face. Josh smoothly stepped to the side, gripping the man's wrist, and twisting it up behind the man's ear as his momentum took him past Josh. Turning his body, Josh forced the man's wrist past his ear and down towards the mat, the man's body falling backwards landing heavily onto the mat. The Sergeant's back hit the mat with a grunt as the force drove the wind from his lungs.

Josh pressed his knee against the shoulder of the arm he still held firmly in his hands at the wrist. The man slapped the mat in pain as Josh held the position for a moment and then released him.

"Very good," Grayson grinned. "Again," he nodded.

The Sergeant got to his feet once more and pressing the attack throwing punch after punch. This time Josh blocked with his forearms and moved quickly from side to side deflecting each strike past his head, the breeze felt by either ear.

Josh stepped through the man's advance and drove a hand into the middle of his chest sending him sliding across the mat on his back.

Josh stood motionless, hand extended, knees bent, poised in the follow through of his strike. He then drew back into a balanced position, hands in front, ready for the next assault. The Sergeant stood slowly, the last encounter taking something out of him. He slid his feet together, and bowed deeply, hands pressed together before him.

Josh retuned the respectful gesture, turning to Grayson, Swanson, and the teens. The two adults smiled knowingly as the teens showed a mix of surprise and excitement, for they understood each could accomplish what Josh had.

"Cali," Grayson turned to the girl. "You're up."

She grinned nervously to him, giving a quick glance out of the corner of her eye to Josh who gave her an encouraging nod.

She stepped before the Sergeant and readied herself in a balanced stance, her hands hanging lightly by her sides. She looked back at Sydney for a moment and then the Sergeant attacked, swinging for her face with a powerful right hook.

Cali deftly pulled her torso back away from the blow as his fist missed her face by a fraction as she grabbed his arm and brought her knee up, striking him in the stomach causing him to groan loudly as the air rushed from him. He fell to the mat as she stepped behind him, still holding his wrist and twisting his arm to his back straddling him.

"Very nice," Grayson clapped.

"Sydney," he turned to the girl.

"I'm not sure I can do this," she said hesitantly.

"Let your instincts take over. Don't over think it," Grayson encouraged.

"It comes naturally," Cali said as she released the Sergeant's wrist, looking to check on the man's condition.

He nodded up at her as he pushed himself from the mat and she walked over next to Josh, flashing him an excited smile.

Josh gave her a thumbs up, grinning.

Sydney moved to the center of the mat as the man stretched out the shoulder Cali had wrenched on. He hopped on the balls of his feet, moving smoothly from side to side.

"I can't do this," Sydney said turning her back to the Sergeant as she looked at Grayson, her hands held palms up, arms away from her sides.

The Sergeant moved in quickly, taking a hold of Sydney with his arm around her throat and pulling her right arm around behind her back.

Sydney looked shocked at Grayson who merely nodded with his eyebrows raised.

The man cranked upward on her arm behind her back, causing her to cry out in pain.

"Well, Sydney," Grayson questioned, "are you going to remain the victim and allow this terrorist to kill innocent Americans while you decide if you want to do anything about it?"

The girl's lips tightened as her jaw set and eyes narrowed. She exploded into motion so quickly it made her first movement impossible to discern. She jumped nearly straight up twisting her body around, releasing the pressure on her arm and prying her neck free from his arm with her shoulders and striking the Sergeant across his chin. She neatly came down on her feet as the Sergeant fell backwards to the mat. He lay motionless for a moment before he sat up slowly, shaking his head to clear the fogginess caused by the blow.

Josh and Cali stared at each other in shock as they turned together to Tal who stood white as a sheet. Tal's first exposure to their new physical abilities left him at a loss.

"Wow," Ms. Swanson shouted. "I've never seen that maneuver before. Where'd that come from?"

"Just thought it up," Sydney shrugged as she knelt beside the Sergeant to assure he would be alright.

"It made sense," Josh added. "I was thinking the same thing, sort of. You could have gone completely over him and turned the restraining hold back on him."

"That would have worked too, but what about not going so high, but spinning more around him than over him and you shorten the time you're vulnerable in the air," Cali said pointing at the Sergeant as she spoke.

"And how are you thinking of these moves?" Grayson asked.

"They're variations in the patterns the martial arts videos showed, combining and adapting them to our superior strength, speed and agility," Tal said as they spun to face him. He stood with his arms crossed over his chest nodding his head. "With our superior strength, we could easily overpower the Sergeant no matter what hold or attack he decides to use on us."

"He's right," Josh said as they looked to him. "I think what we should concentrate on is how quickly we can neutralize an assailant with the least amount of energy and sound. That would best suit our mission design. Tal, would you like to show them?"

Tal nodded as the Sergeant stood shaking his arms, legs and rotating his head in a large circle upon his neck, his ears touching his shoulders as they passed.

"This will not hurt you, Sergeant," Tal said stepping onto the mat. The tallest of the teens, over six feet, but his muscled arms and slender legs showed his power and speed. He held his hand up in front of his chest, trying to reassure the man he wasn't going to harm him.

The man glanced to Grayson who nodded, and the Sergeant charged Tal with such force, he covered the distance between them in an instant. Tal side-stepped much like Josh did in his encounter, but this time, Tal used an open handed karate style chop at the base of the man's neck, crumpling the soldier to the mat in a heap.

Swanson and Grayson gasped as the Sergeant hit the mat and skidded for a short distance, driven by his own momentum. The soldier lay there, out cold, his chest rising and falling evenly with every breath.

"He's fine," Cali said as they gathered around the man. "Tal's strike hit a nerve which rendered him unconscious. He'll have a horrible headache when he comes around, but he'll be fine."

Grayson and Swanson stared as Cali looked flatly at them and then joined Josh and Sydney patting Tal on the back in congratulations.

"Perfect," Josh smiled widely. "You struck at the optimum time." Josh said.

"Wow, that was so quick," Sydney praised.

"I never saw that coming," Cali joined in.

Seeing Josh's confused look, Cali stopped, looking at him and soon all three teens curiously observed the boy.

"What is it?" Cali asked.

"I can't believe what we're becoming," he said making eye contact with each of them as the realization came to them. "We're becoming trained soldiers, but even more than that. Soldiers learn how to fight, defend, and attack. We're learning to adapt the techniques we've been exposed to and make a hybrid form of martial arts according to our own unique strengths."

The others nodded their agreement.

"We should be able to choose when we use deadly force and we don't," Cali pointed out.

"With our understanding of the body and where the vulnerabilities are, we could ideally, never have to kill," Sydney said with realization.

"Or we can choose to kill at any time we feel the person is too dangerous to live," Tal added as the others spun on him.

"That would make us judge and jury," Cali protested.

"But with our new knowledge and insight, who better to decide than us?" Tal argued.

"Tal, you can't be serious," Sydney scolded.

"But he is," Josh said softly. When the girl's cold stares fell upon him, he took a few steps back with his hands raised before him in defense. "Tal spoke of the choice. We all know we won't make that choice unless it's absolutely necessary. But he's correct in saying we can kill in a blink of an eye and that gives us power to be judge and jury. Unless we're not given that flexibility of judgment?" he added turning to Grayson and Swanson.

Grayson pointed to Swanson. "It's our belief you should never leave any witness if possible. That's the doctrine of our unit. If there's a terrorist or combatant who, if left alive, will endanger our unit's secrecy, then you must consider eliminating that threat."

"So if a terrorist can clearly identify us, we must kill him?" Cali said throwing up her arms over her head.

"If any of them find out who we are and where we come from, not only you, but all of your families and loved ones, not to mention the entire town of White Water would be in danger of attack," Grayson emphasized.

"Now we're a unit of assassins?" Sydney asked incredulously.

"You're all forgetting we are the good guys here," Swanson emphasized.

"We're only going to expose ourselves to the terrorists who have chosen their path willingly," Grayson added.

"Listen to us," Tal sighed. "We're already worrying about killing someone when we haven't even gotten out of the hanger yet. Why not wait until we have a terrorist in our sights before we concern ourselves with killing him or not."

Everyone turned and stared silently at him. Josh began to chuckle and then Cali and Sydney joined in and soon they were all laughing loudly.

The Sergeant moaned on the floor, and they turned to attend to him, their laughter dying out. He looked up at the smiling faces with curiosity.

"I surmise the training is a success and I can return to base?" He looked to Grayson.

"Yes Sergeant and a job well done. Remember the level of security required here," Grayson said somberly.

"Yes Sir," the man saluted. "Only the president himself is cleared for this information besides those at this base today."

"That is correct, dismissed." Grayson saluted back and the man strode off solidly at first but then began to sway. The four teens rushed instantly by his side, supporting him, and helping him over to the Humvee he walked toward. The man turned his head from side to side in shock, taking in the four teens. When reaching the vehicle, they opened the back compartment and set the man in the seat.

"Wait here," Josh said and hurried away.

"I'm fine," the Sergeant protested, but the teens would hear none of it, removing the man's shirt and wiping the sweat beading on his forehead with Tal's fatigue shirt.

Josh reappeared with a canteen of water and a dampened towel. He handed the towel to Cali who continued wiping the Sergeant's face, neck, and head. He then gave the man the canteen. The Sergeant drank deeply and gave a sigh.

"How are you feeling now?" Josh asked.

"Much better, thank you," the man grinned.

Grayson and Swanson came over after observing from a distance.

"Sorry, sir," the man said trying to come to his feet, but forced back down by Tal and Sydney.

"Quite all right Sergeant," Grayson smiled. "It is nice to know they also have compassion."

"We're right here," Cali shot him a look. "You don't need to talk about us like we're some lab animals in your little experiment."

"He didn't mean it like that," Swanson soothed.

"Then how did he mean it?" Tal glared.

"It's very hard to know how your personalities will develop over the years and we're never sure who we will end up with," Swanson explained.

"You talk like you have been through this before. Are there others like us?" Josh questioned.

"No, nothing of the sort," Grayson interrupted. "Sergeant, agent Kelli will take you to the airport if you're able."

"Yes sir, I think I can make it now," the man nodded feebly.

Agent Kelli appeared as if on cue and helped the man into the passenger side of the Humvee, climbed into the driver's seat, and drove off as the teens stepped away from the vehicle.

Cali turned to Grayson, but he walked away without a word. As she looked to Swanson, she also refused to make eye contact and began walking.

"So now you think you can walk away without any explanation?" She shouted as her words echoed around the hanger. "Have you done this before? Are there others like us?" She cried with her arms extended above her head.

"They aren't going to tell us," Josh said as he moved over, putting a comforting hand on her shoulder.

Cali brought her arms down around his shoulders and laid her head on his shoulder. "I don't know if I can do this," she whispered.

"We're all in this together," he said, looking to Tal and Sydney who nodded. "As long as we stick together, we can make it through. You saw what we can do, all of us. We need to remember the reasoning and cause for what we do is just. We're the ones who have to choose how we go about doing it that matters. We have control over that and always will."

"You're right," Tal sighed. "We can't forget they do have a gun to our head. If we don't do this, our families will be put in prison. I'm not going to let that happen." The boy set his jaw and the look in his eyes made the others draw back slightly.

"Do you really think they've done this before?" Sydney asked.

"Why wouldn't they, the technology has been available since the sixties," Cali nodded.

"You're only speculating," Josh insisted. "Until we have proof, we need to concentrate on what's ahead of us, comrade," he added with a heavy Russian accent."

The teens began to laugh as they walked to the elevator waiting for them to go back into the facility. They knew they needed to be at Chatterly for class in two days and every minute of training could prove crucial for the survival of those teachers and students.

"Happy Birthday Tal," Cali said as they entered the elevator. "At least for another minute or so, she said looking at the digital clock on the elevator wall."

"What I wouldn't give to be fifteen again," he groaned as the others moaned in agreement.

The elevator whirred quietly down into the recesses of the air base, coming to a jerky stop. The doors opened and there stood Swanson and Grayson waiting for them in street clothes.

"We have a few more things to do and then we need to get on the plane for the East Coast." Grayson said motioning for them to step out.

They headed down the hallway to the classroom and as they entered, they noted small boxes on the tables before their chairs. They each took a seat and waited as Swanson came around to stand in front of them. Each teen looked curiously at the small plain box before them.

"You may open the box in front of you and wait once you have finished." she instructed.

The teens did so to reveal small, black contact cases. They looked questioningly at Swanson who spoke, gesturing with her hand at the cases. "These are contacts specially made for you. They are experimental and haven't been used anywhere else. They tap into your genetic abilities and allow you to do things normally requiring much larger equipment. Please put them in."

Josh slipped one in and raised his hand. Swanson nodded him to continue. "Do we take these out when we're not on a mission or at night?"

"These can remain in your eyes and shouldn't give you any of problems normal contacts do. We used your genetic DNA to create the lens from your own tissues. The only reason you need to remove them is on the rare occasion they are damaged. If you leave them in while they are damaged, they will repair in time." She smiled at the shocked expressions on the teenager's faces.

Josh slipped the other lens in and looked around expectantly. He could see no difference. Amazement spread across his face as he realized he couldn't feel the lenses in his eyes.

"So what are they supposed to do?" Tal asked looking around the room.

Grayson turned the lights off and the room went pitch dark.

A gasp came from the students as they looked around the dark room. Josh could see everything in the room as if the lights were still on. "Are we able to see with night vision?" he laughed.

"That's correct," Swanson answered. "Think of thermal imaging and the lenses should allow you to see the thermal image of people and objects in the room with different heat signatures from the surroundings."

Josh did as she suggested and sure enough, he saw the differences in heat of the people and objects around him. The giggles and laughs from the others told him they also were able to make the contacts change.

The lights came on unexpectedly and a surging pain flashed across Josh's brain for a split second as the lenses changed from night vision back to normal.

"Owe," Cali complained.

"Yeah, that hurt," Sydney agreed.

"What the hell was that?" Tal added.

"It takes a split second for the contacts to make the adjustment from total darkness to light again," Swanson explained. "That instant, you let in more light than your optic nerve can handle, and it created a moment of pain."

"Small price to pay for such a great advantage," Grayson grumbled.

"There are a few more benefits to the contacts," Swanson interrupted giving Grayson a dirty look. "You will be able to focus at very close distances or very long distances, similar to binoculars or magnifying glasses. They will also lessen the effect of certain gasses that are designed to incapacitate a victim through blinding."

"That will come in handy if I were ever pepper sprayed," Tal said sarcastically.

"You will be glad you have them if it happens," Grayson shot back.

"It's been a long evening, we need to get on the plane, and you can get some sleep," Swanson interrupted their exchange. "Get your things together and meet top side."

After getting into their street clothes and collecting their possessions, the teens rode the elevator back to the hanger. As the doors slid open, a sleek passenger jet sat in the hanger, the door open and steps down awaiting them.

Grayson and Swanson stood on either side of the steps as the youths stood with their mouths open.

"Get inside, we need to be off," Grayson herded them onto the jet.

They boarded with a gasp, the luxurious jet impressing the teens as they entered, finding plush leather seats.

Cali and Josh sat next to each other as Tal and Sydney sat further up on separate sides of the plane. Cali stretched her arm over to Josh's seat, taking hold of his hand as it sat on his leg. He turned, smiling wearily at her as she grinned back.

"At least we are doing this together," she whispered.

"I wouldn't have it any other way," he squeezed her hand as she gripped it back.

Swanson walked past; taking a seat by Tal and then Grayson closed the door and strode by, pausing next to Josh and Cali, glancing irritated at their hands on Josh's knee.

Cali began to pull her hand back, but Josh held fast, glaring right back at Grayson defiantly. Cali stopped struggling and looked at Grayson as well.

"Humph," he grunted and then turned, striding into the cockpit.

Chapter 16

Soon the jet's engines were whirring, and the plane jerked into motion. It pulled from the hanger and rushed down the deserted runway with lines of lights leading the way. As they pulled up from the earth, the teens peered out the window at their training facility to see the lights on the runway wink out.

"It's been a busy week," Swanson spun in her chair to them. "Get some sleep. The chairs recline completely and there are pillows and blankets under the benches on the side.

"Let's be sure to concentrate on getting some rest and nothing more," Grayson added over the intercom.

Tal and Sydney turned towards Cali and Josh with knowing grins, but Josh refused to relinquish Cali's hand.

"I'll get you a pillow and blanket," he said unbuckling and getting to his feet to step over and lift the bench on the seating against the window. He tossed a blanket and pillow to Tal and Sydney before gathering two more for him and Cali. He began to move back to his seat, but then hesitated, grabbing one more blanket and pillow to offer to Ms. Swanson.

Ms. Swanson looked curiously down at the pillow and blanket before her, and then up at Josh in surprise. "Well, thank you Josh," she said.

"You're welcome," he smirked and went back to his seat.

The sounds of constant breathing mixed with an occasional snort or snoring filled the cabin. But Josh Taylor gazed out the window, wondering where this all would end. Were they really up to this challenge, this soon? He watched the clouds scroll by the window and the sun disappear in the distance, giving the clouds the appearance of mountains covered with snow.

A soft touch on his hand as it sat on the chair arm, outside the blanket that covered him brought his attention to Cali as she sat with her chair reclined and her head lolled to one side so she could study him.

He smiled softly and leaned over to kiss her lips with a feather light brush. He began to pull away, but her hand came around to cradle his head and pull their lips together in a passionate kiss. A soft moan escaped her lips as his tongue flicked out to touch hers through the slight separation in of their lips. She held him there a moment longer and reluctantly released him.

"I'm glad you are with me," she said staring deeply into his eyes.

Her green eyes glistened, catching the dimmed lights of the cabin, and reflecting them at Josh, making them glow.

"Me too," he nodded, unable to turn away from the incredible image of Cali at that moment.

"I'm scared," she whispered.

"We all are a little unnerved by what's ahead of us, it's natural," Josh tried to sound confident not only in tone, but by the words he chose. But he didn't have much confidence. Actually, the prospect of not knowing what to do in a crucial situation terrified him.

"What, are you becoming Grayson now, you sure sounded like him right then," Cali giggled as she reached over and poked him in the ribs with her finger.

"Yeah, right," he chuckled. "Get some sleep."

Cali nodded and turned her head away as she closed her eyes, forcing her nerves down and finally fell asleep.

Josh looked past Cali, out the window once more, unable to calm himself. Being the leader of this unit, he wasn't sure he knew where to lead them. A short time later, he finally succumbed to sleep.

Josh woke in darkness as the plane landed. He stared out the window seeing trees lining the runway silhouette by the runway lights and they taxied to a hanger. They entered and the door was closed behind them, leaving them in darkness until the interior lighting flickered on.

Grayson stepped into the cabin as the rest of the occupants woke, stretching and rubbing the sleep from their eyes.

"Try to get your heads on straight. We've landed in a secluded airstrip close to Chatterly in Virginia." He nodded his head out the window. "We'll be taking you to the private prep school with your supplies in the predawn darkness, to avoid detection of your arrival and keep the suspicion down. We will be going in pairs."

"Since the dormitories are not coed, you will be less likely associated if we send one male and one female in today and then the other two in tomorrow," Ms. Swanson said as she stood from her seat stiffly, putting a hand to her back in pain.

"Josh and Cali will go in first," Grayson said looking irritated at Ms. Swanson. "We will drop you off in separate cars at each dorm."

"You've been registered with your cover identities, and everything should be set," Ms. Swanson said, oblivious to Mr. Grayson's glare. "We've chosen names that should be easily covered, but important enough to keep suspicion to a minimum."

"Remember, you do not know each other, and you must keep it that way while you're undercover," Grayson pressed.

"Josh, you are Dmitri Plotchin and Cali, you are Cali Ascalla." Ms. Swanson handed them passports and other identification cards. "You must try and blend in with the other students while observing, as well as taking note of anyone else in the school who might be a threat. Our intelligence says there are at least three people inside who are planning to help with the assault." She stood staring at the teens, assuring they comprehended her briefing.

"You are to neutralize anyone you deem poses a potential threat to the school and the students," Grayson stepped between them and Ms. Swanson. "Do you understand?"

"Find the threats and capture them," Cali nodded.

"Or kill them," Josh added as all heads in the cabin spun on him. "What?" he shrugged as they looked at him with a myriad of emotions on their faces.

"He's right," Grayson nodded. "If the suspects can identify you as their captor, then you will need to remove that possibility.

Sydney turned on Grayson, but a raised hand with an extended index finger silenced her with her mouth gaping open. "Those are your orders, Sydney. Not following them could create grave consequences affecting your lives and those of your families. These people would love to know the identities of special covert operatives."

"He is correct in this," Swanson emphasized the last to words as she addressed the teens. "Not only you, but your friends, family, anyone who ever had contact with you are in harm's way if these people have that vital information."

"Time to go," Grayson said as he opened the door and dropped down the stairs. "Here are your bags," he said picking up a backpack. "They have the clothing and supplies you will need. Don't let anyone riffle through your things. Great care has been taken to assure there is nothing to jeopardize your identity, but you have some 'special' hardware hidden in the lining to assist in your mission." He tossed the bag to Josh and then picked up the other one to toss to Cali. "Luggage trunks were shipped to the school ahead of you."

Cali paused at the door, looking back at Sydney and Tal who gave her a nod. She nodded and stepped out of the plane and onto the pavement of the closed hanger.

Josh stepped down beside her as they paused staring at two long black limousines. Grayson moved beside them as the teens turned to him questioningly.

"You are the children of powerful men; you will be expected to travel as such. You will find your bag contains the most expensive apparel and items money can buy. Try and act like you've lived this way your entire life."

Swanson stepped down from the plane beside them, placing a hand on each of their shoulders. "I will begin as an English teacher tomorrow so you will see me in class. Cali, you have the first limo and Josh, you take the other. Let's get a move on." She clapped them on the back and went to the first limo, taking Cali along with her.

Josh followed after, stopping behind them as Ms. Swanson turned in surprise.

"I'd like a moment, please," Josh said sheepishly.

Ms. Swanson nodded and walked back to stand next to Mr. Grayson.

"I guess this is it," Josh said kicking his foot at something unseen on the hanger floor and looking up at her uncomfortably.

Cali reached out, pulling him into her hug and held him tightly. "Be careful sounds so cliché," she smiled up at him as his face turned down to hers.

"How about, catch ya later?" Josh said just before Cali reached up with her hand behind his neck and pulled his lips onto hers.

She held the kiss for a time, letting go of his neck in the middle and then he pulled away, their eyes meeting, the affection pouring forth. "Catch ya later," she whispered, stepping into the limo's open door.

Josh shut the door and walked dazedly to his limo, tossed his bag in, and then ducked inside. He began to pull the door shut, but a resistance on the other side made him pause. He expected to see Grayson's frowning face over the exchange of feelings. Instead, Ms. Swanson climbed inside with him, drawing the door closed as she took a seat across from him facing the rear. He looked curiously at her, and she shrugged.

"I need a ride to the school as well. The teachers sometimes board on school grounds if they come from out of the area to teach." She said. "That was something; I thought Grayson might burst a vein when you two kissed." She chuckled.

"It didn't bother you?" Josh asked.

"I could see the connection long before now, but Grayson, he's old school and emotions never enter into it with him."

"Oh, don't think I condone it, but it didn't surprise me," she said dipping her head and looking up at him. "It is never wise to mix duty with personal, never."

"But we liked each other before you and Grayson came along," Josh protested.

"Doesn't matter," she shook her head. "It compromises the missions and instead of concentrating on what needs to be done, the two of you will be concentrating on each other."

"Isn't that what's supposed to happen when we become a team," Josh argued. "We watch out for each other. Why is this any different?"

"It just is. You are too young to understand, but losing a buddy is entirely different than losing a lover," she folded her arms across her chest then reached up and tapped on the dividing window and the limo began to move.

Josh sat stoically, jostling from side to side as the car winded its way to the male dormitory of Chatterly Prep School.

Chapter 17

Cali didn't enjoy her ride either. Grayson stepped in the car and proceeded to glare at her in silence until she couldn't stand it anymore.

"What?" she finally asked.

"We told you about becoming involved. It's highly frowned upon, being emotionally involved with someone in your unit."

"I knew what you meant. It happened before we became a unit and you won't take it away from me," she shouted. "You've taken the rest of my childhood. I refuse to let you take my first love from me." She stopped, stunned. Did she just say "first love?

She stared back at Grayson who gave no indication of emotion on his face.

"I mean, he was my first kiss, not necessarily my first love, but he *was* my first kiss." Is that what she meant, or did she really feel more for Josh?

She didn't have any time to contemplate it as the limo pulled to a stop outside an enormous staircase leading to deep brown block walls accented with light tan blocks in the arch and up the stairs on either side. The stairs led to large double doors made of dark wood with thick metal hinges fastened by straps extending almost to the other edge of the door.

Grayson handed her bag to her as she sat staring out the window, causing her to jump with a start. She looked down at the bag and then back at him.

"I'm not sure I can do this?" She waffled.

"You've been designed and trained to do this. It will get easier once you get into it. Just pretend you're back at White Water High the first day of school."

"You don't realize how horrible that day was." She looked at him with an anxious expression.

"Remember, you are Cali Ascalla, daughter of a wealthy diplomat. You need to act like all these other students are beneath you and stay a little stand offish until they've done something to impresses you enough you can see they are worthy of your attention."

"I'm not like that," she complained.

"But Cali Ascalla is exactly like that," Grayson said raising an eyebrow.

"Fine," she sighed.

Grayson tapped the glass between them, and the driver and her door swung open as a large man in a dark suit towered over her when she stepped out. Darkness still engulfed the campus, and the lighting gave the grounds a very elegant feeling, something out of a story she may have read about the rich and famous.

As soon as she cleared the door it slammed shut. The driver slid back behind the wheel and pulled away before she could turn around.

There she stood before the girls dorms of one of the most prestigious prep schools in the world. If the mission wasn't so dire, she may have enjoyed seeing how the other side lived, but now she needed to find the seedy side of the political landscape shaping the world today and root out the bad elements.

She slowly climbed the steps to the large doors. Lifting the old antique handle she found it locked. A note behind a plexiglass plate mounted to the side of the door told her to ring the bell and she pressed the button with no apparent result, hoping it actually did something unseen or unheard inside.

She didn't have to wait long as a man stuck his head out, looked her up and down, and then motioned her in silently. She stepped in without a word and waited as he closed the door behind her and checked to assure it was secured properly.

He turned to her, his large build stuffed into a tight uniform topped off by a military style haircut and piercing blue eyes. She noticed an earpiece in his right ear and a firearm at his side, a Beretta 9mm.

"Ms. Ascalla, I will show you to the House Mother's room. The rest of the girls have turned in for the night and it is only ten minutes before lights out." He didn't wait for a reply but took the bag from her shoulder and strode down the hallway. She scurried to catch up to his large strides, certain he enjoyed making the girls hurry after him like they were chasing him. He glanced over his shoulder from time to time as they walked down the tiled hall and then into a room where the door stood open, and light shone out into the hall.

A woman sat reading in a luxurious upholstered lounge chair beneath a floor lamp reaching over the back of the chair and extending a bit, the glass shade in the shape of a rose gave off an eerie red hue to the rest of the room except to the woman who sat beneath.

She wore a black silk robe over similar pajamas and looked up as they entered the room lined with bookcases, filled with books. The woman smiled widely, placing her marker between the pages, and set the tome down on a table beside her. She slid her feet off the chair, setting her slippers lightly on the tiled floor.

"You must be Cali," she greeted extending her hand.

Cali began to speak, but then caught herself, adjusting her thoughts to speak as if English was her second language and Arabic her primary. "Yes," she said with a slight accent, smiling back at the woman. If she were a diplomat's daughter, she would have been schooled in English from birth, so the accent must be presented, however, subtle.

"Welcome to Chatterly," she took Cali's hand, her short red hair swinging around as her small, slender body, nearly bounced out of her slippers. "I am Ms. Patterson, the House Mother. I am so pleased you are here. You must be exhausted, do you need something to eat, or would you rather get to your room?"

The guard stood awkwardly for a moment and then cleared his throat making Ms. Patterson aware of his presence.

"Oh, Rolland, I nearly forgot you were still here. You can leave her bag here, I will see to her now. Thank you."

The man nodded, glancing one last time at Cali, who nearly thanked him as well, before she remembered what Grayson told her. This man was beneath her. He turned without a word and went out into the hall and strode off.

"I think I shall go to my room now," Cali said looking back to Ms. Patterson even before Rolland vanished down the hallway.

"That will be excellent; your roommate will not be disturbed after lights out that way."

Cali froze. She hadn't counted on having to deal with a roommate. "I have another person sharing my room?"

"Why yes, all the girls share a room. It is a way we develop a sisterhood at Chatterly that will last a lifetime."

Cali didn't move, staring at Ms. Patterson in disbelief.

"My dear, I know you come from a very wealthy and privileged family, but here we help you develop as a woman who is worldly. You will come to enjoy it, I'm sure." With that, Ms. Patterson stooped down, retrieving Cali's bag from where

Rolland had left it, and motioned for Cali to go out into the hall before her.

Once in the hall, Cali waited for the Ms. Patterson to come out and lead the way. They turned onto a staircase and began to climb, Cali noticing the stairs going down deeper under the building as well. They went up two flights to the third floor and stopped before a door with light shimmering out from underneath spreading out like a fan across the tiles.

Ms. Patterson tapped on the door, and it swung open quickly, as if the person on the other side had been waiting with their hand upon the doorknob when the knock had come.

Before Cali stood a girl about half her height, long brown hair falling to her waist and deep brown eyes. She blushed, closing her bright blue bathrobe around her, and tying the robe's belt in a bow. Her slender snow white face contrasted her dark hair making it seem even lighter.

"Stephanie," Ms. Patterson began. "This is Cali. Cali this is Stephanie."

The girl extended her hand to Cali who looked at it for a moment, and then took it in her own, shaking it slightly as she looked around the room with a bored expression on her face.

Stephanie turned to Ms. Patterson uncertain, but a nod from the woman gave her reassurance.

"I'm so happy to meet you, Cali." Stephanie nodded and shook Cali's hand firmly.

"You too...," Cali began and then paused as if unable to remember the girl's name. She looked to Ms. Patterson who cleared her throat uncomfortably.

"Stephanie," she whispered.

"Yes, Stephanie," Cali said forcing a smile.

"Well, I'll let you girls get settled in for the night. Good night," Ms. Patterson said closing the door behind her.

Cali and Stephanie stood there awkwardly, Cali scanning the room and then coming back to Stephanie with her gaze.

"Oh, I nearly forgot, they dropped your stuff off for you earlier today," Stephanie said pointing at a large trunk to one side of the room. The trunk sat next to a bed neatly made with a light green comforter and golden throw pillows with tassels.

Cali took in the trunk with surprise as she walked over and stood in front of it. Her name, or the name of the person she portrayed while at Chatterly, embossed on the front. She pulled the envelope attached to the top, tearing it open. The single sheet of paper held only a four words. "Open with a finger."

She looked at the trunk, finding a latch with a small flat screen on it. Pausing a moment, she placed the index finger of her right hand against the screen. A ribbon of light slid from top to bottom on the screen and the latch clicked open. She slid the two doors apart to expose expensive clothes like she had never seen before, except if you wanted to count on TV with the celebrities walking the red carpet.

Stephanie gasped behind her, and Cali turned to see the girl with a hand to her mouth and her eyes wide with amazement. Cali looked back at the clothing to be sure there wasn't anything else catching the girl's attention. Assured Stephanie's awe came from the clothing and not some covert operative weaponry. She pulled the fabric of one of the dresses out to see it better. The shimmering black fabric felt light and airy, sliding effortlessly through her fingers.

"Your uniform is hanging on your side of the closet," Stephanie told her, pointing to the closet in front of them.

Cali nodded as she went to the closet and pulled out one of five identical uniforms hanging there. A white blouse with a navy tie, navy skirt, and a navy blazer with the emblem of

Chatterly Prep School on the pocket and navy shoes with white socks neatly set out below each complete uniform.

"They're not the clothes you're used to, but they're of the finest material. We all get used to them over time."

"What am I to do with my other clothes?" Cali said disappointment heavy in her voice.

"We only wear the uniforms during school hours, and then we can wear whatever we want. You'll get plenty of use out of your nice clothes. We go out on the weekends, with a chaperone of course."

A soft tone came in through a speaker mounted in the corner of the room. Cali looked up at the speaker over her shoulder and then back at Stephanie.

"Lights out, hurry and change into your pajamas and get into bed. We're allowed to use our reading lights, but the main lights go out in only a few minutes." She skipped across the room and hopped into her bed decked out in bright blues and reds.

Cali pulled her bag over closer to her new chest and began to search for something appropriate. She found some silky pajamas in a deep green and slid them on, keeping her back to her new roommate. She pulled the top on over her head as the lights went out. She stood for a moment as her contacts changed into night vision automatically. She saw Stephanie reaching for the lamp on her nightstand and closed her eyes to avoid the pain from the sudden light. The light clicked on, and she waited.

Cali slowly opened her eyes, testing the change to normal vision and smiled with relief when the pain didn't explode in her head.

"Hurry up and get in bed," Stephanie said motioning with her hand. "I'm dying to hear about India. You know I had to convince Ms. Patterson to allow me to be your roommate.

There were three other girls, who wanted to as well, but I've been here the longest and she gave you to me," Stephanie cringed as she said those last words.

Cali turned away so Stephanie wouldn't see her smile. She regained her composure and turned back to her with a weary expression. "It's been a long flight, and I really would prefer to get some sleep. Maybe tomorrow night we can share the gossip?"

Disappointment spread across Stephanie's face, making it nearly impossible for Cali to keep her eyes from tearing up. She felt the urge to apologize but remembered her cover. She turned away before Stephanie could see her empathy, pulling the covers up over her shoulder with her back to her new roommate.

"Night Cali," Stephanie said her disappointment apparent.

"Good night Stephanie," Cali replied. She pulled the covers tightly against her chin as the girl shut the light off. As she lay in the pitch blackness of the room, she couldn't help but wonder how Josh faired in the boy's dorm.

Chapter 18

Josh stood outside the looming dormitory building as the limo pulled away, leaving him on his own. He swung his bag up over one shoulder and headed up the granite steps and to the large wooden doors. He pressed the lighted bell after pulling on the handles of the large door proved fruitless.

Waiting for a brief moment, a large man with a crew cut and black t-shirt stretching across an abnormally muscular chest leaned out the door.

"Master Plotchin?" The man asked as his hand slid back to rest reflexively on his gun.

Berretta, Josh thought to himself, and the specs of the gun flashed in his mind. "Yes," he replied with a heavy accent.

"Follow me please. Do you need any help with your things?"

"No, I'm fine," Josh replied.

"The trunk with your possessions is already in your room."

Josh nodded as if he understood, but it confused him. Grayson must have thought it wasn't worth mentioning.

They walked into the entrance where they paused while the guard secured the door again. Another guard nearly identical in build stood at the side of the door. Josh looked up at him, but he didn't make eye contact, staring straight ahead.

"This way," the first guard said and started off down the tiled hallway lit by only a few wall sconces every so many feet. The incredible architecture with its intricate details and carvings lining the walls left Josh in a state of awe.

"Must be very old," Josh said as they walked.

"That's what they say," the man replied without looking back.

They walked on a little further, stopping at a door where the guard knocked softly.

"Enter," came from the other side and the man opened the door, motioning for Josh to go first.

Josh nodded, walking into a room lined with bookshelves filled with books. A little man with only a hallo of gray hair framing a white, bald head looked up at Josh and smiled, making his reading glasses balance precariously on the end of his nose. He stood quickly, causing the book he read to fall onto the floor with a bang. The man jumped, and then bent to retrieve the book, coming up with his head bright red with embarrassment.

"That will be all Russell," the man said, and the guard nodded, leaving them alone as he shut the door behind him.

"Welcome to Chatterly, Dmitri," the man greeted extending his hand.

Josh gripped the man's small, sweaty palm, shaking it firmly, raising an eyebrow at the man curiously.

"Oh, yes, my name is Mr. Burslie. I'm the dorm supervisor. If you need anything or have any issues, you should contact me."

"Thank you Mr. Burslie," Josh said. "It's been a long trip." Josh said, waiting.

"Of course, I will take you to your room," he said pulling his gray robe around him and scuffing to the door in his black slippers.

Josh followed as they went down the hall to the end and took a flight of stairs up to the next level. They walked down a few doors, music and televisions wafting into the hallway from the other sides, before pausing at a dark wooden door with the number 218 on it in silver numbers.

Mr. Burslie put a key in the door and the latch clicked open as he turned the knob and swung the door inward. Reaching around the corner, he flicked on the light and took a few paces inside.

"We're very lucky here, in that, all our residents have a room of their own. There is a bathroom off of each room you will share with one other student, but over at the girl's dorms, they share rooms and have four rooms to a large bathroom facility. It is much nicer here with more privacy."

Josh looked at him as he wondered why the boys got it so much better. The curiosity must have shown on his face as Mr. Burslie turned and began to explain.

"This originally held the teacher's quarters and Chatterly an all-male school. Now the teachers are much better paid, only a few reside here in a new facility across campus. The boys then moved here, and the girls brought into the underclassman dorms nearly fifty some years ago." He beamed proudly.

"You must want to get some sleep. Breakfast is in the dining hall starting at six and the first class is at 7:30am. You schedule is on your desk," he said motioning to a large built-in desk and a heavy wooden chair. "There is a map of the campus as well, but I'm sure you won't need it once you meet some of the other boys. Calisthenics are at 5:30 am."

Mr. Burslie gave a curt nod, stepping out of the room and closing the door behind him. Josh stood in his new room taking in the bland white walls and tan drapes standing open, showing the black night outside. He walked over to the window, pulling the drapery shut and then checked the bathroom door. He glanced in as the light from his room lit the dark bathroom. Two sinks, a shower and toilet, pretty plain. He shut the door and latched the lock testing it was secured with a quick shake. He then went to the main door and did the same. He didn't want to be surprised by someone curious about the new kid from Russia.

He tossed his bag on his bed made up in a dark blue bedspread and several pillows and stepped over to investigate the trunk. An envelope on the top bore his new name and he pulled it off, tearing it open and read it out loud. "Use a finger to unlock your chest."

He grinned as he placed his finger onto the smooth pad next to the latch. A bar of light slid from the top of his finger to the bottom and the lock clicked open. He stepped back, drawing the door to the chest open, exposing the contents inside.

Clothes hung neatly on hangers spanning the width of the trunk. Josh pulled a shirt out and smiled. He and his dad could never afford designer clothing. He took the shirt and slid the door to his closet back, surprised to see five sets of navy slacks along with five matching white dress shirts, five navy ties, and five navy blazers with the Chatterly emblem embroidered on the pocket. There were five pairs of polished black shoes along with five pairs of navy dress socks. He hung his shirt next to the uniforms and then emptied the rest of his trunk.

When the trunk stood empty, he stepped back, staring at the inside. Something didn't add up. He walked around the side of the trunk and then around the back to return to the front and gaze inside once more. He reached around, tapping on the side of the trunk and then the back. He noticed the difference in tone of the knock right off. His eyebrow cocked as he sucked in part of his lower lip and bit down lightly as he studied the luggage.

He happened to glance down at the touch pad lit with a solid white light. He placed his index finger against it once more and another clicking sound reached his ears as a latch inside the trunk opened. He slid the false back towards the open door of the trunk to expose a cache of 'spy stuff.'

Something caught his eye, and he reached inside and pulled a device resembling a handgun, but with a much larger muzzle opening. As he turned it in his hands, the information of a grappling hook launcher came to him. He grinned and placed the item back in its slot. Next he removed what appeared to be a small dish on a handle. He pulled his iPhone from his coat pocket and plugged the item in. The screen lit up and soon sounds from outside the room, became amplified and began being processed for voice recognition in the CIA database. He turned, allowing the instrument to scan in different directions. When nothing came back as identifiable from the database, he switched off his iPhone and returned the receiver to the trunk.

He glanced at the other items ranging from concussion grenades to an assault rifle. Who packed this trunk? He noted the sections of a sniper rifle and infrared sensors to be placed around the campus to detect activity which may remain undiscovered by normal means.

A soft tone came from a speaker mounted in one corner. Josh glanced up at it and then at his wristwatch. Ten, he thought. He pulled his bag open on his bed and drew out some shorts and a T-shirt to sleep in. He quickly dressed and climbed into bed.

He would get some rest tonight and get a lay of the land in the morning before venturing out on campus at night. The lights went out without further warning and his eyes adjusted to night vision as his contact lenses activated. He wasn't sure he liked the lenses just changing on their own, but he liked it at this moment. He noticed his trunk open and climbed out of bed, missing his shoes he kicked off in the middle of the floor, and shut the door tightly. The latch fastened with a click, and he got back into bed.

No roommate, he noted. He wondered how Cali fared with her roommate. He touched his lips with his fingertips, remembering her kiss before they left the hanger. He hoped they could complete this mission quickly. He didn't want to be so close and yet unable to share his affection for her openly, not that Grayson would approve. He rolled over with a sigh and closed his eyes, falling asleep.

Chapter 19

Cali woke to a buzzing alarm as Stephanie scurried from her bed, slapped the top of her clock on the desk and wrapped her robe around her.

Cali looked questioningly at the girl as five o'clock shone on the digital clock. Stephanie smiled as she gathered her toiletries in her arms.

"Good morning roomie," she grinned. "Breakfast is from six to seven and the first class is at seven thirty. We share a bathroom with six other girls and if we don't get down there early, we have to wait on the others and they'll make us miss breakfast or be late for class, neither of which I'm ok with. So get up and at it." She shuffled out the door and Cali could hear a door down the hall slam shut.

How could she act superior when she had to share a room and a bathroom? She decided right then that she needed to act stand offish, but not cruel, aloof, but not too arrogant. If she could pull it off, she may be able to get close enough to the other girls and gain insight into anything out of the norm for Chatterly and thus narrow down potential players in this conspiracy.

She hopped to her feet with a nod, confirming her course of action, and pulled her bathroom supplies from her bag. Curious as to how they knew what she needed when they packed it for her. She opened the door to an empty, dimly lit hall. She followed the sound of running water to the door leading into the bathroom. She nodded her approval as the accommodations pleasantly surprised her. Instead of an open shower room that she dreaded, she found neatly curtained showers divided by tiled walls. Each shower stall contained a sink and mirror on one end and a fairly expansive shower on the other. Four toilets stalls lined the opposite wall.

She walked past the stall she assumed Stephanie occupied, jumping as the girl stuck her sudsy head out suddenly.

"The one right next to mine is the best for hot water. The others on the end can be a little spotty," she said and then pulled back in.

Cali didn't have time to reply as her head disappeared behind the curtain in an instant. She climbed into the shower, noting this outdid her bathroom at home. After a relaxing shower she stood in front of the mirror drying her hair and then putting on her makeup. The quality makeup she from her trunk overwhelmed her, but if she were a diplomat's daughter, she would have the best of everything. She felt a little guilty at enjoying the pampering.

After getting into her perfectly tailored uniform, she moved over to the mirror in her room, taking some special makeup from her bag. She placed a small red bindi on her forehead with her fingertip. She never wore one before even though she had Indian decent, but she felt being a diplomat's daughter from India, she would be in the habit of wearing one. She leaned back from the mirror, admiring her artwork. Smiling confidently, she wiped the remaining cosmetics from her finger and turned to see Stephanie standing behind her, staring.

"I've always thought those were so elegant," the girl sighed.

"It's a custom in my culture. The bindi is said to give strength and concentrate power. You should try it sometime," Cali smirked.

"Maybe when we go out this weekend," Stephanie grinned. "I notice you have so many beautiful Sarees, could you show me how to wear one sometime?"

"Sure, we can wear some out this weekend," Cali said before thinking. She realized she might be acting too nicely, but the better they got along with her roommate, the easier it would be obtaining valuable information about the school from her.

"We better get to breakfast," Stephanie said looking at the clock on her desk. She grabbed her backpack, swung it over her shoulder and headed for the door.

Cali took the empty backpack from her things and followed after. They walked down the stairs past the first floor where she came in the night before and down into the basement. They followed along narrow corridors with dark stone blocks lining the walls and then began to ascend another flight of stairs. Shiny subway type tile lined the walls and Cali could tell they now walked in a different building.

"Where are we?" she asked Stephanie.

"We took the tunnel from our dorm to the main hall where the dining hall is. All the buildings are connected with tunnels, so we don't have to walk outside during the colder months. It's a lot faster to get around." She spoke over her shoulder as Cali followed behind.

They walked down a marble tile corridor and then turned left into a large cafeteria. Tables upon tables set in rows with high-backed wooden chairs filled the room. They moved over to one side of the room and entered a food line. They picked up trays and went through, receiving helpings of food from the staff standing behind a large counter where the food sat steaming in trays. Glass separated the students from the staff and food as they pointed to what they wanted and moved on to the next selection.

Cali followed Stephanie's lead and stopped at the end where a large woman with gray hair covered by a white hairnet sat on a stool. The woman's gray dress covered by a white apron streaked with grease and food remnants made Cali cringe with disgust.

"So this is the newbie?" she asked Stephanie.

"Cali, this is Grace, the head cook," Stephanie introduced.

"Like to be out here to see the ones I feed, India huh," Grace grinned with crooked teeth.

"Yes," Cali said, trying to act superior.

"You just let me know if there is anything special you would like me to add to the menu, dear. Grace will make you feel at home, at least in the cafeteria." She smiled again, adding a wink.

"Uh, thank you," Cali said, unable to hide her smile.

"Don't mention it. I do it for all of you. You might come from mighty *special* families, "but you're still kids down deep and most of you get homesick."

Cali followed Stephanie to a table and sat next to her.

"She's very nice, but don't tell her you won't eat her food, she really hates that," Stephanie leaned in and whispered.

Cali took a bite of her pancakes as she took in her new classmates entering the hall. They came from different parts of the world, but the identical uniforms they wore seemed to overshadow their ethnicity. Here, Chatterly was the *only* group they belonged to.

She had her doubts that any of the terrorists were students at Chatterly, so she began to observe the kitchen help as she ate. There were a total of six of them, including Grace, four men and two women. The men from differing nationalities; two appeared to be Middle Eastern, one Hispanic, and the one woman and Grace, Caucasian. The other woman appeared to be of Asian descent. They all wore white aprons and ridiculous looking hair nets. Cali felt positive it would be difficult to identify them without those nets on in street clothes.

Anyone could be a conspirator and she needed to begin ruling possible suspects out.

She then noticed there were only a few other female students in the room and none of the boys were there yet.

"Where are the boys?" She turned to Stephanie.

"Wow, you don't waste any time, do you?" Stephanie said with a smirk. Seeing that her comment did not amuse Cali, she cleared her throat nervously. "They have calisthenics before breakfast, so they get here about seven. Most of the girls will be here in the next few minutes and the boys should be close behind. I like getting here early while the food is hot, and I don't have to wait in line."

Cali glanced at the line of a whopping three girls now, wondering how long the line actually gets.

In a few minutes, the line swelled to a steady ten, the girls moving through smoothly keeping the number constant. When the girls all went through, Cali glanced up at the clock on the wall. Seven, she thought, when would Josh, Dmitri, she corrected, get here?

Chapter 20

Josh jolted out of sleep as a loud solid tone from the speaker in the corner of his room rang out. He jumped to his feet, stunned, scanning the room for the disturbance. When he realized the noise came from the speaker, he relaxed, recalling calisthenics this morning.

The bathroom door connecting his room to his neighbor slammed and he unlocked his side, cautiously opening the door to reveal a tall, slender boy, blond hair gnarled on his head as it stuck out in every direction. The boy stood in nothing but his boxers, hand against the wall before the toilet with his back to Josh who quietly shut the door, waiting patiently until the toilet flushed. He then knocked on the door and listened. Something dropped to the tile floor with a metal clang and a few cuss words echoed off the tiled walls, but then the door cracked open.

A pair of deep blue eyes peered out at Josh through the small opening. "What ya want?" The boy asked.

"What's the alarm about?" Josh asked with a heavy accent.

"Oh, ya, you must be Dmitri," the boy said opening the door wide.

Josh could see a can of shaving cream, the foam sprayed across the mirror and counter, and onto the floor beside. The boy held a razor in his hand and half his face covered in cream.

"Ya," Josh nodded.

"We have exercises every morning with Mr. Burslie on the front lawn. From the time of the tone, we have ten minutes to get down there." He paused staring at Josh. "I shave and brush my teeth before I go down. Speeds things up afterwards so I can get to breakfast in time to eat it."

Josh groaned at the thought of doing this every day.

"Don't worry," the boy chuckled. "It isn't too tough. Some sit-ups, push-ups and jumping jacks. We run around the building twice, but it only takes about fifteen minutes." Realization crossed the boy's face. "Better hurry up, we don't want to be late or else Burslie gives you an extra lap at the end." He nodded and shut the door.

Josh went over and put on some wind pants and a sweatshirt while he waited for the bathroom. When he heard the door open on the other side, he went in. He cleaned up, brushed his teeth, and relieved himself.

A knock came at on the door and he opened it to see the same boy, dressed in sweatpants and a sweatshirt with a stocking cap pulled over the messed head of hair.

"Ready to go?" he asked, walking out the door leading from the bathroom to the hallway without waiting for an answer.

Josh followed behind as they went down the stairs and out the door on the opposite side of the building Josh entered last night. Many other boys moved in that direction, and they entered the flow of the crowd and soon stood in lines spaced apart in rows. The boy from Josh's room stood next to him, giving a shrug.

Josh looked around, noticing a few of the boys pointing and whispering to each other. Josh wondered how many times he needed to be the new kid in school this year because it was getting old already.

His attention drifted to Mr. Burslie standing in front of the group blowing a whistle, black stocking cap covering his bald head, black sweatshirt with the Chatterly emblem on it, and black wind pants.

"Jumping Jacks," he shouted. "Fifty, begin."

The entire group, Josh estimated around one hundred boys, burst into motion, counting off as they went. He grinned at the thought of his superior physical abilities as he went through the motions.

He studied Mr. Burslie as he exercised. Could he one of the plotters? A disgruntled employee upset over his treatment here at Chatterly? He couldn't rule anyone out.

The group dropped down on their backs to do sit-ups and then rolled to their stomachs to continue with push-ups. They got to their feet and began two laps around the dorm. Josh could easily outdistance everyone in the group but jogged along with his newest acquaintance.

"What's your name?" he asked as they jogged.

"Trevor," the boy gasped, trying to catch his breath.

"Nice to meet you, Trevor," Josh smiled. "Thank you for showing me around."

"No problem," Trevor wheezed. "We have all our classes together, so you were set up as my suite mate."

They finished their second lap and walked back into the dorm and up the stairs. Before entering their rooms, Trevor stopped.

"If it's ok, I'll jump in the shower first and let you know when I'm finished. We'll head over for breakfast when you're ready, but we need to get there fast if we want to have hot food and time to eat."

"Fine," Josh said as they each entered their rooms.

He hurried inside, being sure to lock the door behind him and also lock the bathroom door as well. Quickly unlocking his trunk, he pulled out the small listening dish and plugged it into to his iPhone once more. He moved to the window, aiming it to the exercise grounds they just left. A few people visited on the lawn and Josh pointed the device, listening to the conversation and letting the program check for any recognizable voices. The lights flashed on his iPhone as the program ran. None detected, blinked on the screen.

The handle on the bathroom door rattled and then stopped. Josh held his breath as he looked to the door. He placed the instrument back into the trunk and slid the false panel closed over his spy paraphernalia.

He crept to the door, hand drawn back ready to strike as he unlocked the latch and opened the door.

Trevor's face poked into view as Josh dropped his hand to his side and forced a smile.

"Shower's all yours dude," the boy nodded and walked out the door leading to his room in nothing but a towel, his hair soaking wet, water still dripping down his back. He shut the door behind him without another look.

Josh gave a sigh as Trevor shut his door. Glancing at the clock on the counter, his eye shot wide. He only had a few minutes to shower and get ready. He jumped into the shower realizing too late the absence of hot water and the shower head sprayed nothing but cold water. He shampooed his hair and lathered his body as his teeth began to chatter uncontrollably. He hopped out of the shower, ran a hand through his hair and raced into his room wrapping a towel around his dripping wet body.

He swung open his door to discover a man leaning over his trunk, dressed in all black, like the guards from last night, tapping curiously on the side and up the back of the trunk. When he glanced up and saw Josh enter, he threw the duffle bag he held at Josh and broke for the hall door.

Josh flung the bag from his face, lunging for the man, but the he slipped out the door before Josh could reach him. Bursting into the hall, Josh found himself surrounded by other students, the man nowhere in sight.

The boys laughed and pointed as they passed, Josh realizing he only wore his towel. He felt the heat of embarrassment reach his face and stormed back into his room, slamming the door behind him.

Josh retrieved the duffle bag the man threw at him only to discover it was his own. Upon inspection of the trunk, noticeable marks scarred the trunk where the man tried to pry the false back open. He placed his finger on the touch pad and the panel popped open. After seeing everything still rested safely in its place, he removed a small video camera and found a good place to keep an eye on his trunk while he attended classes. On the intercom speaker in one corner, he could see the entire room on his iPhone receiving the signal.

He smiled confidently as he quickly dressed. He bent over tying his shoes when Trevor knocked on his bathroom door.

"Come in," Josh said looping the last lace and fastening it neatly.

"Ready?" Trevor grinned, hefting his backpack higher on his shoulder.

"Let's go," Josh nodded, grabbing his empty backpack, and following after.

They took the staircase next to their room and exited the dorm in the back by the exercise yard they used that morning. They followed the cobblestone walk through neatly manicured lawns and gardens lined with perfectly trimmed hedges.

Josh imagined stepping back in time to the fifties or sixties. Everything seemed architecturally authentic from the arching windows to the copper roof lines. He could only imagine a time so long before his time. He still found it intriguing as he gazed in amazement.

They entered a large hall and proceeded to the cafeteria where he stepped into a place in a short line as he followed Trevor.

"Stay away from the scrambled eggs," Trevor warned. "By this time in the morning, they've been sitting in the heating pans for at least an hour. Dry as a popcorn fart."

"Thanks," Josh laughed. He asked for whatever Trevor requested ahead of him and stood waiting to give his name to a large woman sitting on a high stool. He observed the kitchen workers as they moved around behind the stainless steel counter and glass.

The small Asian woman stared at him for a long time, giving him a seductive smile that couldn't have been less appealing with her white apron, grease streaks, and other messes on it, and topped off by the unbecoming hair net.

Josh gave a half-hearted smile back and turned back to the woman on the stool as she glared impatiently at him.

"Dmitri?" she questioned holding his attention.

"Yes," he answered.

"Welcome to Chatterly. If there is something you would like us to make for you special, you just let old Grace know and I'll be sure to get it for you." She glanced back at the Asian woman. "Anything that makes you feel better about being away from home," she added turning back to him with a suggestive grin.

The offer wasn't lost on Josh who blushed as he did a double take, first at Grace, and then at the woman who smiled widely and batted her eyes at him.

"No, I'm fine," he stuttered. He saw Trevor motioning for him to hurry up and he nodded awkwardly and walked away.

"Don't let Grace bother you," Trevor whispered as Josh sat down next to him at a table. "She tries to drum up extracurricular activities with everyone, but she's harmless.

Some take her up on it and others don't. It's no big deal," he added with a shrug.

Josh sat with his mouth open looking at Trevor.

"How long have you been at Chatterly?" Josh asked.

"Too long," Trevor chuckled. "This is my," he hesitated looking up as if the number resided on the inside of his skull, as he counted with silent lips, "sixth year. Been here since seventh grade," he grinned stuffing some French toast in his mouth, the syrup dripping down his chin as he continued to smile.

"That's a long time to be away at school. Don't you miss your parents?"

"Not anymore. Dad is a CEO of a large company and mom is busy with all her fund-raising. I'd much rather come here instead of having the private tutor. Besides, at least here I get to have some friends." He shrugged and continued eating.

Tyler looked around the cafeteria, a strange sense someone watched him. Then he saw her. Her navy uniform unable to disguise her uniquely individual beauty as she stared at him, her green eyes filled with emotion. He looked away from her, his feelings racing to the surface.

He glanced back at Cali as she looked towards him again after turning her head away. This wasn't the way they were supposed to act. They needed to behave like they didn't know each other. He couldn't help but gaze at her, unable to divert his eyes.

"Wow, you have an admirer already," Trevor said as he reached across the table to nudge his shoulder. "I don't remember her, she must be new too. She's hot," he added with a lustful smile.

"Uh, yeah, I guess," Josh said, trying to decide how to handle this. "Don't we have to get going?"

"Shit, yes," Trevor said looking at his watch. "We're going to be late." He got to his feet, grabbed his tray after slinging his

171

backpack over his shoulder and sped for the window to drop his tray.

Josh scrambled to get to his feet and hurried after him, giving a sigh of relief at getting away from Cali and his uncontrollable emotions with her around.

They moved swiftly down the hall, turning abruptly into a classroom with the door standing open as they passed a confused looking teacher headed towards the door. He paused as the boys sped in, watching as Trevor slid into a desk, motioning for Josh to sit in a vacant seat next to him.

Once they were seated, the teacher stepped into the hall, coming back into the room as he pulled the door closed behind him. He waited with his back against the closed door observing the students visiting in the room, his gaze lingering a moment on the new student, before striding to the front of the room.

Chapter 21

Cali couldn't help but stare as Josh sat in his navy-blue uniform and tie. Mesmerized by the way the light filtering in the cafeteria through the arching windows caught the shine of his hair and the glint in his eye as he surveyed his new environment. Cali knew he scanned the hall for any possible suspects just as she had done upon entering.

Their eyes met and she knew she should avert them from his, but something held her, entranced in his gaze, unable to look away. Thankfully, the boy across from Josh drew his attention away and the moment passed.

She now walked down the hall with Stephanie by her side. They entered a classroom not far from the dining hall and sat down at a series of tables slid together making circle. A large, oversized leather chair sat in the middle with the back facing them. The top of a blonde head lifted over the high back slightly, exposing the occupant's presence.

The chair swiveled around, causing Cali to gasp inadvertently. Stephanie turned to her curiously, looking from Cali to the person in the chair.

"Do you know her?" Stephanie asked, looking to the woman sitting in the center of the room.

Cali stared at Ms. Swanson for a moment longer shaking her head looking back to Stephanie. "No, I thought she might be somebody else."

Cali glanced back at Ms. Swanson and then down at the table as she took her seat.

"She's a sub. Ms. Crocket is out on maternity leave. They told us to expect someone else today. Seems like there are many new faces at Chatterly today," she smiled.

"Who else is new?" Cali asked distracted by Ms. Swanson's presence and not looking at the girl.

"There has been a big change over of security these past few weeks. A lot of those guys had been here since I came to Chatterly two years ago."

"How do you know that?" Cali asked turning her full attention to Stephanie.

"You kinda get to know the guys when they're around that much. Most of them are really nice. The one's that aren't usually don't stay here long." She pulled her books out of her backpack and jotted down something in her notebook.

"Good morning class," Swanson addressed them. "I'm Ms. Cutlage. I will be your Sociology professor until Ms. Crocket comes back from her parental leave. I'll keep you updated on her condition and the condition of her baby when she delivers. She wanted me to send her greetings with the hopes you will push yourselves like you do when she is here.

"I'm staying in the teacher housing on the west side of the campus. If any of you need extra assistance, please feel free to contact me through the switchboard or stop by and get some help in person." She looked around the room at the twelve students as she spoke, pausing for a second longer on Cali and then continued on.

Cali noted Ms. Swanson's location on campus and how she could be reached.

Cali leaned close to Stephanie as Ms. Swanson spoke. "Can I borrow a piece of paper?" she whispered.

Stephanie slowly tore a piece out of her notebook, trying not to make too much noise. She handed it to Cali who pulled a pen from her backpack's pocket.

Cali scribbled a few words down and folded the sheet in half. She pushed it under her backpack and turned back to Ms. Swanson addressing the class. Cali glanced over to Stephanie who stared at her questioningly.

"I don't want to forget to ask Ms. Cutlage how I'm supposed to catch up with the class work. I can't stand being behind."

"I know what you mean," Stephanie chuckled.

Cali waited impatiently for the class to get over as it seemed to drag on and on. When Ms. Swanson finally dismissed the students, Cali waited for them to file out. Assuring Stephanie waited for her out of earshot in the hallway, Cali approached Ms. Swanson. She handed the note to her, pausing for a moment as their eyes met, and then turned, walking out of the room.

****

Ms. Swanson watched the girl leave and then unfolded the paper. "Security Detail" met her widening eyes. She hurried behind her desk, pulled her purse from a drawer, and rummaged through it until she found her cell phone. Pressing a button, the tones of the number speed dialing filled the air. Placing the phone to her ear, she heard a familiar voice.

"Check the records of the security detail. We suspect they have been compromised," She quickly hung up and put the phone back into her purse as the first students for the next class filed in.

****

Josh and Cali passed in the hall exchanging a casual glance as they followed their respective guides to the next class. Josh had sat through the biology class barely able to keep his eyes open, hoping this would allow him to fit in with the other students in his class having the same problem. He observed the room's occupants finding nothing out of the ordinary, scanned the entire text the next few minutes, and could have instructed the class himself as he sat the next 45 minutes waiting for it to end.

They now entered a room with a man obviously of Middle Eastern decent standing impatiently at the front, watching each student file in. When his eyes fell on Josh, they narrowed slightly, following him to his seat next to Trevor. Josh could feel the man's eyes on him as he sat down and pulled a notebook and paper out. He raised his eyes to meet the man's stare, causing the man to clear his throat and turn away uncomfortably.

The teacher strode around the desk and pulled a large map down in front of the whiteboard. The map highlighted the areas of Israel, Iraq, Saudi Arabia, Iran, Egypt, Afghanistan, and Kuwait.

"Dmitri, I would like to welcome you to Middle Eastern studies," the man smiled as he turned back to look at Josh. "I am Mr. Abdalann." He lifted a textbook off his desk and proceeded to the table where Josh sat, setting it down in front of him.

"Here is the textbook required by Chatterly, but as the other students can attest, we deal here with more realistic views of what is happening and what has happened in the Middle East. Namely, we look directly at the imperialistic approach of America and its allies to systematically control and rape the region for their own purposes."

Josh scanned the classroom as the students nodded their agreement to Mr. Abdalann's comments. He looked back to the Abdalann, standing in front of him, waiting for a response.

"Uh, we too feel the west has often forced this region into an impoverished state only to allow for extraction of cheap energy recourses. I feel America has been allowed too much leeway when dealing with these countries and has protected the invalid existence of the Israeli state."

"Very perceptive, Dmitri," Abdalann grinned. "You're going to fit in very nicely, very nicely indeed."

Josh turned to Trevor who looked at him with a disgusted expression. Trevor glanced out of the corner of his eye as Abdalann moved back to his desk before he leaned in closer. "If I had known how you felt about us imperialists, you could have found your own way around."

"I said what he wanted me to say," Josh whispered. "Why would I come to America if I hated you? It's the optimism of what's possible in America that brings my father and me here, not your history of control in the Middle East. We see what you do as powerful, and we respect that. But please keep that to yourself, else I'll have far more enemies than friends here."

Josh and Trevor held each other's gaze for a moment longer before Trevor gave a slight nod of concession and sat back in his chair.

Josh leaned back as Mr. Abdalann proceeded to rant about the horrors brought down upon the people of the region by the United States and its allies. Josh observed the student's reactions as well. A mix of every nationality you could imagine filled the room, Trevor seeming to be the exception. After Abdalann mentioned certain atrocities the west perpetuated upon the Middle East, several students turned a judgmental eye to Trevor and a little blonde girl sitting a few chairs down.

Josh noticed the girl staring at him when he followed the looks of some of the others to her. She beamed sweetly, giving him a slight nod. He smiled back with a nod and turned back to Trevor who wore a sheepish grin.

"What?" Josh whispered leaning closer to him.

"Cindy Halstrum," Trevor whispered back. "The hottest girl in school, except for the new one you saw this morning, maybe. What has them falling for you the first time they see you?"

"I couldn't tell you," Josh shrugged as he shook his head.

"Must be the Russian charm," Trevor elbowed him with a chuckle.

They sat listening to their professor rant on and on about the oppression of the people by the west and how Jihad is justified by the actions of the west and any extreme actions taken are justified after what has been done to them.

Josh grew more and more uneasy as the hairs stood up on the back of his neck. Someone with these strong feelings would have no problem helping terrorists take over a school and make the arrogant west pay for the centuries of evil perpetuated upon the downtrodden of the Middle East.

He carefully reached into his pocket and pulled out his iPhone, keeping it hidden behind his backpack sitting on the table in front of him. Only Trevor could see him using it and he grinned with a raised eyebrow.

Turning the voice recognition on, he allowed the ranting flowing from the professor, to input into the processor and waited. "Inconclusive information" showed on the screen. Inconclusive? What did inconclusive mean? Either it identified him, or it didn't.

He sat pondering the response until movement out of the corner of his eye caught his attention. He quickly pulled the iPhone off the table into his lap, tapping the touchpad rapidly.

Abdalann stood in front of him, hand extended towards him, palm up, his face a mix of anger and resignation as he stared down at him. "The item you are rudely playing with instead of listening to our lecture, please Dmitri," he scowled.

Josh reluctantly drew the iPhone from under the table and handed it to him, glancing at the screen, hoping his attempts cleared any incriminating evidence from the screen. To his relief, the image of a map of the Middle East, news headlines scrolling across the small map showed on the screen.

The professor stared in shock at the images as his mouth dropped open. Holding the device above his head, he screamed, causing everyone to jump in their seats.

"This is exactly what I've been talking about for weeks, class. Dmitri has tapped into the type of information we should be using every day to affirm the atrocities constantly perpetuated by the western civilization upon the most ancient cultures in our world." He handed the iPhone back to Josh, giving him such a smile that it sent chills up Josh's back.

"Thank you for bringing new life into our class, injecting us with new reasons and information to reinforce our views. What we're doing here has meaning and we should develop our ideals to fend off complacency in our lives and work for the greater good." He strode back to the front of the room, tall and proud of what he believed. Looking at the clock over the whiteboard, he stopped to stare down at his papers.

"Class is dismissed," he said with his back to them. "Thanks to Dmitri, you will not have any assignment for tomorrow." He gave a wave of his hand in dismissal and the students got to their feet, filing out the door.

Before Josh could leave, Abdalann took him by the arm, pulling him aside.

Josh looked to the man, ready to act, if necessary.

"Please don't let me find that device in class again," he said calmly, but somewhat distracted. "We have an after school group on Middle Eastern Studies you might be interested in. Think about it. We're meeting after school every Tuesday and Thursday." He smiled with a pat on Josh's back.

Josh nodded without a word and nearly bumped into Trevor in the hall waiting for him as he stared back at the professor.

"What did he say?" Trevor asked as the headed for their next class.

"He doesn't want me to bring my iPhone to class anymore." Josh told him.

Trevor nodded. "Most of the professors don't like that."

"He also mentioned a club he wants me to join."

"You're kidding," Trevor stopped, spinning on him with a stunned look on his face.

"No," Josh said. "He said it meets Tuesdays and Thursdays."

"He never asked anyone but students with Middle Eastern backgrounds to be in that club. He must really like you."

"I'm not sure it's a good thing," Josh sighed and started off again as Trevor hurried to catch up.

"It will make getting through his class a lot easier," Trevor pointed out. "Besides, it was cool the way you changed your iPhone to that web site under the table without looking. How'd you do that?"

"I don't know," Josh said concerned Trevor saw the screen before he cleared the information from it.

"I didn't mean to look, but I saw a green screen and then you pulled it out of from under the table, it was on the site. I couldn't do that without looking, but good thinking." Trevor cringed as Josh looked at him. "Really, I didn't mean to snoop. I'm sorry if I ticked you off."

Josh glanced up at Trevor's face distractedly, realizing from the boy's expression he frowned deeply. "No, no, it's ok. I was thinking about something else. I'm not mad."

"Whew, that's good, because you looked really pissed off."

"Sorry, I'm a little confused by Abdalann, that's all. He seems a little radical for a school with all rich kids, most with diplomatic ties."

"None of us know how he got in with all of his extremist views, but the dean assured us it's good to have diversity with differing beliefs. He says it will make us better leaders."

Josh nodded half-heartedly as he thought on this while they walked down the sparsely populated hall. The dean agreed to Abdalann. He needed to find out how much the dean agreed with him and the extent of their radical beliefs. Maybe they were in on the plan together.

They walked into the classroom and sat at a table arranged with others in a circle around a large leather chair. Josh only half glanced at the teacher in the chair, but then froze, looking over at Ms. Swanson sitting casually smiling back at him and then turning her attention to the other students taking their seats.

"Welcome students," she greeted them as the last girl took her seat. "I am Ms. Cutlage. I will be your professor until Ms. Crocket comes back from parental leave. I will also keep you updated on her condition and the condition of her baby when she delivers. She wanted me to send her greetings with the hope you will push yourselves like you do when she is here.

"I am staying in the teacher housing on the west side of the campus and if any of you need extra assistance, please feel free to contact me through the switchboard or stop by and get some help in person." She looked around the room at the fourteen students as she spoke.

She stood from her chair, walking over in front of Josh and placed a textbook down on his table with a smile. "There are some interesting sections on your country on page 264, if you want to take a look, Dmitri. I've marked them with a slip of paper."

She moved back to her chair without another glance and spun the chair away from his side of the room as she began her lecture on the developmental requirements of society to ensure harmonious existence.

Josh checked to see Trevor looking at Ms. Swanson out of the corner of his eye and when he felt sure no one watched him, he opened the book to the page marked with a small piece of white paper. He opened the folded paper containing three words, "Security Detail Questionable."

He folded the paper over once more and closed his book. He then turned his outward attention to Swanson's lecture, but playing over the possible suspects in his mind as her voice wafted through his head as background noise.

Professor Abdalann sat at the top of his list thus far, but with this new information, he recalled the thief in his room that morning.

He pulled out his iPhone and tapped on the application turning on the camera in his room. There sat his trunk, just as he had left it. He changed from the live view to the recorded images from earlier. Pressing the fast forward button, he watched as the trunk sat alone in his room all morning. Suddenly, an image flashed across the screen. It lasted for just a second and then vanished. He rewound the recording and the figure flashed by again. Hitting play, he watched as the same man crouched in front of his trunk, trying to find something. His face, obscured by the shadows in the room and possibly by something else, maybe a scarf, remained indiscernible. The man tapped and pressed all around the outside walls of the trunk. When nothing happened, he returned to trying to get into the luggage.

The man paused, pulling something from his pocket. Flipping open a large knife, he tapped the trunk with his ear pressed against the sides. Drawing back his hand holding the knife he drove it into the trunk. At least that was the idea. The information of the trunk's construction flashed in Josh's mind as a smile split his lips and he watched the knife twist in the man's hand after coming in contact with the Kevlar reinforced trunk wall. The man's mouth flew open with a silent cry of pain as the deflected blade came back and impaled his hand.

Cradling his injured hand against his body, he gathered the weapon from the floor with his functional hand and scampered out of sight of the camera.

Josh watched a while longer disguising his grin as deep consideration to what Swanson discussed.

He could now identify this suspect, even though his face wasn't visible in the recording. The man wore the clothing of the security detail and Ms. Swanson's note made perfect sense to him now. He needed to search for the security officer with an injured right hand. The injury would identify his thief and give him a place to look deeper. He needed to check into the security detail and with Professor Abdalann Tuesday afternoon at the Middle Eastern Club meeting.

Placing his iPhone back in his pocket, he smiled openly as Ms. Swanson turned towards him as she spoke to the class. Her facial expression didn't belie her thoughts, but Josh noticed the expectation in her eyes as she read the confidence across his face. He felt confident that he was well on his way to finding the conspirators before they had a chance to spring their trap and carry out their plans.

Chapter 22

Cali sat calmly in Middle Eastern Studies as Professor Abdalann ranted, going on about the unparalleled evilness of the United States. She fought every urge in her body, keeping her emotions under control as he accused America of extortion, terrorism and strong handed politics that cost innocent people their lives. She concentrated on the students in the class, looking around at their reactions and looking for anything to indicate their depth of agreement with this extreme professor.

Out of nowhere, Abdalann stood in front of her table and slapped his hand down with all his might. The bang reverberated in the room causing Cali and everyone around her to jump in their seats.

She glared up at the man with anger as he glowered over her, pleased by her reaction. Her eyes shot up to meet his and he took a step back as her anger consumed her.

"And why would you feel it necessary to behave in that manner?" she grit her teeth.

"This is my classroom, and I will behave in any manner I see fit, Ms. Ascalla."

"You will not speak to me in that manner," Cali fumed. She was a diplomat's daughter and to be given the utmost respect throughout her life. She needed to live up to that image.

Cali came to her feet. She felt the heat radiating from her face, her hands clenched into fists. "You're nothing more than a servant to the students here whose parents pay for your services. Don't ever deceive yourself that you can reach the status to speak disrespectfully to me."

Abdalann had his hand raised, finger pointing, ready to dive into a tirade, but a man dressed in security detail uniform interrupted as he stood behind Cali. The man had a hold of Abdalann's raised wrist as they stared venomously at each other.

"You've been warned about your temper with the students before," the man whispered, belying the anger boiling underneath his calm exterior.

Abdalann flexed his arm, trying to free it from the man's grasp which held him firmly. Abdalann finally relaxed and the man released him.

An uncomfortable silence filled the room until the man turned to Cali. "Ms. Ascalla, if you would accompany me, I believe we need to speak in private."

Cali nodded, stunned, getting to her feet robotically and walking out before the man as he gestured her to lead. They entered the hall but not before the man turned one last time to Abdalann and wagged his finger at him, closing the door behind him.

He motioned with his arm to proceed, and Cali began walking down the hall as the man stepped in beside her.

Cali remembered the warning she shared with Ms. Swanson earlier. This man was in the security detail of the school. The same detail Stephanie said changed out most of its longtime personnel recently.

She glanced at the man as they walked. He never looked down at her, but proceeded with his eyes straight ahead, scanning the hall as he moved.

They turned down a smaller hallway and then into an office on one side. She entered the office ahead of him, noticing the plain wood walls, large mahogany desk and a few leather chairs filling the remainder of the tight space. No outside window and only an American flag and the words, honor, duty, courage underneath hung on the wall.

He motioned for her to sit as he shut the door and stepped around the other side of the desk to sit in a high backed executive chair.

As he sat, he reached up to turn down the sound on a television sitting on his desk. The television appeared to be tuned into some kind of talk show. No, not a talk show, she smiled, Abdalann's class. The realization made her look up at the man in shock.

He finished turning the sound down to a whisper and looked over at her as she stared in surprise. Looking at the monitor and then back at her expression, he grinned and cleared his throat.

"Yeah, well Professor Abdalann is the most radical and controversial teacher here. It's a benefit to Chatterly to keep very close tabs on him." The man ran a nervous hand through his thick gray hair.

"Then why not get rid of him?" Cali questioned.

"I guess they feel it's a benefit to have all types of views at Chatterly. They say it creates better members of society." He shrugged and crossed his arms, leaning back in the chair.

"And what do you think, Mr. ...?" Cali asked.

"Mr. Broderick," the man said, "the Officer in Charge."

"In charge of spying on radical professors?" Cali pressed.

"Not just that. In charge of your protection while you are here at Chatterly," he stammered, fidgeting in his chair, uncomfortable under her scrutiny.

"I'm so pleased you are here to protect me from some pompous professor who thinks too highly of himself," she rolled her eyes. "Do you protect me in other ways, Mr. Broderick?"

"Total security of the campus is carried out by highly trained officers whose main responsibility is to ensure no harm comes to any student here at Chatterly." Mr. Broderick puffed up behind his desk. "This is just one of the nuisance assignments I watch over since I'm in my office more than the rest of the men."

"Do you feel Professor Abdalann poses a danger to me?" Cali asked.

"You pushed his buttons really well, but he never crossed the line of being a windbag to someone who actually might carry out any harm to anyone." He chuckled to himself. "He wouldn't be here if we felt there was a chance of that."

"People slip through the cracks all the time, what makes you sure he isn't one of those people," Cali asked and regretted the question as the words came out.

"You seem to have a lot of questions for someone here less than twenty-four hours. Who did you say your father was?"

"I didn't," she said, forcing a syrupy smile.

"Please enlighten me. To be sure you aren't one of those people slipping through the cracks." He leaned forward in his chair, placing his palms on the desk before him.

"I'm Cali Ascalla, daughter of the Ambassador Ascalla from India, Baracatt Ascalla. He decided I'm old enough to join him here in the United States, instead of staying behind with my younger siblings, to experience the world we live in." She fluidly recalled the intelligence information on the Ambassador provided to her on the limo ride and held no doubt Grayson developed her cover completely.

"Well Ms. Ascalla, I have never seen anyone stand up to the professor before. Most students will let him degrade them and then get out of his class as quickly as possible. What made you decide to stand up to him?"

"If I didn't, who would? I was raised to respect myself and others. I will not be treated like some dog on the street."

"Remember I'll be keeping an eye on the professor in case he gets out of hand, but he should settle down after I report this to the Dean, and he gets a talking to." He looked down at his watch and gave a nod. "Time for your next class, what do you have?"

"I think I'm at lunch now." Cali sighed at the thought of only half a day behind her.

"Do you think you can find your way to the dining hall, or would like me to escort you?" He smiled standing.

"If you would please," she said as she stood. "I'm not too adept at navigating my way yet," she lied.

"Very well." He walked to the door, opening it, and letting her walk ahead.

They walked quietly down the hall past the classroom doors with their doors swung wide and the rooms standing empty. All the students already dismissed for lunch.

"Does everyone eat at the same time?" Cali asked casually.

"The two younger classed eat earlier while the older three eat at the same time. The younger students have a wing to themselves in order to nurture them along a little more," Broderick said smiling down at her.

"Here we are," he said as they came to stop outside the dining hall.

"Thank you Mr. Broderick. I feel much safer knowing that you are in charge of my safety,"

"I take that as a very large compliment, Ms. Ascalla," he replied nodding his head slightly. "Have an enjoyable lunch." He turned and walked back down the hall the way they had come.

Cali stood watching him move away. His body flexing under the tight uniform, giving glimpses of the deadliness of his training. She had a good feeling about Mr. Broderick, but she was far too green at this to rely on her intuition before she ruled them out as possible perpetrators.

Stephanie burst out of the dining hall's doors slamming them into the hallway walls, snapping Cali out of her contemplation.

"There you are. Boy did you get Abdalann angry. That was the first time any of us can remember that Mr. Broderick intervened in a classroom altercation. What was he like? Where did you go? He is so dreamy."

Cali turned back to where Mr. Broderick had disappeared down the hallway. She guessed he was good looking, she thought as her hand came to her mouth, covering her smile.

Stephanie stood staring at her expectantly. "Well? Spill it."

"Oh, uh, maybe later tonight, I'm kind of hungry now." She brushed by a speechless Stephanie on her way into the dining hall, the grin spreading freely across her face.

As she walked into the hall, she spotted Josh. He sat with a group of boys, many of them talking to him excitedly as he appeared to be sharing information about his cover identity. His eyes lifted and followed her across the hall as she went to the food line. She tried not to look at him directly but watched him out of the corner of her eye.

Chapter 23

Josh saw Cali enter the dining hall as he shared the details of his cover with some of his new classmates. He made sure not to hesitate this time as she came in, only keeping track her with his peripheral vision, amazed at how much he could see on either side while looking straight ahead. He focused his thoughts on Cali and the image of her sharpened as the people in front of him lost a little clarity. He wondered if this due to his heightened abilities or the result of the contact lenses he wore.

The thought of White Water made him pause contemplating how his father held up with him gone? He was shocked at the lack of thought given to his father until this point.

His thoughts were interrupted by the conversation in front of him. Trevor leaned closer speaking softly to a blonde haired boy next to him about Cali.

"She really checked out Dmitri this morning at breakfast," he said turning to grin at Josh. "Her name is Cali Ascalla, a daughter of the ambassador from India."

"She's so fine," the boy grinned with his head down, trying not to be too obvious as he followed Cali's progress through the lunch line.

Josh looked over at him as the other boys at the table agreed and snatched glimpses of Cali.

The boy looked back at Josh and his amused expression turned fearful. "Dude, I didn't mean anything by it. She's just hot, you know. You don't have to bust a gasket that someone else thinks she's hot."

Josh realized by the looks on Trevor's and the other boy's faces, that he was glaring at them menacingly.

"Ah, sorry," he said shaking his head to clear his thoughts and hopefully shake the expression from his face. "I was thinking about something else," he tried to cover.

"No problem, but if you want first crack at her, you got it," the boy said grinning nervously. All the other boys at the table, including Trevor, nodded their agreement.

"Thanks, but I think she is out of my league," Josh said, truly meaning it.

"Are you nuts," Trevor joked. "He had Cindy Halstrum's eye this morning in Mad Abdalann's class."

A round of oohs erupted from the table of boys, just as Cali passed. She blushed and rushed to the table where Stephanie waited with some of her classmates, taking a seat beside the girl.

"She was just being nice," Josh protested as his face turned shades of red.

"Cindy doesn't look at anyone unless they're making a fool of themselves, or she's interested in them," the blond laughed. "I know. I've been on the foolish side of things a few times. She usually only dates the older boys, but if Trevor thinks she has eyes for you, you should feel lucky."

"Ya, but her last boyfriend's dad was a big shot on Wall Street, and he lost everything, guess if you don't have the money, you don't get no honey," another boy said laughing and running a hand over his short brown hair.

The table burst into laughter as a solid tone sounded over the intercom system, sending the dining hall into motion as the students headed over to drop their trays off at the drop window and head back to class.

Josh followed Trevor as they went past Cali with her back to him, finishing her lunch at the table of girls. She didn't look up as he glanced down at her, but kept her head turned. As he lifted his eyes, they were met by a pair of deep blue eyes staring purposefully at him. He nodded politely and continued to walk past Cindy, but she reached up, grabbing his arm, and pulled him to a stop before her. The line of boys trailing behind Josh bumped into him, protesting loudly as all eyes turned to Cindy and Josh.

Josh looked over to see Cali staring as well. He turned his attention back to Cindy as she smiled sweetly up at him.

"I usually don't date boys younger than me, I am a junior you know, but with you I think I will make an exception. Meet me in the courtyard in front of Old Main Hall after classes today and we can talk." She stood, giving him a small peck on the cheek, and walked off, leaving Josh blushing deeply.

The boys behind him finally pushed him forward as Trevor came back to pull him to drop off his tray and then out of the dining hall.

Trevor turned to him excitedly, hardly able to contain himself. "That is so awesome. My suitemate is going to date Cindy Halstrum, daughter of the director of the CIA."

Josh stopped in his tracks, looking at Trevor in shock.

"Did you say the director of the CIA?"

"That's right, he is the leader of the most mysterious agency in the government, and you are going to be dating his daughter. I hope you don't have any secrets, I mean ANY secrets, because they won't be secret for long once Cindy tells her daddy about you," Trevor babbled on.

Panic flooded Josh's thoughts making everything go blurry. Or perhaps terror? This could expose him, Cali, and the entire team. Grayson had said that only the current president knew of their existence. What would happen if the director of the CIA found out about them? Would they be taken over and controlled even more by the agency? The more people who knew about them increased the chance that the enemy would find out about them and retaliate against anything they accomplished here or in the future.

He pulled out his iPhone and tapped out a message on the special communications application installed just for them by Grayson and Swanson. "Cindy Halstrum has taken an interest in my cover and may compromise that cover if she has father check into it further." He pressed send as an image of a mailbox appeared and verified that the message went through.

He slipped the iPhone back in his pocket and followed Trevor into his next class. This net three hours of classes may prove to be the longest three hours of classes he had ever experienced. Maybe he could devise a plan to avoid Cindy other than not showing up and drawing more suspicion upon his cover. He walked in and sat down heavily next to Trevor.

"This has been the best first day anyone could ever have," Trevor said smiling widely at him.

"Yeah, the best," Josh said trying to fake excitement. Really great.

Chapter 24

Cali could hardly believe her ears when the little blonde girl declared Josh her boyfriend right in front of her. She kept her head down so no one could see her jealously and blow her cover. As the girl made her announcement, Cali glared out of the corner of her eye. She thought she was something, laying claims to him like he was a piece of meat.

After the girl finished her declaration, Stephanie turned back to the table with the rest of the girls as they all began talking excitedly at once.

"I can't believe she did that," Stephanie said to the girl across from her.

"I know, that wasn't like her at all," the little red head squealed with excitement. "Imagine Cindy Halstrum going out with an underclassman."

"Who is this Cindy Halstrum?" Cali asked Stephanie.

The entire table went silent as every girl's eyes were on Cali.

"She just got to America yesterday," Stephanie explained as all the girls nodded understanding.

"Cindy Halstrum is the most popular girl in school and has been ever since she arrived here three years ago. She is also the daughter of the director of the CIA, the most powerful intelligence agency in the world," Stephanie explained.

The look on Cali's face betrayed shock mixed with fear, but luckily the girl took it as amazement, because she nodded excitedly.

"Yeah, it is incredible that someone who just came to Chatterly and is only a sophomore could get Cindy's interest," Stephanie added.

"I hope his father isn't involved with the Russian mafia, because after Cindy's dad gets done with a background check on him, he might wish she had never noticed him," the red head laughed.

Oh my god, Cali thought. This could ruin everything. She reached for her iPhone tucked away in her backpack as the girls got up from the table. As Stephanie stood up, Cali looked up at her as her friend looked at her questioningly.

"Could you please take my tray for me, I have to do something before we leave," Cali asked.

"Sure," Stephanie said, taking the tray with hers.

Cali opened the communications program and typed in a quick message, "Josh's cover may be compromised, please advise." She exited the program and tucked the iPhone away again, hoping that Grayson or Swanson could figure out what they should do next. She felt a slight tinge of resentment for Josh as she got up from the table and slung the backpack filled with her new textbooks over her right shoulder. If he hadn't flirted with this girl, she would not have taken an interest in him and now the mission wouldn't be in jeopardy.

She stopped, realizing she was blaming him for a girl taking an interest in him? If Cindy was attracted to him, it wasn't Josh's fault.

The vibrating of her iPhone in her backpack buzzed against her back. She swung the pack from her shoulder, stopping just outside her next class's door.

"Just go in, I have to do something first," she told Stephanie who looked questioningly at her and then nodded before entering the classroom.

Cali touched the iPhone and opened the communications page. "Meet with Swanson at teacher's housing, five sharp." She turned the devise off and walked into class as she tucked it away. Five seemed so far off; she frowned as she took her place next to Stephanie with a sigh.

****

Josh puzzled through his last three classes before the students were released for the day. Trevor elbowed him as they packed up after the last class, a knowing grin across his face.

"What?" Josh frowned.

"You know what," Trevor smirked. "I expect details, you hear? Details."

"Nothing is going to happen the first time we meet," Josh assured him.

"She likes you, that's what matters. She'll let you know how much she likes you pretty quickly."

Josh hoped not. He wanted to distance himself from her without being too obvious about it. He needed to figure out how to do that with the most effect. Should he tell her he wasn't interested and bring a huge amount of skepticism, or he could approach it another way?

He nodded goodbye to Trevor after assuring him he knew how to get back to his room and walked to the courtyard in front of the Old Main Building at the center of the campus. It wasn't hard to miss. The large, dark stone building stood out majestically as the cornerstone to the entire campus. He walked nervously towards the towering building, wiping the sweat from his hands on his pants.

He came around the corner of a building and there she sat, the warm fall sun shining brightly down on her golden hair as she leaned her head back to feel the warmth on her face and neck. Her uniform was unbuttoned scandalously low, and the sun shone brightly off her white flesh. She sat on a garden wall with her feet next to her and her knees bent before her.

When she saw him coming, she tilted her head slightly as a devilish smile curled her lips that sent a shiver up his spine. He questioned his decided course of action for a split second but then threw caution to the wind and dove in, so to speak.

He slid up behind her as she leaned back against him and took hold of her long blond hair, tilted her head forcibly back and pressed her lips tightly to his.

A cry of surprise escaped her lips for a split second but turned into a moan of passion as their tongues met and she ravenously kissed him back.

Josh's eyes shot wide in shock at the response as she took the lead, reaching back to hold his head in place and kissing even more deeply. He closed his eyes as the moment took hold of him and his desire swelled in him as her tongue drove his desire higher with its staccato flicking.

She finally released him and they parted, gasping and looking to each other intensely.

"I never would have guessed that from you," she purred. "You look absolutely harmless, but underneath, you're an animal, Dmitri."

"There is just something about you that won't allow me to stay in control," Josh said with his heavy Russian accent.

"And that accent, it is so adorable," she giggled.

Who knew, Josh thought, that she would be so easily smitten by him? After all the hype everyone had for her, she had fallen for him?

"I am sorry Cindy, but even though I find you incredibly attractive, I cannot see you," he said turning away. Time for plan B, he thought.

"Excuse me?" she said dropping her feet from the ledge and swinging around to him, placing her head on his shoulder, and pressing herself against his turned back.

Josh turned slowly around to face her as she looked up at him with a mix of pain and anger.

"I did not know who you were when we first met, but knowing who your father is, I cannot be with you," Josh said compassionately and then turned away again.

"My father, what does my father have to do with this?" she shouted, coming to her feet.

He turned back to her, taking her hands in his and pulling her down next to him on the ledge again. Looking into those incredible blue eyes, filled with pain, he thought he could care for her if the circumstances were different.

"He is the director of the CIA, no?" Josh asked.

"Yes, he is the director of the CIA, what does that have to do with us?" She questioned.

"I am sure he has means of finding out any secret about anyone he wishes, no?"

"Yes, yes he does, he can find out pretty much anything. Why is that a problem..." she stopped in mid-sentence as she realized what he was implying. "You have something to hide that you don't want him to find out."

Josh turned away, dropping his eyes from hers shamefully. "I would not be able to live with you finding out about my family's past. I would prefer we be friends if that will keep your father from digging up the past sins of my family." Josh worked some tears up in his eyes as he turned back to her.

Cindy looked at him as her eyes filled with tears of their own. "My father can be a hard man, but I know he would understand that the sins of your family are not your sins," she comforted as she placed her hand to his cheek, wiping away a tear.

"Even though my heart fills with desire at the sight of you, I am afraid that my past sins weigh far too heavy on my soul to allow you to be hurt by my past and that of my family." He searched her eyes for a sign of acceptance, but when he found none, he changed tactics slightly. "Although, if you could promise me your father needn't know about us and our relationship, then he would have no need to find those sins of the past."

Cindy leapt to her feet, clapping her hands before her. "I will not tell him you and I are involved. Actually, I won't mention you to him at all and that should allow us time to decide how to approach him when he does find out."

"How do you know that this will last at all, we have just met?" Josh questioned.

"I know these things, and no one says no to me." She grinned and then dove on top of him, kissing him deeply and driving him down against the ledge.

His initial pain of the hard ledge pressing into his back gave way to a flow of passion through his body, filling him with a feeling of guilt as Cali came to mind, but then he allowed himself to be swept away by the rationalization that he was protecting his cover, nothing more.

Chapter 25

Cali went to her room with Stephanie and changed. She threw on some jeans and a sweatshirt and headed out the door.

"Where are you going?" Stephanie asked.

"I thought I would go for a walk and then I need to speak with Ms. Cutlage before dinner. She said she would make sure I was up to speed on my coursework if I stopped by."

"Then don't you need your backpack?" Stephanie pointed to the pack on the floor.

"You're right," she grinned. "I would have been coming back for that."

She walked over and slung the pack onto her shoulder and headed out the door. She hurried out the back door towards the center of campus and Old Main. She wanted to see what Josh and that Cindy girl were up to.

As she sped along, she felt sorry for Cindy and what Josh must have said to her. Maybe he had let her down with the, "I have a girlfriend back home," line and technically that wouldn't have been a lie.

She grinned to herself at the thought of that brash girl being knocked down a peg or two. Would Cali find her crying on Josh's shoulder as he comforted her in her moment of embarrassment? He was thoughtful like that.

As she came around a large grouping of shrubs in the garden, she stumbled over her feet at what she saw.

Josh and Cindy sat making out ravenously, Josh on his back on a small retaining wall ledge and Cindy full on top of him locked onto his lips with hers, moaning grotesquely. Rage burst through Cali as the sight caused it to shoot right past her control. A loud cry of disgust escaped her lips causing the two lovers to suddenly stop and look around.

Josh heard a person's cry, but thought it sounded more like an animal in distress than a human. He and Cindy shared startled stares as he sat up, pushing her off him to a sitting position. He looked where the sound originate from, but there was nothing there but a fluttering of leaves from a large grouping of shrubs.

Josh stood slowly as his contacts focused in on the dark object in the shadows of the shrubs. When the image became clear, he wished it hadn't. There, hidden in the greenery to all but his special vision, Cali sat seething, not taking her eyes from his. Shame washed over him as he couldn't take his eyes from hers.

"What is it?" Cindy asked, taking a hold of his hand.

"Uh, nothing," Josh said distractedly. "We should be going. I have to change before dinner and get some things done."

"Meet me at my dormitory and we can walk to dinner together," Cindy told him, reaching up and pulling his head until he finally relented in to letting her give him one last French kiss and then scurry away.

Josh stood there, still looking at Cali long after Cindy had gone. Realizing Cali had no intention of showing herself, he retrieved his backpack and walked over to the shrubs. Standing next to them, he looked in at Cali as she turned away in disgust.

"I needed to play along so her father wouldn't do a background check on me. The director of the CIA will eventually find out who I really am." He waited for a response, but when none came, he continued. "I'm sorry what I did caused you pain, but if I didn't do this right, it would have only drawn suspicion on me. Cindy promised she wouldn't mention me to her father and hopefully we can accomplish our mission before she does."

Cali sat stewing in the foliage as she shot icy glances at Josh. She had lost control of herself but regained it in time to hide before anyone saw her standing there. She was furious with Josh but wouldn't give him the satisfaction of showing it to him. Somehow she knew he already realized the extent he had hurt her, but she wouldn't vocalize it, at least not here, not now.

Josh turned his vision into thermal imaging and could see Cali's temperature in her face and ears shine a bright red. She was angry and when he changed his vision to register her vital signs, which he didn't realize he could do, her heart rate was elevated and blood pressure on the high side.

"I'm sorry, but it appears I need to continue the charade of being her boyfriend, at least for now," he said leaning into the shrubs slightly and then walked away without looking back.

Cali sat there a while longer to be certain that no one would see her step from the shrubs. Brushing herself off and pulling her iPhone from her bag, she realized she needed to meet Ms. Swanson and hurried to the west side of the campus and the teacher's quarters.

As she walked, she fumed over the approach Josh decided to take in order to deal with this possibly mission ending situation. He could have chosen a number of different paths, but he chose to play along with being the boyfriend of the prettiest girl on campus, how convenient.

As she neared the large brick teacher housing complex, someone walked up beside her, slipping a hand through the crook of her arm and drew her down a path alongside the building instead of the main entrance.

Cali spun defensively on the figure only to find Ms. Swanson staring straight ahead and walking briskly along.

"So good to see you again, Cali," she nodded at her as they walked.

"You too, Ms. Cutlage," Cali replied.

"Let's sit down here for a while and go over the questions you have for me," Ms. Swanson said coming up to a cement bench alongside the walk.

They sat down, both surveying their surroundings for possible observers and when none were found, they turned to each other.

"I got your message and so did Mr. Grayson," Ms. Swanson began. "We 've been trying to reach Josh for the past few hours and haven't had any luck. We're trying to get directions to him as to how to proceed with this. This is a very delicate situation." The worried look on the woman's face drove home the seriousness to Cali.

"I saw Josh and Cindy Halstrum in the garden by Old Main on the way here." Cali said looking at her hands in her lap.

"You did?" Ms. Swanson said in hushed concern.

"They were making out when I came upon them unexpectedly," Cali admitted.

"Did they see you?"

"Only Josh. I hid in some bushes until the girl was gone." Cali sighed.

Ms. Swanson leaned closer, taking Cali's hands in hers, causing the girl to look up at her. "This is always hard when you have feelings for your teammates as you do for Josh," she commiserated. "But sometimes you will find yourself in such a predicament and you will have to decide if you are willing to do something that sickens you in order to protect everyone involved with the mission."

"But Josh could have done something different," Cali protested even as Ms. Swanson looked at her skeptically.

"Like what?" Ms. Swanson pressed raising an eyebrow.

NORTHERN LIGHTS CODED TO KILL

"He could have told her he wasn't interested in her, or that she wasn't his type, or that he had a girlfriend, or maybe..." Cali began her protest strongly, but as each option came out of her mouth, she could hear how foolish it sounded and lost a little conviction with each one.

Ms. Swanson tipped her head from side to side with each suggestion and patiently waited for Cali to finish.

"Cindy Halstrum is the most popular girl on campus, and some might argue the most attractive as well. If Josh had turned down such an invitation to be her boyfriend, his cover would have been compromised by people questioning his reasons for turning her down. I'm not only talking about the student body, but everyone who would hear about it. Teachers, security officers, dorm supervisors, and the list would go on and on. Josh would be considered strange for his decision and thus limit his ability to fit in on campus. By choosing to be Cindy's boyfriend, he has instantly become the most popular boy on campus and with that; he will be accepted almost without question."

Cali's eyes filled with tears as the logic and the reality of what Swanson said became clear. Josh had no other choice. She began to feel sorry for the way she had treated him, but then she stopped, wiping her eyes, and setting her jaw she looked right at Ms. Swanson.

"He didn't have to enjoy it so much," she shot back.

"I'm sure when you speak with him, that he didn't," Ms. Swanson assured her as she grimaced. "I once had to seduce a very handsome Russian general. I thought I would come to like the mission, but he was just someone I needed to become close with in order to complete my mission. Josh will feel the same way with Cindy. No matter how attractive and desirable she is, she is just an obstacle to eliminate in order to complete the mission."

"I understand, but do you have to keep reminding me how beautiful she is?" Cali laughed painfully.

"I'm sorry, but you know I am right. Now is there anything else you need to report as I don't think we should meet up again unless it is absolutely necessary. It is too dangerous when we still don't know who is involved," Ms. Swanson pointed out as she looked cautiously around.

"Professor Abdalann is a complete nut job," Cali blurted out. "Mr. Broderick, the OIC had to remove me from his class today to diffuse a volatile argument we were having. It wasn't my fault," she added seeing Ms. Swanson disapproval. "He verbally attacked me and seeing as who my father is supposed to be, I felt it wouldn't be believable if I just took it."

"Josh thought Abdalann was a bit out there as well," Ms. Swanson said putting a thoughtful hand to her chin. "We will keep him high on our list. How is Broderick?"

"He seemed very much in charge and very nice. It would be hard for me to see any possible connection he would have with the plot," Cali admitted.

"He did come out squeaky clean in our check, but with his authority and access to the campus, we need to be sure, so keep an eye on him too, anyone else?"

"There are some questionable characters in the cafeteria staff," Cali pointed out.

"We are checking their records even as we speak, which reminds me, I need to check out the Dean's office tonight and get into the private employee files. That means you better get going to dinner," she finished and stood.

Cali came to her feet, wiping the sweat from her palms.

"You're doing fine," the woman reassured her.

"When are Tal and Sydney coming in?" Cali asked.

"We aren't sure yet. With the impact the two of you have made, there might be other areas they will be looking into with Mr. Grayson."

"Like whom is the outside support for the assault when it comes," Cali stated.

"That's right," Ms. Swanson smiled. "Every plot needs an outside support team in order to keep the assailants on the inside apprised of the response that is coming at them from the authorities. Mr. Grayson is having them scour information on possible accomplices with connections to the school, but don't work or go to school here."

"See you in class," Cali said giving her a nod.

"Watch yourself, and Josh if you can," Swanson said as she squeezed the girls shoulder.

Cali went out the same direction they had entered, but Ms. Swanson exited the back of the walkway between the buildings.

Cali hurried to the dining hall, all the way steeling herself to the actions and appearances that would greet her when Cindy and Josh exhibited their PDA for all to see.

She paused in front of the large doors entering the dining hall, collecting her thoughts. With a deep breath, she swung the door open and saw something she could have never prepared herself for.

Chapter 26

After the scene in the garden, Josh hurried to his room, pulling out the iPhone along the way and checking for messages. Twelve messages popped up on the device. He skipped through the first eleven and quickly opened the twelfth. "Do not engage the subject if possible. Avoid direct interaction if possible. If in your judgment, that will not be effective with subject, continue the charade as love interest, avoiding possible detection by the Director."

Josh sighed as he tucked the iPhone into his pocket. He wished he had avoided contact, but he was doing this for the entire team. He frowned as he played Cali's reaction in his mind again. He hoped she would forgive him.

A mob of classmates surrounded him before he could unlock the door when he reached his room. A mass of boys inundated him with questions about the meeting. He shrugged them off and slipped inside, pushing the door closed against the pressing bodies.

As the door latched closed, he flicked the deadbolt and slid down with his back against the door to come to a rest on the floor.

Then he remembered his intruder from the video earlier that day. He stood, tossing his pack to the side and approached the trunk cautiously. The trunk appeared to be intact without any signs of penetration into the hidden compartment in the back. He recalled the knife and the apparent injury the man suffered when trying to get into that compartment.

Josh moved over and flicked the light on as the sun set in his large windows overlooking the exercise grounds. He circled the trunk and spotted a small splatter of blood from the man's injury.

He placed his thumb onto the trunk's security pad and the false back popped open. He retrieved a device that looked like a scanner from the grocery store. Plugging the item into the iPhone he pulled from his pocket, he placed it close to the blood. A soft whirring sound came from the device as it drew in a small amount of the blood and the words, "Processing Sample Please Wait," appeared on the screen of his phone. Below the words, the time ticked down from ten minutes.

Josh set the iPhone down on his bed and unplugged the scanner, tucking it back into the trunk and closed it again.

He used the time to change into some jeans, a t-shirt, and a pullover sweatshirt. He slipped on a pair of tennis shoes when a slight ping sounded from the iPhone. Walking over, he lifted it so he could read the screen. "Subject Identified," flashed in red letters on the monitor. "Please push button for complete file," scrolled across the bottom of the screen.

He pressed the button and the words, "High Risk – Proceed with Caution," flashed at him in red. Then the image of a man came up as the information rolled across the screen. Sarcassi Natolei, ties to al-Qaida, very dangerous. Information already sent to team leader.

Josh stared in disbelief at the screen. The man on the screen didn't look like a terrorist, nor did he look foreign. He appeared to be anyone he would have run across in the little town of White Water, MN. The man had short dark hair, light skin and a dark beard trimmed short. Josh couldn't see any discernable markings on his face, and none were listed in the file.

He touched the continue button and the information scrolled across the screen. Natolei was believed to have been the orchestrator mind behind many of the suicide bombings in Iraq and suspected of helping plan the 911 bombings. He was listed as highly dangerous and whereabouts unknown.

Josh now knew who broke into his room. Natolei hid in plain sight posing as a security officer. His clothing matched the security detail Josh noticed on campus.

But the main question puzzled Josh. How could this man pass all the background checks all the security forces were required to undergo?

A knock at the bathroom door interrupted his thoughts.

Josh quickly tucked the iPhone into his sweatshirt pocket and opened the door to find Trevor standing there with a disappointed look on his face.

"What's the matter?" Josh asked.

"I would have thought you could have at least stopped over when you got back and filled me in on the juicy details," he said flashing a grin from his feigned frown.

"There's nothing to divulge," Josh said as he turned away walking into his room.

"Oh, come on," Trevor groaned following after him. "You had to have done something; you were gone nearly two hours."

Josh glanced down at his watch. "Already five?"

"Why, were you supposed to meet Cindy for dinner?" Trevor ribbed.

Josh turned back to him, not amused.

"You were," Trevor chided. "That is rich. The new guy lands the hottest girl at Chatterly his first day and you nearly had two."

"What do you mean two?" Josh turned back to him with a raised eyebrow.

"That Indian girl sure thought you were something. She couldn't take her eyes off you at breakfast and lunch." Trevor pointed out.

"Huh, didn't notice," Josh shrugged.

"You are the only one who didn't," Trevor pressed.

"I've got to get to the dining hall," Josh said as he closed up his trunk completely and secured the latch. "Coming?" he asked turning to Trevor.

"Yeah, let me grab my sweatshirt," he said and raced through the bathroom into his own room and quickly returned.

Josh stuck his head out of the door looking both ways down the hallway. Seeing the crowd no longer waited outside, they walked out and down into the tunnels and soon climbed the stairs in the building holding the dining hall and most of the classrooms.

They moved through the large wooden doors where Cindy greeted them with a contingent of friends. The girls swarmed around the two boys as Cindy slid her arm through Josh's and leaned against his shoulder.

"Cindy, this is my friend Trevor," Josh introduced.

"Oh, you are precious. Of course we all know Trevor," Cindy cooed. "As a matter of fact," Cindy released her grasp on Josh for a moment to pull a cute little red headed girl from the throng of girls surrounding them. "This is Stacy; she is dying to meet Trevor." Cindy grinned.

Stacy smiled widely as she blushed and moved over next to Trevor with a lot of nudges from her friends.

"Hi." Stacy grinned sheepishly.

"Hi." Trevor blushed.

A smaller grouping of girls whisked Trevor away with Stacy and Josh lost sight of him as they entered the dining hall with the remaining girls.

Josh glanced up and noticed the large sign hanging at the far end of the dining hall. In big navy blue lettering it read, "Welcome Dmitri and Cali."

Josh's mouth dropped open as he turned to Cindy in shock.

"What's the matter, honey," she purred as she laid her head on his shoulder.

"No one has ever welcomed me like this before," Josh said as his voice cracked.

"We felt we needed to welcome you and Cali to our school and make sure you understand how happy we are that you are here." Cindy rubbed Josh's back comfortingly.

Just then the doors behind him flew open and everyone spun to see Cali standing there, tears in her eyes. She hesitated a moment as she read the sign and then zeroed in on Josh and Cindy.

Josh saw her anger soften as the sign touched her as it did him. Being welcomed and accepted by these people they deceived was almost more than he could stand. He fought back tears of his own and did the only thing that could refocus both of them on their mission in one fell swoop.

Grabbing the back of Cindy's head, he pulled her to his lips and kissed her deeply. He snuck a look at Cali as Cindy kissed him back with her eyes closed. Cali's expression changed from one moved by the gesture of the welcome, into fury.

He closed his eyes, assured that Cali would now be able to concentrate on the task at hand and not be swept up in the goodness at Chatterly.

Cali stormed by them roughly and joined the group of her girlfriends waiting at a table.

Josh peeked as she passed and then pulled away from a speechless Cindy who looked at him in shock.

"I'm glad you have no problems with PDAs," she said, catching her breath.

"I thought that was what you liked," Josh said, still watching Cali sitting down at a table with her back to them.

"Yeah, I do, but I thought you might not be too open to it."

"Whatever makes you happy," Josh said smiling down at her, "makes me happy."

****

A flood of emotions hit Cali at seeing the sign welcoming her to Chatterly. She had never been welcomed anywhere like that before. White Water shunned her until Josh arrived and now Chatterly students welcomed her to this prestigious prep school.

Tears filled her eyes as her gratitude overwhelmed her. That lasted a short moment until Josh reached over and pulled Cindy to him in a deep kiss. Anger and jealousy shot through her like a lightning bolt as her reality surged back into her. She was playing Cali Ascalla, the daughter to the Indian Ambassador to the United States. Pretending to be something she wasn't to do her mission. Guilt mixed with her anger as she realized these students were only pawns in this game of espionage.

She saw Stephanie at a table waving her over and pushed passed Josh and Cindy, still lip locking, to join her pretend friends.

"What's the matter, don't you like it?" Stephanie asked.

"Yeah, it's great," Cali said trying to sound convincing as she forced a smile.

"This dinner is prepared in your and Dmitri's honor with food from your country. We had the Dean look up your favorite dishes from home and Grace and her staff prepared it for you two," Stephanie explained.

"It's incredible, thank you," Cali said, trying to sound more upbeat.

"What's up with you and Dmitri?" Stephanie asked.

"What do you mean?" Cali spun on the girl suddenly.

"I, I, I mean you seem to have a thing for him, that's all. I didn't mean anything by it," Stephanie stammered.

"He's cute and I was hoping to get a chance to meet him," Cali recovered, calming her facial expression.

"Well, it's too late now that Cindy got a hold of him," A brunette sitting across from them said.

"Yeah, whatever Cindy wants, Cindy gets," a blonde agreed rolling her eyes.

"You haven't told us about your meeting with Mr. Broderick yet," Stephanie questioned, remembering the encounter.

"You were the one he took out of Mad Abdalann's class today?" the brunette cried, leaning in closer across the table.

Cali shook her head.

"Tell us, what he is like in private?" the blonde giggled.

"Is he as gorgeous close up as he is from a distance?" the brunette asked excitedly.

"I'm sure you all know more about him than I do. I only got here last night," Cali protested.

"But he has never done that before," Stephanie pointed out.

"Never?" Cali questioned.

"Never," all the girls at the table chimed in.

Cali's eyebrow shot up. This was unexpected. Why did he intervene on her behalf after never doing so before?

"How long has Broderick been here? Stephanie said the security officers have been changed out recently for no apparent reason," Cali prodded.

"They have been, all except for Mr. Broderick," Stephanie explained.

"He is so reclusive that we hardly ever see him around," the brunette added.

"How about the rest of the officers, I haven't seen any on campus since last night," Cali asked.

"They guard the outer walls and only a few patrol the dorms during the night," Stephanie told her.

"Why are you so interested in the security at Chatterly?" the blond asked suspiciously.

"In my country, we are always taught not to leave anything to chance," Cali covered.

"You don't have to worry about Chatterly," Stephanie boasted. "Our security is the best in the country, some say even better than the president gets from the secret service."

"Enough of this kind of talk," a freckled red head scolded.

"Yeah, this is your welcome to Chatterly party, let's have fun." Stephanie agreed. She stood up and walked over to a table set up in the corner which Cali hadn't noticed until now. There was a boy sitting at the table with electronics equipment strewn all over it.

Stephanie whispered into his ear, and he nodded, giving her two thumbs up. She strode back confidently as Cali's favorite song began to play over the speakers set up all over the hall.

When Stephanie reached their table, Cali leaned in, shouting in her ear over the music. "How did you know 'Tangled Up In Me' by Skye Sweetnam was my favorite song?"

"Like I said, I have connections with the Dean. Dinner can wait, let's dance," she said helping Cali to her feet as they all got up to dance.

****

Josh sat down at a table with Cindy and her friends. Trevor and his new girl sat with a few people at a table across from them. Josh kept himself from steeling a glance at Cali, for fear of giving either of them away, but when a song began to play, he somehow knew it was her favorite song. He couldn't put his finger on it, but it seemed to fit her to the tee.

He could see Cali's table empty as the girls got up to dance and listened closely to the lyrics as Cindy kissed his neck. "I'm the girl that's sweeping you off your feet" echoed through the dining hall and his mind, as Cali's face burned into his brain.

Chapter 27

He was in such a trance with his thoughts and the music; he almost missed the person walking along the edge of the dining hall, behind the group of dancers along the wall. The face wasn't really a match to Natolei, even after his contacts zoomed in closer, but when the man reached to adjust his black baseball cap, the bandaged right hand sent a chill through him.

Josh jumped to his feet, nearly knocking Cindy over. Ignoring her complaints; he rushed through the crowd, trying to keep an eye on the man. The man exited the hall while Josh still pressed his way through the dancers trying to get to the door.

Josh burst through the doors, slamming them against the walls sending echoes through the empty corridors. He scanned to his left, and then his right, pressing his vision to its limits. He spotted nothing, no one in sight, even with night vision and thermal imagery.

A sound echoed down the hallway directly in front of him and he burst into motion, racing down the dark corridor, night vision turned on. He moved silently across the granite tiles, scanning the classrooms through the window of their closed doors as he hurried past.

Footfalls running down steps drew him to the stairwell, and he after them taking two and three stairs at a time, trying distance between him and his quarry. He found through the tunnel leading towards the boy's climbing the stairs to the main floor. the doorway entering the first floor hall as the . He slid along the wall to the corner until eye out to see the corridor. Establishing no one occupied the hallway, he slowly moved along trying to pick up a sign from the suspect.

He walked with his back to the stairwell leading to the tunnels when Mr. Burslie bumped into him coming out of his office.

Startled, the man jumped at Josh's presence, nearly dropping the pile of paperwork in his arms.

"Oh, Dmitri, you scared me. What are you doing back here so soon? Don't you like your welcome party?"

"It's very nice of everyone, I just wanted to be sure I had locked my room," Josh said, still turning his head scanning for the other man.

"Well, you don't have to worry about that. Security patrols the dorms twenty-four seven," Burslie reassure him.

"Then why don't I ever see them?" Josh questioned.

"They are trained to blend in. We don't want to make the students uneasy by their presence," he explained.

"You better get back. Don't want to keep them waiting for one of the guests of honor. You wouldn't want them to think you are rude," Burslie said as he ushered Josh to the stairwell and then continued on down the hall.

Josh took a step back, watching the man walk down the hall and then looked the other way. Where had the other man gone?

By the time he returned to the dining hall, the music played softly in the background as everyone ate and visited.

Cindy gave Josh a scolding glare after he got some food and sat down next to her.

"I'm sorry, I needed to go back to my room for something," Josh tried to explain.

"Something you will need to learn if we are going to be together," she leaned in whispering intensely. "You never leave me without a kiss goodbye."

Their eyes locked as she pulled away and Josh knew she wasn't kidding. He could only nod as he stuffed another forkful of beef stroganoff into his mouth. He continued nodding as he chewed, scanning the room until he spotted Cali and then averted his eyes as to not draw Cindy's suspicions.

****

As Josh rushed out of the room, his movement did not go unnoticed by Cali as she danced with her new friends. She cocked an eyebrow curiously as he slipped out of the dining hall.

"What is it?" Stephanie asked.

"Nothing." Cali dropped her eyes and shook her head as she swung her hips to the music.

"Oh my god," Stephanie whispered as she came close to Cali, grabbing her by the arm.

"What?" Cali lifted her head to see what upset Stephanie.

"Don't look." Stephanie pulled Cali into a crouch, so they were hidden within the dancers. "Mad Abdalann is here."

"Mr. Abdalann? Is that normal for a teacher to come to a student function like this?"

"No, I've never seen him in the dining hall before. The guards come and go, but no teacher is ever around here."

"What do you think he wants?" Cali asked as she waited for an alternative explanation than the one forming in her mind.

"He has to be looking for you," Stephanie whispered as she rose up slightly to spot the teacher.

"Me, why me?" Cali posed, feeling she already knew the answer. She showed the man up in his own classroom. Even if he had nothing to do with the terrorist plot, he would want to have the last word, as all men did.

218

Stephanie rose up once more and then ducked down quickly, but not quickly enough as Mr. Abdalann stepped through the crowd right next to Cali.

"A word if you would, please, Ms. Ascalla," he said politely, taking hold of her arm between the elbow and her shoulder, pulling her after him towards the exit.

Cali thought about taking this moment to remove his hand from her arm and twisting his hand to flip him onto his back, but she refrained, concerned of the questions that would arise from such an action.

"What do you want, Mr. Abdalann?" she questioned, letting him lead her to the door.

"Just a word," he said with a smile that made her skin crawl. "Not you Ms. Watson," he turned to Stephanie following close behind.

"But I don't think I should..." Stephanie began, but trailed off as Abdalann stared her down.

"That's alright Steph," Cali said giving her a slight smile; "it will be ok."

Stephanie stopped as Abdalann opened the door and nudged Cali through as he followed, not releasing her arm from his grasp.

Once the door clicked closed behind them, Cali took hold of Abdalann's little finger and twisted it, forcing him to release her with a cry of pain.

He spun on her angrily, fire burning in his eyes as he came up so close to her face, she could see the pores of his skin as perspiration seeped through.

"I have had enough of your disrespect for one day, young lady," he hissed.

"And how have I been disrespectful, professor, by defending my beliefs and by removing your hand from my person?" Cali glared back, the initial uncertainty caused by his arrival now gone.

"You have no right to contradict me in my classroom in front of my students, do you understand me?" he said, flailing his arms wildly over his head. "It undermines my authority and diminishes my effectiveness as a teacher."

"As a tyrant, more like," she interjected.

This sent him into another tirade, and he spun back on her after having taken a step away.

"This is not over, not by a long shot," he warned. "If you continue this course of behavior, I will not go easy on you."

"Why Mr. Abdalann, that sounds like a threat," Cali said closing the already small gap between them so now she could feel his breath on her face as she looked up slightly at him.

Mr. Abdalann's face went blank, void of emotion as he looked down at Cali.

Fury boiled in her and she fought the urge to teach him a lesson right there and then.

He turned deathly white and stepped back as if able to read her mind, raising his hands as he backed away, looking at her with a glazed look.

She then realized that Abdalann no longer looked at her, but past her. Cali spun her head to see Mr. Broderick standing behind her. The man had a baton drawn holding it firmly in his right fist and smacking it into his left palm.

"Mr. Abdalann thanks you for your time this evening, but he must be on his way," Mr. Broderick said slowly, staring at Abdalann.

"Uh, yes, thank you for taking the time away from your activity to speak with me Ms. Ascalla. I look forward to seeing you tomorrow in class." Mr. Abdalann said with a breathy voice laced with fear.

"Mr. Abdalann misspoke about tomorrow, Ms. Ascalla," Mr. Broderick said softly. "He will not be in class for a few weeks due to some unforeseen developments in his personal and professional life. Isn't that right, Mr. Abdalann?"

"That is absolutely correct, Mr. Broderick. Something has come up that requires my immediate attention. I need to leave tonight and as a matter of fact I am late packing for my journey. That is why I came by tonight, to try and assure you that I hold no grudge against you speaking your mind in my class," he lied.

"Then you better be off," Mr. Broderick said, adding a loud snap of the baton hitting his palm for effect.

Abdalann gave a quick nod and scurried off down the hallway and into the stairwell leading to the tunnels under the campus.

Cali watched him go, listening to his footfalls until they faded into nothing. She turned to Mr. Broderick, but she stood alone in the corridor. She spun around, looking for the man, but he was nowhere in sight.

She stood there processing what just happened when the doors to the dining hall burst open and Stephanie came rushing out with her group of girlfriends.

"Where did Mad Abdalann go?" Stephanie asked.

"He had to leave," Cali explained. "He wanted me to know that he held no hard feelings, but he needed to take some time to get some personal matters in order."

"You had better get in here. Grace has announced that the food is ready, and she made your favorite Indian dish, Chicken Pakora and Mutter Parathas bread."

Cali grinned at the mention of the traditional Indian food. Her father loved to cook for her and her mother before he returned to India and those were indeed her favorite dishes.

"Does she have a big pickle to go with the Mutter?" Cali asked excitedly.

"We can ask her, but I bet she does. Grace doesn't forget much when it comes to food," Stephanie grinned. She took Cali by the hand and pulled her into the dining hall as the rest of the girls trailed behind.

They got their food and were enjoying it immensely when Josh slipped back into the hall. Cali didn't suspect anyone other than Cindy and a few of her friends noticed his return, but she watched him go through the line and move over to take his spot next to Cindy.

Just like a lap dog, Cali sneered. She wasn't going to let this get to her. She needed to get done eating and do some investigating tonight after Stephanie went to bed. She pulled a piece of the Mutter bread off with her teeth and grinned softly. She thought she might check out Mr. Abdalann's quarters in the teacher's housing and maybe check up on Mr. Broderick while she was at it. She fidgeted in anticipation and chewed her bread.

Chapter 28

Josh enjoyed the stroganoff and planned to leave so he could do some recon, but Cindy had other ideas. The two left the dining hall and walked back towards the girl's dorms, arms wrapped around each other's waist. The other girls went on ahead at Cindy's insistence so they could be alone.

Josh looked around anxiously as he anticipated what Cindy might have on her one-track mind. Natolei kept playing on his mind. He was in front of Josh one minute and then the next, he was gone, vanished. He needed to find him, and soon. He felt certain Natolei played a part in the plot to take Chatterly, but how did he get into Chatterly past their security and how long had he been there laying his plan out?

As they walked up the large steps in front of the dorm, Josh looked at the top of Cindy's head, disgusted by the pain his actions caused Cali. He needed to make it up to Cali, but later, after he completed his mission.

He stopped at the top step and opened the door for her to go inside. The sun disappeared behind the large, ancient trees and the lights on the campus began to flicker with their automatic sensors clicking on and their halogen hum filling the grounds.

When he paused and didn't follow Cindy into her dorm, she turned and stepped back out.

"What are you doing? Aren't you coming up?" she asked.

"I'm really tired after my long journey last night and I have a lot of homework, especially in Abdalann's class," Josh explained.

"Didn't you hear? Abdalann is taking a few weeks off and we will be having a substitute teacher. I'm sure the teacher won't expect you to have it done," Cindy said with a smile, pleased with her logic for him to stay.

"I'm still very tired," Josh countered shaking his head. "I will see you at breakfast?"

Cindy looked up at him with puppy dog eyes and sticking out her bottom lip in a pout. "I suppose, but do I get a goodnight kiss at least?"

Josh leaned in to give her a soft peck on the lips, but Cindy had other ideas. She wrapped her arms around his neck as she pressed her lips tightly to his and then jumped up to wrap her legs around his waist. Josh would have cried out in shock if Cindy hadn't had her tongue halfway down his throat, preventing this.

She held herself wrapped around him and kissed him deeply even after he began to untangle her from himself.

Josh set her feet back on the step and pulled her arms from around his neck and finally separated his lips forcibly from hers with a loud sucking sound resulting.

"I've got to go," Josh said, his red face shining in the dim light. He took a few steps down the stairs and then paused to look back up at her.

Cindy smiled devilishly as she watched him go, giving him a little wave goodbye accompanied by a giggle.

Josh turned and hurried off, his head spinning with emotions, both good and bad as he felt guilty for liking Cindy on some level and admitting to himself that he liked the affection. He shook his head angrily at the thought as he stormed along the sidewalk. He couldn't betray Cali or the mission by actually having feelings for the girl and enjoying their sexual encounters.

He took the stairs outside his dorm two at a time and came to an abrupt stop as two guards stood just inside the door. The men asked for identification and Josh handed one of them his student id he received that morning.

The guard studied the card and then Josh up and down, nodding as he handed it back to him.

"Very good, sir, thank you for your assistance," the man said waving him into the dorms.

Josh tucked the id back into his wallet, thinking that getting past this security post seemed way too easy. Why was security so relaxed around here? He hadn't seen any guards on patrol. He still mulled this over in his head when he came to the landing between the first and second floors, glancing out the large windows as he proceeded up the stairs.

He stopped on the second step of the next flight and slowly turned back to the windows. He walked back down to stand in front of the huge panes as the sun could still be seen in the distance. His mouth dropped open as he saw one Humvee after another; loaded with weaponry a front line soldier would have killed for, roll along just inside the outer rock fence of the campus. Soldiers in black manned each Humvee turret wearing night vision goggles while he could see other men in the vehicle using electronic surveillance equipment.

Of course, Josh grinned. Why have guards on the campus when you can secure the campus from the perimeter? Chatterly was fortified like a prison, electronic fencing added to the top of the old block walls humming in Josh's ears when he concentrated on listening for them. He looked closer and his contacts changed into the thermal vision setting with a thought to see the glow of electricity pulsing through the wires.

He sighed with relief as he felt more confident that an attack would be more difficult than any terrorist would expect.

"Beautiful sight, isn't it?" A voice from behind him made him jump.

Josh turned to see Mr. Burslie, hands clasped behind his back, watching the movement of the security detail with immense pride.

"Ah, yeah, I guess," Josh finally said.

"You should feel very safe knowing that all precautions and safe measures have been taken to ensure you safety." Burslie smiled, the setting sun reflecting strangely off some of his teeth more than others.

Josh's brow furrowed with curiosity as he studied the man's teeth.

Burslie glanced down at Josh, catching him studying him and frowned, "What is it? Why are you looking at me that way?"

"Your teeth don't have the same enamel. Some are natural while others are manufactured. Did you have an accident as a child that caused you to have a plate put in?" Josh asked.

"No, you must be mistaken. These are and have always been my own teeth," he said pulling one of his hands from behind his back to nervously touch his mouth.

The white bandage held Josh's gaze for far too long as Burslie looked at Josh's expression and quickly drew his hand back behind his back.

"A letter opener slipped this morning and cut my hand. It is minor, but I didn't want to get blood anywhere," Burslie explained.

Like my room, Josh thought as he nodded, drawing his lips into a grin in a sign of his understanding.

One of the guards from the front door came up the stairs, panting a bit from the climb.

"Yes?" Burslie said as the man stopped before him.

"We've been informed that Mr. Abdalann will no longer be allowed on campus until further notice," the guard informed him, but then stopped when he saw Josh.

"If you would excuse me Dmitri, but we have some official business to attend to," Mr. Burslie said with a slight bow of his head as he forced a smile.

"Oh, yeah, no problem," Josh said as he moved past the two men and went up to the second floor and turned down the hall towards his room. He rounded the corner and then pressed himself against the wall, sliding back to the corner of the wall by the stairwell.

He listened as he pulled his iPhone out of his pocket, tapping it for external microphone and easing the device as close to the stairs as he dared. He touched the voice recognition button and waited.

There was silence for a long while, but then a loud slap could be heard.

"You idiot, you are never to speak to me about information like that in front of anyone else. Luckily, he has no concept of what is going on, but you shouldn't be taking those chances." Mr. Burslie's voice whispered with intensity.

"Broderick removed Abdalann for two weeks after he was too aggressive to a female student who stood up to him," the guard told him.

"Fool," Burslie spat. "Abdalann was supposed to keep suspicion on him while we carried out our plans behind his rhetoric."

"Now what do we do?" the guard asked.

"Continue the preparations as planned. We are almost ready to proceed. Only a few more items need to be put in place and we shall be prepared." Burslie told him.

"Did you ever find out what was in the Russian kid's trunk?" the guard questioned.

"No," Burslie sighed. "What did the scan show when you brought it through security?"

"Just a blank spot, but there was a lot of space where there was nothing," the guard explained.

"Maybe it was his father's trunk, and the boy didn't even realize it had a false back. Wouldn't the scan have shown you if there was something in the space?" Burslie reasoned.

"Not if it was lined properly," the guard pointed out.

"Do you suspect him of anything?" Burslie asked.

"No, not really, just a dumb rusky," the guard chuckled.

"I don't either," Burslie agreed, "he was running around here tonight like he was lost. I don't think he has his mind on anything but his new girlfriend."

"He's the one who is dating Halstrum?" the guard said amazed.

"The girl's taste is turning bad," Burslie laughed, their voices fading off as they went down the stairs.

Josh clenched his teeth against the insults, letting the iPhone do its job. He looked down at the screen as it flashed "Voice identified, Sarcassi Natolei, wanted for terrorism."

He quickly tapped out a message to Cali, Ms. Swanson, and Mr. Grayson about his discovery. He felt confident that Mr. Burslie was indeed Sarcassi Natolei and at least some of the guards had aligned him.

The mention of Mr. Broderick implied he wasn't part of the plan since he removed the misdirection of Mr. Abdalann from the plot. An uneasy feeling that the plot went far deeper than just these two crept through Josh's thoughts.

Josh hurried into his room leaving the lights off, careful not to make a sound to alert Trevor to his return. He eased the lock into place on the door to the bathroom from his side and pressed his thumb against the touch pad as the light scanned his print illuminating his face in the dark room. The latch clicked open, and he pulled open the back compartment.

He changed into the black attire needed to do some recon undetected and fastened a sheathed knife on one hip and a silenced revolver on the other. He had no intention on having a firefight tonight or even encountering a conflict at this point. He needed to discover the goal of the plot and ascertain the extent of the preparation thus far.

He moved to the window, undoing the latch, and pushing the pane outward. He stuck his head out examining the narrow ledge running the entire side of the building. He slipped out onto the ledge but only walked along it as far as a copper downspout and then shinnied down to the ground, dropping behind the shrubbery along the foundation.

He headed for the teacher's housing on the far side of campus, keeping to the deeper shadows created by all the landscaping. It may look good in the day, but it was a haven for those who wanted to remain undetected at night. After checking out Abdalann's quarters, he would move over to the security officer's quarters and see if he could discern any other accomplices in the plans.

Chapter 29

Cali waited for a time after the sun set for Stephanie to go to sleep, but the girl insisted on staying up to talk. Finally, Cali convinced her to have a pop, slipping a light sedative undetected into the drink, sending her off to sleep none too soon.

Stephanie snored deeply as Cali's dark figure slipped out the window and crawled down the wall, using her fingers to grip the mortar lines in the brick wall to lightly land in the greenery surrounding the dorm.

I think I have been in the foliage a little too much today already; she frowned and then crept from shadow to shadow until she crouched outside the teacher's housing. She stood outside the main entrance to the building, pressed in the shadows of a corner of the ornate architecture. Leaning forward against the rail, she peered through the glass window at the mailboxes along the entrance wall. Focusing in closer with her contacts, she made out Abdalann's name on apartment 308.

Leaning back, she looked up at the towering building three stories above her. With a sigh, she started to climb up a steel waterspout running down from the gutters, glad that the building only had three floors, since she felt sure that Abdalann's apartment would have been at the top floor no matter how many the building had. Such was her luck.

After reaching the third floor, she moved slowly across the small ledge, taking care to move as quickly as she could past lit windows, of which there were only a few, until she came to a window leading into a hallway. Reaching down, she pulled on the window, but it wouldn't budge.

Taking a small item that looked like a pen from her pocket, she lined the pen up with the latch through the window. Flicking a switch a small laser shot out of the pen, melting the latch, and allowing her to slide the now unlocked window open.

She moved down the lit hall, too aware of being fully exposed, even though she wore a hood over her head. Her lips curled up at the irony that if she were discovered, she would appear exactly like the terrorists she came here to stop.

Cali found 308 and with pen in hand, prepared to destroy the lock, but then she hesitated and reached up, trying the knob to find it unlocked. It turned in her hand and the door swing open slightly.

She got low as she crept into the room, her eyes changing to night vision as she entered the dark room almost without a thought. She found the room in complete disarray as articles and items lay strewn everywhere.

A noise came from another room, and she slid up next to the wall separating the kitchen and the living room, listening intently. The sound of shuffling papers and a drawer being opened reached her ears again.

She peered around the corner as a dark figure, even with night vision, crept into the room. The figure spotted the open door and immediately dropped down into a defensive position and moved over closer to the open door.

Just as the person eased past Cali and her darkened hiding place, they threw a fierce punch at her head.

Cali ducked the blow striking the mid-section of the figure as it fought to remove its hand from the hole in the sheetrock.

Cali struck again, but the person nimbly jumped over her outstretched arm and landed next to her, taking a hold of her neck, but then hesitating for a slight moment before it twisted her head for a quick kill.

Cali used this hesitation to grasp the arm around her neck and throw the attacker over her shoulder and onto an overturned couch in the center of the room. She moved quickly towards the figure lying prone on the furniture and then stopped, perplexed.

The figure shook as it lay across the couch... laughing.

Cali stepped over to flick a light switch and there lay Josh, hand on his ribs, laughing hysterically. She glared down at him, hands on her hips, and a disapproving frown on her face.

"What?" Josh asked as he raised his arms and grimaced at the pain in his rib as he did so.

"I could have killed you," she whispered angrily.

"But you didn't. Does that mean you are too soft for this spy stuff," he teased.

"When did you know it was me?" she asked.

"When I had you around your neck, there was something about your perfume I remembered."

"Why didn't you say something before I threw you?"

"I didn't have time." He grinned. "That move was awesome."

She walked over, quietly shutting the door, and then came back and sat down next to him as he righted himself stiffly.

They looked at each other and he held her gaze, the sincerity visible in his eyes. "I'm sorry about the way the Cindy thing has turned out," he said and then turned away from her.

"Ms. Swanson explained it to me, but just because I can understand it, doesn't mean I have to like it. Does it?"

"I was protecting all of us and the mission," he continued.

"I said I get it," she said irritably. "Why did you wreck Abdalann's apartment?"

"I didn't. It was like this when I got here," he explained.

"Did you find anything?" she asked.

"It was a real mess in here, but I did find a notebook that had some codes written on it and then the top sheet had been torn off. They looked like some kind of launch codes," he added.

"What would they do with launch codes?" Cali asked skeptically.

"To launch something," Josh said shrugging indicating he didn't know.

"I know what they would use them for, but have you found anything that they could launch?" She sighed rolling her eyes.

"It could also be an activation code for a bomb, I suppose," he said raising an eyebrow at his spoken thought.

"A bomb? Did you find a bomb or any component for a bomb?" She leaned closer.

"No, but it would make perfect sense. They take the school hostage with the children of many important diplomats and leaders of industry. You demand the release of the prisoners at Guantanamo and while everyone is running around trying to free the hostages, you have a bomb that will make as big a statement to the world as 911 did. The terrorists would have a twofold victory." Chills ran up Josh's back as he laid out the possible scenario.

"So they free the prisoners and then kill all the hostages," Cali got to her feet. "We know they're all martyrs, so dying during the takeover would not even be an issue for them."

"We have to tell Ms. Swanson," Cali said as she grabbed Josh's hand and pulled her after him. She stopped before the door. "I don't know what apartment she is in?"

"303 down the hall," Josh noticing her impressed look. "What, I checked before I came in?" He shrugged.

They slipped out of the apartment and silently crept down the hall to Ms. Swanson's apartment.

Cali reached up to knock on the door when Josh took a hold of her hand. She looked at him, irritated.

Josh put a finger to his lips and motioned with his head to the door.

Cali looked at him curiously for a moment and then leaned in closer to the door placing her ear just inches from the wood. The faint sound reached her ears as muffled crying and then a sudden sound of flesh being struck, and bones being broken followed by a silenced cry of pain.

Josh pulled the pistol out of his hip holster and Cali drew her knife strapped to her waist. Taking the pen she used before, she melted the lock and they looked to each other, Josh holding up three fingers and together they nodded a count of three.

Bursting into the room, they discovered four men dressed in black security uniforms surrounding a battered and beaten Ms. Swanson tied to a chair.

Without hesitation, Cali sliced the throat of the man nearest her, and Josh proceeded to put a bullet into the head of the remaining three, their pistols dropping harmlessly out of their hands as the men fell dead on the floor.

They rushed to Ms. Swanson, Cali cutting her bonds and Josh untying the cloth holding the gag in her mouth. Blood ran from her ears, nose, and eye. Bones protruded from her skin on her right arm and left leg. It looked as if they broke every finger and toe. She sat in only her bra and panties. Cigarette burns covered her legs, arms, neck, and breasts.

Ms. Swanson slunk heavily into Josh's arms as he carefully lowered her to the floor. He sat holding her as Cali checked for vitals, looking horrified at Josh as she held her hand to the woman's neck checking her pulse.

"Call 911," Josh told Cali.

As the girl rose to get the phone, the soft words wafted to her as she froze, not believing her own ears.

"No," the words came again, this time a little louder than the first.

"Ms. Swanson," Josh whispered in as soothing a voice as he could muster. "You're going to be ok. Let Cali call for help and you will be ok."

"No time for that, I'm afraid," Ms. Swanson said and began to cough up blood. "They've punctured my lungs, those bastards."

"That is why we need to get you to the hospital," Cali pleaded.

"They suspected me from the start," Swanson slurred her words. "Abdalann was watching me, and something tipped him off. They wanted to know who I was working for and who else was undercover here."

"That's alright," Josh assured her. "We found some of the players and think we have an idea what they might be up to."

"A bomb," Swanson said as her eyes closed heavily. "They are going to kill everyone within a block of Chatterly with a bomb. They were so proud of their plan; they kept telling me over and over, sons of bitches. Once the prisoners from Guantanamo are released, they are going to kill everyone."

"We have to get word to Grayson once we get you to the hospital," Josh said, nodding to Cali to get the phone.

"Stop," Swanson said pulling Cali up cold. "I am going to die, we all know that." She looked hard at Josh and then painfully turned to stare at Cali. "I knew the dangers when I joined up, and you know that it is always a possibility, and now it was my turn. If you take me to the hospital, you will blow your cover and give the terrorists the upper hand. With you two still in place, we have a chance to stop this from happening."

Swanson stared into Josh's eyes, the pain rolled beneath her blue orbs as the end drew nearer. "I never wanted to hurt you kids, but you are in a position to help so many innocent people. I'm proud of you all and only wish that you could have been mine to enjoy for the first sixteen years of your life as I have enjoyed you for the last few weeks of mine."

She closed her eyes, and her breathing became labored as Josh drew her battered and bloodied body close to his, pressing his cheek to hers. Josh's eyes shot wide with surprise and then a lone tear rolled down his cheek.

He held her for a moment longer and then stood with her in his arms and walked robot like into her bedroom with Cali close behind. Josh laid Ms. Swanson on the bed, covering her up to her face with her bedspread.

Josh turned and Cali wrapped her arms around him, holding him tight without a word.

"Malory," he whispered in her ear.

"What?"

"Her first name was Malory."

He pulled away from her embrace and strode out of the room.

Cali looked back one last time on Malory Swanson and then followed Josh. She found him pulling his black hood back up with the cloth covering everything but his sad eyes.

"We need to get back to our rooms and act like nothing has happened," he told her. "I'll contact Grayson and they should find her soon. Let's hope we have enough time to find the bomb before they put their plans in motion. Because like it or not, we will be as much hostages as the rest of the students when it reaches that point."

He turned and walked out the door, then put his head back in before shutting it behind him. "Mr. Burslie and some security officers are in the middle of this. I heard him say that Broderick was getting in the way. Maybe we can use Broderick to our advantage down the stretch." He nodded his head as he processed his own words and then closed the door behind him.

Cali drew her hood up as well, haunted by Josh's sorrow filled eyes. Something about them made her very uneasy. It was what she saw behind that sorrow which really terrified her, revenge.

She slipped out the window and into the night, racing to return to her charade of Cali Ascalla, Chatterly student.

Chapter 30

Josh raced back to his dorm, the tears flowing down his cheek in a steady stream. He at first attempted to brush them away as he went, but the futility of it just made him angry as he wiped them away with the back of his hand, over and over. Each attempt becoming increasingly violent until he stopped, leaning against the corner of a building in the shadows, crying uncontrollably.

The old wound of losing his mother lay bare and exposed. The slightly healed wound torn open by the loss of Malory, the woman who always tried to reason with the teens and show them compassion while Grayson played their driving force.

He crouched down lower in the shadows as two men on patrol walked by. He reached into his pocket and tapped his iPhone, letting Grayson and the others know of Malory's fate. Turning the device off, he slid it into his pocket and stared out as the men rounded a corner of a distant building.

He skirted another building and shinnied up the drainpipe that ran next to his window. He lifted himself to swing inside when something caught his eye and he stopped, pressing firmly against the block wall, and peering into the room. At first he saw nothing, but as he convinced himself he saw nothing and relaxed his stance to go in, a slight movement in the corner drew his attention as his contacts changed to night vision. A man dressed in black crouched in the corner, waiting patiently.

Then it struck Josh. The man waited for him. He waited where the door would swing open when a normal student would return. But Josh wasn't a normal student. He studied his assailant and a glint of a blade caught Josh's eye.

Josh contemplated waiting the man out, but then a slight tap came at the door and the latch clicked open. Josh's eyebrow rose curiously as he peered through the window at the door sliding silently open.

The man came slowly to his feet, hands raised, at the ready, a blade in one and an open palm with the other.

Josh pulled his silenced pistol out of its holster and carefully took aim as Cindy's blond head slipped in through the doorway. Just as the man flexed to strike, Josh put a bullet in the back of his head and he crumbled to the floor, falling against the door, and slamming it shut on the girl as she tumbled into the hallway with a cry muffled by the closing door.

Josh scurried through the window, grabbing a towel hanging on a chair and wrapped it firmly around the dead man's head to slow the bleeding. He then hefted the man into the closet and closed the door quickly. He took another towel and wiped up the blood splatter and the blood that spread across the tile and tossed it into the closet with the dead man.

Another tap came at the door as he spun from the closet and he opened the door, yanking off his hood and mask at the last second, stuffing them into his pocket as he pulled his shirt down over his holstered gun and sheathed knife.

"Cindy," he said rubbing his eyes as he feigned sleepiness, "what are you doing here?"

"I came over to surprise you, but you slammed the door on me and nearly took my head off," she said with her hands upon her hips.

"I didn't know it was you and I had to throw on some clothes," he said, not letting her move past him as she pressed against the door he held ajar and leaned out from behind.

"I heard a lot of noise in there," she craned her neck to see past him into the darkened room. "Are you sure you don't have anyone in there with you?"

"Not a living soul in here but me," Josh said looking down as he saw a small line of blood slowly flowing out from between his feet, under the ajar door and into the hall by Cindy's feet.

"I'm really beat and took some sleeping pills tonight, so can we do this another time?" he said, quickly looking away from the tell-tale blood back at her.

"I thought you would want me to stay with you tonight," she wined, sticking out her bottom lip and frowning.

"You know I do, but I want to be awake and able to give you the attention you deserve when you stay with me for the first time." He smiled sheepishly, lifting his eyebrows.

She stared at him for a moment and then her eyes brightened, and she smirked devilishly. "You're right. I want our first night together to be something we can remember always."

"Exactly my thoughts," he shot back.

"Good night, Dmitri," she said, leaning close to give him a soft kiss.

"Good night, Cindy," he said as she pulled away.

She gave him one last look, mixed with attraction and doubt, and then flashed another seductive smile. "I hope you know what you missed," she opened her coat to reveal a lacey teddy underneath and then closed it quickly and strode off.

Josh watched her go, contemplating going after her to make sure she got to her room safely, but decided to figure out what he should to do about the dead man in his closet and determine to what extent Mr. Burslie suspected him.

Josh grabbed a towel hanging on a hook, quickly wiped the blood easing into the hallway, and backed into his room shutting the door and locking it. He slid down the door to a sitting position with his back against it. As he pulled his iPhone out, he recalled somewhere in all the things he read in the past few days, a method for destroying all kinds of evidence.

He glanced at the screen as a message came in from Grayson. "Sorry to hear about Ms. Swanson, we will be sure to eliminate any evidence of the occurrence. Be advised, external support for terrorist mission has been identified and will be eliminated by the remainder of the team."

He texted an accounting of his incident with the man waiting for him when he returned to his room and voiced his concern as to how he could dispose of the body.

The light blinked on as a new message came in. "Use 'garbage bag' to dispose of unwanted rubbish. Then proceed with caution until you ascertain the extent to which you are under suspicion." Grayson replied.

As he read the message, he recalled the item Grayson referred to. He walked over to his trunk and released the hidden compartment. He drew out a thick black bag, unfolding it many times until it was twice the size of him. He then unzipped the bag and laid it out on the floor. Returning to the closet, he pulled the dead man from his hiding place and centered him on the black plastic. He began to zip the bag shut, and then paused to toss the extra towels in.

He zipped the corpse into the bag and then taking some electrical leads extending from the corners of the bag, attached them to his iPhone.

The screen showed the bag and a drop down list of articles that were inside. Josh chose the appropriate items, towels, body, clothing, knife, and pressed the dispose button.

The bag puffed up like a balloon and a faint odor reached Josh's nose reminding him of popcorn in a microwave. He vowed then and there to never eat popcorn again.

A slight hissing sound came from the bag through a vent on the side. The air soon escaped plastic and the bag lay as flat as it had before the body resided inside.

"Remove metals" flashed on his iPhone and Josh unzipped the bag, expecting to see ooze or gore left over, but the blade from the man's knife and the zippers from his clothing remained, not even ash. Josh detached the wires from his iPhone and folded the bag into a neat square once more.

After placing the bag back in its hiding place, Josh returned his gun and knife along with the dark clothing to their rightful spots in the trunk and slid the false back into place.

He lay down on his bed, pulling the covers over his naked body, shivering uncontrollably. He wasn't cold, but he couldn't stop shaking. He glanced at his iPhone as the clock showed 3:00 am.

A message light blinked, and he touched the face of the device, the glow lit the room with an eerie haze. "Ms. Swanson home now, others disposed of."

That was it. Nice and sterile, the way Grayson liked it. No emotions, just efficient.

Josh lay awake, thinking of his next move. He decided to use this situation as an opportunity to root out the others involved. He should be able to tell the players by their reaction to him still being alive.

Mr. Burslie is actually Sarcassi Natolei, he thought. How was that possible when the two men didn't looking anything alike? He pulled up the files of the men, bringing their pictures onto the screen next to each other and studying each over and over.

He finally shook his head, deciding that Natolei must have had plastic surgery to prepare to take over Mr. Burslie's position at Chatterly. But then, where was the real Burslie?

The thought had to wait as his alarm sounded and he drug himself out of bed, exhausted both physically and emotionally after the night's activities.

Slipping into some wind pants and a sweatshirt, he headed to the exercise field, conscious of each person's reaction to his appearance.

Most of the guards he passed paid him no mind, but there were a few who stopped in their tracks, watching him pass when they saw him. None held quite the expression that Burslie did though. The man went deathly white, and his jaw dropped open as he stood at the front of the exercise formation of students.

It took Burslie several minutes to regain his composure and begin the morning calisthenics. A short man in security fatigues ran up and whispered into Burslie's ear and shot nervous looks towards Josh. The man nodded, staring at Josh as Burslie spoke in his ear and then ran back into the dormitory.

Josh and Trevor finished their laps and returned to their rooms. As Josh entered, he found his room ransacked and his belongings strewn everywhere. He always carried his iPhone and his trunk had been locked, but that held little consolation as he saw the trunk was gone.

He locked the door as he quickly tapped out a message on his iPhone. "Room searched, trunk gone, afraid cover compromised."

He began looking for anything he could salvage out of the mess as a message came back almost instantly.

"Mission in jeopardy, remove yourself from site immediately."

He lifted a finger to type his respond to the affirmative but then realized he would be leaving Cali at Chatterly by herself. "Negative," he replied. "Will find vantage point to remain on campus to offer support to team member," he pressed send and waited impatiently.

"Not advisable, but understandable, confirmed," the response came back.

Josh was ready to argue his point, feeling Grayson would never allow him to stay, but instead, stood staring at the text in shock.

He gathered what clothing he could, shoving it into his backpack and headed out the door. He thought he would have liked to have his supplies at this moment as he stopped suddenly, remembering information about the trunk. Touching his iPhone, he touched the icon labeled 'tracking.' Holding his breath as the menu for the program came up, he grinned with a sigh as one of the selections read, 'equipment container,' on the screen.

Choosing the item, a flashing red dot showing the location of his supplies on a map of the campus appeared. The only problem was the trunk appeared to be in the very room where he now stood. How could that be? He stared dumbfounded at the screen for a moment, but then it hit him, and he began to move. He went out the door, not bothering to close it after him as he spun quickly down the stairs, following them to the ground floor. He stopped, moving over to where the dot flashed on the screen. He moved over to the door, turned the knob, and pushed the door inward. He stared in disbelief as the room was a storage closet with nothing but boxes lining the walls.

Turning away from the room, he followed the stairs further down into the tunnels, finding himself standing in the middle of a tunnel with no trunk in sight. He wandered through the side tunnels until he wound back towards the red dot, finding a spiral staircase twisting down into the depths beneath the dormitory.

He paused, listening for any indication of someone down there with him. When he felt satisfied that he was not being followed and no one approached, he continued on as the lighting in the tunnels became less frequent and he often found himself in complete darkness.

As his eyes adjusted, his night vision became even less effective in the tunnel devoid of any light. He reached out, using the wall to guide him, not willing to touch his iPhone and allow anyone looking in his direction to see the device glowing in the pitch black.

He finally stopped by a bend in the tunnel, covering the iPhone with his shirt pulled up over his head so he could see his progress of locating his trunk. The screen glowed softly as the red dot showed to be not more than thirty feet to his left.

Tucking the iPhone back into his pocket, he moved along the wall, seeing a light up ahead accompanied by the sound of voices.

The language Josh heard was a mix of Arabic and English as the men fluctuated between the two randomly. From the sound of it, there were at least four of them and they were working at getting something open, not having much luck by the sounds of their curses.

Josh moved close enough to an opening in the tunnel to see it widen into a large room where the men bent over his trunk, two with crow bars, another with an acetylene torch, burning brightly in his hand.

Josh's hand moved slowly to his hip, grasping for his handgun that wasn't there. His left hand felt reflexively for his knife with no more luck. He stood peering into the room, the men in black security uniforms all much larger than him, wondering what to do next.

One of the men turned towards Josh and he slipped back into the tunnel further, trying to press against the wall and blend into the darkness as much as possible. As he pressed, a door behind him opened and he stumbled backwards into a darkened room. He scrambled to his feet as his eyes adjusted to the dim light and he slipped behind a large looming object.

The man who turned while Josh observed them trying to open his trunk stuck his head in the room, holding a flashlight in front of him, the sudden light blinding Josh for an instant as he ducked down lower behind the object. The man scanned the room and then pulled the door closed behind him as he left.

Josh heard the unsettling sound of the door being secured from the outside with the click of a padlock being closed. A lump formed in Josh's throat as he thought of his predicament.

The voices next store became louder as the men argued over what to try next to open the trunk since the crowbars and torch hadn't done the job.

"Natolei wants us top side," one of the men told the others. "We are nearing the time."

Josh heard the men file out and secure the door as they did the one to the room he now occupied.

Their footsteps faded into silence as Josh strained to listen. He flicked his iPhone on and shone the light around for a better look of the room. He stared in disbelief at the object he hid behind. Eight large Plexiglas cylinders stood nearly as tall as him filled with thick liquid while a central container holding white powder towered over him, nearly four times the size of the other cylinders.

Josh found the bomb but was now locked in the room with it. He tapped out a text to Grayson, telling him he had located the bomb. He pressed send and waited as the thin blue line on top raced across screen at first but then froze. He stared a moment longer before seeing that he had no connection to any type of network down here, well below the surface of the campus.

The light blinked out on the screen, timing out in a power conserving setting. As the lights went out, Josh felt his hope go out as well.

Chapter 31

Cali slipped in through her window, checking to see that Stephanie was still sleeping soundly.

She got undressed, carefully returning her clothing to the secure compartment in her trunk. As she slid the black attire into its place, she paused, looking at the drops of blood on the dark fabric. Impossible to discern whether the blood came from the terrorists or Ms. Swanson, the thought of it made her stomach roll. She raced for the bathroom wearing nothing but her bra and panties as she emptied her stomach into the porcelain bowl.

When she felt fairly sure her stomach emptied its entire contents, she leaned back against the stall's wall, wiping the perspiration from her forehead. The image of Ms. Swanson crept back to her thoughts, forcing what remained in her stomach out into the toilet. She sat back once more, trying to force the events of the night from her mind.

She sat there for a while, wondering what to do next, uncertain as to how they were expected to find a bomb in such a short time. The terrorists must now realize that something hadn't gone right with their plan, even if they didn't find the bodies of their comrades, as Josh assured her Grayson would take care of. Eventually, they would notice them missing. That would force the terrorist's hand and they may move their plans ahead, giving her and Josh even less time to locate the bomb before they were taken hostage.

When she crept back into her room, Stephanie snored softly with her back to Cali. Cali slipped between the sheets of her bed and let out a soft sigh, closing her eyes.

She woke with a start, sitting straight up in her bed as the alarm sounded on the stand next to her. Stephanie groggily reached to press the snooze bar on the clock as she slowly sat up and stretched.

"You look like hell," Stephanie said, rubbing her eyes as she glanced at Cali.

"It wasn't a good night, last night," Cali said weakly.

"You can call the dean and tell them you're sick," Stephanie suggested.

"No, I need to go to class. It's only my second day." Cali smiled wearily as she slid her legs over the edge of the bed and Stephanie stood up stretching.

That was when Cali noticed the light blinking on her iPhone sitting on the dresser. She picked it up and touched the screen. A red warning flashed across the screen, "for your eyes only," caused her to look over at her roommate and assure she wasn't near enough to see.

"You coming?" Stephanie asked.

"Go ahead, I'll catch up with you," she told her.

Cali watched the girl leave and waited a moment to tap the screen, activating the emergency message. "Josh's cover compromised, watch yourself," scrolled across the screen.

Cali's heart dropped. Was he ok? Did they have him? Was he getting out? The questions rolled one after another through her mind.

She typed out a text and sent it, "what should I do?" she asked.

A message came back quickly, "maintain cover and search for bomb."

She turned the screen off and tucked the device safely away in her trunk behind the locked panel. She then grabbed a towel and headed for the showers. She felt confident the day was going to be short for all the things she needed to accomplish.

They showered and walked to the dining hall where the room already buzzed with excitement. Cali watched with trepidation as Stephanie came skipping back from a nearby table where Cindy and her crowd sat chattering.

"Ms. Cutlage left unexpectedly and now we don't have a teacher for first class," Stephanie said between bites of pancakes.

"Where'd she go?" Cali asked hesitantly, cringing as she expected to hear the horrifying news that Ms. Cutlage had been murdered.

"They say her father was taken ill suddenly and she needed to rush to his side in the hospital," Stephanie said shrugging.

"Oh." Cali nodded as she slipped a forkful of French toast between her lips, the syrup dripping down her chin. She wiped her chin with a napkin and glanced up to see Mr. Broderick striding into the hall and stopping right next to her. She glanced up, the white napkin still pressed against her skin.

"I wonder if I could have a word with you?" he asked, leaning down as he spoke softly.

"Yes, of course," she said nodding coming to her feet as he gently took hold of her upper arm and helped her step away from the table. "I'll be right back," she said to Stephanie as the girl stared curiously.

She walked with Mr. Broderick out of the hall and followed him down to his office where they spoke the day before.

He ushered her in, shutting the door behind him and motioned for her to take a seat as he stepped around behind the desk and sat down heavily.

He stared at her wordlessly as he stroked his chin, his eyes often moving to look at the ceiling as he fought to choose his words.

"I have a few questions for you," he started, struggling to steady his voice, and failing.

She nodded her understanding and continued to watch him as he fidgeted in his chair. She crossed her legs, exposing her knee from under her skirt as she did. He looked at the bare flesh and blushed openly, clearing his throat as he looked away.

"Where were you last night?" he began.

"In my room," she replied, looking directly at him.

"How well did you know Ms. Cutlage?"

"I met her yesterday and she was kind enough to help me get on track with my work for her class after school hours. Why?"

"We went to her apartment in the teacher housing when she didn't show up for a staff meeting this morning and we found no sign of her."

"Stephanie said she went to be with her sick father," Cali offered up feeling her palms begin to sweat.

"It said that in a note, but there were some things that just didn't add up when I took a closer look around her apartment," Broderick said lifting a doubtful eyebrow.

"Like what?"

"There were freshly patched holes in the wall as well as pieces of furniture that weren't school issue. You see, the apartments come furnished for all the teachers."

Cali stared right through him as she struggled to discover how he connected this to her.

"I think something happened in that apartment and someone is trying to cover it up," he said flatly.

"Why are you talking to me about this?" Cali asked her pulse racing like a cornered animal.

"You say you were never in her apartment?"

"I told you, we met, but no, we never went to her apartment but sat in the gardens and talked."

"Then how would you explain this?" he said extending his index finger.

Cali leaned in closer to look at the small red dot on the end of his finger as her breath rushed from her when she recognized it. Her hand reflexively went to her forehead where the bindi had been the day before. She neglected to take it off since she wasn't used to wearing one and completely forgot about it.

Their eyes met and he stared emotionlessly back at her as she frantically sought for the right words that now escaped her. She gazed back at him, at a loss.

"What were you doing in her apartment? What happened to her?" He pressed, sitting back in his chair, and tucking the bindi in a plastic bag.

"You have my file." Cali stalled as her mind raced.

"I have a file, yes, but I think you know more than you're letting on."

"I still don't have any idea what went on with Ms. Cutlage. I'm sure there are other girls who wear a bindi at Chatterly," she argued.

"Don't you think I would have checked that out? You are the only one who was wearing a red bindi yesterday. Now what were you doing in the apartment and what happened there?"

"I have nothing to say." Cali crossed her arms.

"I wish you wouldn't take that attitude," Broderick sighed. "I want to help you here. Maybe if you tell me what you know, I will promise to do everything I can to be sure you get a fair deal with the dean."

"What do you think I did?" Cali pressed her hands upon the desk as she leaned forward, her eyebrow raised.

"I think something bad happened in that apartment. I found some traces of blood and think someone was at the very least injured if not killed. You may be a witness and don't even know it, but I'm pretty confident that you were there." He leaned forward bringing his face so close to hers that their noses nearly touched.

They sat there glaring at each other until he leaned back in his chair with a sigh. "Why do you have to be so stubborn?"

Cali stared back at him a moment longer and then leaned back. Should she tell him? Grayson insisted they needed to keep the teams existence secret. He even suggested they kill in order to keep the team's secret.

It wouldn't have been hard to leap over the desk and quickly snap his neck. It would take a second and his questioning would stop. Her mind filled with horror at her terrible thought. How could she think that killing Broderick would be a valid solution? Bile crept up in the back of her throat and she fought the urge to throw up.

"Stay on campus until further notice, I'm not done with you," he said as he frowned at her.

She came to her feet and turned for the door, but stopped with her hand upon the knob, turning back to him as she recalled what Josh had said. "What if I told you I might have seen some of the security guards around the teacher apartments last night?"

"That is pretty normal. We patrol the entire campus," Broderick brushed the question aside.

"Not on patrol, but acting suspiciously," she pressed the point. Why did he have to be so dense? "Are you sure that all your men are who they say they are?"

Broderick opened his mouth to argue but then paused as he turned his eyes up as if looking inside his own head for the answer.

"If you would have asked that a few months ago, I would have had no doubts." He said hesitantly. "But over the last few months, I have been required to replace nearly every man on campus."

"Why is that?" Cali questioned.

"It came from higher than me, out of the Department of Defense. They said there may be a terrorist plot against the school and they were concerned about an inside job. They suggested I turn over my force to ensure that no one got to a man inside."

His face lost all expression as he looked up at her dumbfounded. His job dropped open as he stared at her. "Who are you?"

"Maybe you better worry more about the men you have around you than a little teenage girl?" she said sarcastically and swung the door open, letting it bang against the inside wall as she strode down the hallway without a glance back.

She finally took a deep breath when she reached the door to the dining hall and glanced back to find he wasn't following her. He was suspicious of her, but maybe he would check out some things that would expose the potential threat within the campus walls.

Cali found Stephanie still sitting at the table along with a larger group of students who would have normally been in the class with Ms. Cutlage. They visited amongst themselves as the kitchen staff cleaned the tables and swept the floor.

Cali only gave them a passing glance as she sat next to her roommate. Cindy and her group sat across from them, complaining that Dmitri had not shown up that morning.

"He wouldn't let me into his room last night and then he didn't show up for breakfast before classes," she wined.

"Maybe he was busy with homework," Stephanie reasoned.

Cindy opened her mouth to continue when the intercom let out a long tone and a man's voice came on.

"This is Dean Matson. All students and teachers please report to the dining hall immediately for a special student assembly." A tone came over the speaker again and then went silent.

"What was that about?" Cindy questioned.

"Hard to say," Stephanie said shrugging as she looked up to stare at the students already filing into the hall.

Cali turned one way and then the next as she observed the exits and the appearance of uniformed guards. She quickly got to her feet and slipped into the kitchen and the serving area with the serving line closed off by a door. The kitchen staff were out in the hall cleaning up after breakfast and Cali slipped past Grace unseen as she sat eating her breakfast at her office desk while reading the paper.

Cali eased her head out the door leading to the hallway, immediately pulling back, and closing the door as two guards approached. She watched them move past through the slight crack she peered through. Once the men moved past, she slipped out of the kitchen and down into the stairs leading to the tunnels.

"Hey, stop," a voice called as she slipped into the stairwell causing her to freeze in place.

Chapter 32

Sydney and Tal sat in the Dean's office, waiting for the secretary to finish the required paperwork and have the dean sign off to admit them officially to Chatterly.

Grayson felt uncomfortable about sending them in together, but after the loss of Ms. Swanson, they were running out of time and needed to get back up inside before the terrorists sprung their plan. Otherwise, they would be of little help to Cali and Josh.

As they worked hard at not making eye contact, they listened to the secretary tap on her keyboard and mumble to herself. Her grey hair, cut short, fell forward obscuring her face as she typed. She stopped frequently to wipe her nose with a white Kleenex between the sniffles of a cold, tucking the used tissue in the band of her watch between uses.

The new students each had a large trunk with them, different in design from each other, but containing the same hidden compartments filled with the tools of their new trade.

Sydney glanced at Tal as two men in black uniforms entered the room, coming to stop in front of the secretary.

She kept typing away, not noticing the new arrivals until she paused to dab the end of her nose again. She hesitated with the tissue against her nose as her eyes looked the two men up and down curiously.

"Yes, can I help you?" she asked, her mouth muffled by her hands up to her nose.

"We need to speak with the Dean," one of the men stated.

"Just a minute," she said as she stood and walked into the next room.

She reappeared shortly, pulling the door shut behind her. "He is busy getting the enrollment papers finished for these two students. Could you come back later?"

"No, I don't think that will work for us," the man said looking at the other man and giving a shrug.

"We need to see him right now," the other man said taking the woman by the arm and walking into the dean's office followed by the first man who closed the door behind them.

Muffled voices emanated from the office. Tal and Sydney exchanged suspicious glances as Tal came to his feet, moving over to the door to place his ear against it.

The intercom came on with a long tone and a voice announced, "This is Dean Matson. All students and teachers please report to the dining hall immediately for a special student assembly." Another long tone sounded and then the intercom went silent.

Sydney came to her feet as Tal backed away from the door quickly, pulling her onto his lap as he slid into a chair. She squeaked with surprise as the door opened and the two men came out, guns drawn with amused looks on their faces.

Sydney glanced past them to see the dean tied in his chair with the secretary sitting on his lap facing him, tied tightly to him.

"Maybe these two would like the same treatment," the guard chuckled.

"They already seem very cozy," the other man agreed, waving his gun casually as he spoke.

Sydney saw the opening and took it, diving for the weapon, propelled by Tal coming to his feet with lightning quickness.

Sydney hit the man's gun hand as she flew in front of him, rolling as she landed, coming back to her feet. She spun and swung a kick into the man's midsection as she drove him backwards into the secretary's desk. He toppled over the furniture slamming up against the wall, his head hitting the wall at an unnatural angle with a loud crack.

Tal sprung onto the second man out of the office, taking hold of the gun wrenching it free and tossing it away. Without slowing, he spun the man still holding his wrist, bringing his free arm around the man's neck, and placing his hand on the top of the guard's head. With a sudden flex of Tal's arm, the man's head jerked to one side with a snap and the man fell in a heap to the floor.

Tal turned to see Sydney shutting the door to the office, leaving the dean and his secretary with her back to the door, obliviously safe.

"So much for blending in," Tal grunted.

"Now what?" asked Sydney.

"Now that they've started, we might as well see if we can find Cali and Josh," Tal suggested.

Both opened their luggage and changed into their black fatigues, pulling on matching gloves and hoods with cloth which covered their entire face except their eyes and attaching their iPhones to their belts, plugging in the wires leading from the suites.

Pressing a button on their iPhone, the suit blended in with its surroundings, making the teens nearly invisible.

"That is so cool," Tal laughed. He fastened his silenced pistols in their holsters around his waist and then swung the sniper rifle over one shoulder.

Sydney did the same as her eyes flashed with anticipation. "So we're really doing this?" she said, the trepidation evident in her voice.

"We might as well use what we have," Tal told her. "Besides, who is going to save Mr. All-American?"

"Tal, you shouldn't be so hard on Josh. He feels proud of what he can do, that's all." Sydney turned towards the door, stopping to look back at him. Her eyes flashed to infrared imaging, and she could make him out clearly.

"It gets irritating after a while, him always being the yes man to Grayson and Swa...," he paused in mid-sentence.

"I can't believe she's gone," Sydney whispered.

"Let's get these bastards and get this over so we can go home," he answered and strode past her down the empty hall.

They moved into the tunnels as Grayson instructed. There they would encounter less people, even more so, now with the plot set into motion with the summoning of all students and teachers to the dining hall.

****

Cali stepped into a doorway and waited for the man, grabbing him around the neck as he past, planning on snapping his neck quickly, but she suddenly realized who he was.

She released his neck and Broderick leaned heavily against the far wall of the passage, rubbing his neck, and staring at her in shock.

"What are you doing?" she scolded.

"Me? You nearly choked me to death," he spat and then the realization came to him, and his face went aghast. "That was what you were going to do."

"I didn't know it was you," she said exasperatedly.

"Who did you think I was then?"

"The terrorists taking over the school," she stated matter of fact.

"That's absurd, there are no terrorists taking over the school," he argued.

"How often does the dean gather the students in the dining hall for a student assembly? Don't you have a theatre where you usually meet?"

Broderick's eyes shot wide.

"You really don't pick up on this very quickly, do you?" she said sarcastically.

"I have to get up there and stop them," he said turning and heading back towards the stairs, but Cali took hold of his shirt collar, bringing him up short with a jerk. He spun on her violently.

"What are you doing?"

"You will only get killed or taken hostage like the rest of them." She shook her head.

"It's my job, my responsibility," he argued.

"You won't do anyone any good if you go up there now."

"Then what do you suggest we do?"

"We need to get some things from my room and then we need to get into a position where we can observe the terrorists and monitor their movements," she stated.

"Who ARE you?" He said waving his arms over his head in frustration.

"Someone who is here to help," she said as she turned and headed down the passage.

Broderick shrugged and trailed behind without another word.

****

Josh sat in the dark, letting the blackness caress his mood after getting locked in the room with the bomb. Real smart, he chided himself.

He flicked the screen of his iPhone as the dim light reflected off the clear containers of the bomb's components. A sliver of light shone through an air vent near the ceiling of the room that

260

connected the room where the men attempted to open his trunk.

He located a chair in the room and stood on the back of it to reach the vent. The small vent would never allow him to get through, but he tore the vent off effortlessly anyway. The physical destruction of something made him feel a little more in control of his situation.

Reaching through the vent, he punched the vent cover on the other side leading into the next room off. It clattered upon the cement floor in the empty room.

Hoisting himself partially into the vent, he could squeeze his head and right arm through until they extended into the next room. The dim lighting barely illuminated the trunk as it sat in the middle of the room.

The fabric had been burned off completely, exposing the now signed Kevlar coating that lay hidden underneath. Scrapes bore witness where they tried to pry the false back open, to no avail.

He stared at the trunk for a moment, trying to think of a way to reach the treasures inside that would surely allow him to not only free himself but give him the tools to diffuse the bomb as well.

He pulled back into his dark cell as he stared angrily at the iPhone for some clue as to what to do next. He scrolled through the options and screens, grunting in disgust as he noted the lack of any kind of connection to the outside world.

Not finding anything of help on the screen, he walked over to the bomb, holding the glowing device up over his head as he examined the device which shared his confines. He traced back the trigger to find, to his dismay, numerous triggers that would activate when one was deactivated. It would take nearly five people to diffuse the bomb simultaneously in order to neutralize the threat. There had to be another way. There had to be a trigger somewhere top side that Natolei controlled. He needed to escape his confines and take out Natolei, but how?

He thought hard on what he had learned in his short time as a covert operative that may give him a chance to escape his confinement. He looked casually at the vent opening again and the thought came to him. It was his shoulders that were too large to fit through the opening. He stared at the dark wall before him, contemplating what he was considering and then back up at the opening. It was the only way.

He stood upon the back of the chair again and measured with his hands, bringing them back down to his torso, holding them as steady as he could to get as accurate as he could. He didn't want to do this and find it wouldn't work after all.

As his hands came down to his chest just below his shoulders, he nodded the affirmative as his hands sat slightly wider than his chest. Just as he thought, it was his shoulders.

He swung his arms in circles at his shoulder as they went over his head and round and round. He put the memory of it out of his head, the time when he had wiped surfing and had come down on his board all wrong. He just hoped he had enough force to do the job.

Looking around the room holding the iPhone over his head, he found what he thought were bags of sand, but when he opened them to check, realized it was more of the power he suspected to be inside the large cylinder of the bomb.

His hopes soared as he realized he could change his course of action. He intended on making himself smaller by dislocating his shoulders to slip through the opening, but now with this powdered explosive at his feet, he could make the hole bigger instead.

The only problem, he needed to ignite some of this powder to blow the vent bigger without setting off the bomb. He spun and sat down on the stacked bags and thought. When the solution came to him, he hopped up with excitement and gathered one of the bags in his hands and walked over to set it on the chair.

He lifted the phone over his head to illuminate more of his dark confines searching. He scanned until he found some excess wire in the corner. He raced over to retrieve his discovery and stripped the plastic coating of the wire in one smooth motion. He snapped the wire to his desired length as he measured it against the wall from the vent to the ground.

He then tore a quarter size hole in the bag and spit into the powder several times and then stuck a finger into the hole to pack the wet powder together into a lump. He then coiled up the wire a few times and inserted it into the lump.

He tore some of the cloth from the top of the bag off and fastened the strips around the hole and wire ensuring the wire wouldn't slip out.

Josh paused as he remembered the properties of the explosive powder and lifted the bag in his hands to estimate the weight. He untied the top of the bag and carefully removed a portion and then secured it again. He nodded, satisfied that the amount of explosive remaining could do the job without threatening to set off the bomb.

Taking a deep breath, he inserted the free end of the wire into a port in his iPhone and then took hold of the bag and stepped up onto the chair. He knew he couldn't lower the IED by the ignition wire but needed to drop it and time the ignition just right to weaken the wall.

Hesitating for a moment, he took a deep breath and ran the scenario through one more time. With a less than confident nod, he lifted the bag through the opening and let it go. The wire ran through the opening, and he hit the button on his phone sending current through the wire and into the bag holding the powder.

But where Josh hoped to detonate the explosive in the other room just above the floor sat a bed unbeknownst to him. Josh's perfect timing meant nothing as the bag bounced off the bed and hurtled away from the wall across the room as Josh pressed the button.

A loud explosion erupted in the adjacent room as Josh crouched down on the chair covering his head. The hallway echoed as the steel door of the neighboring room burst open, flying off its hinges and impacted the far wall of the hallway.

Josh's eyes shot wide, not expecting to create such a commotion that certainly would alert the terrorists to his presence. He leapt up to look through the vent as the smoke cleared and the demolished doorway came into view.

"Shit!" Josh spun and slammed down in the chair still a prisoner and a sitting duck for the terrorists to come and finish off.

Chapter 33

Cali glanced back over her shoulder as she ran, Broderick right at her heels. Now she needed to deal with him, she shook her head. She raced up the stairs leading to her dorm room and burst inside. Broderick entered behind her, and she spun on him.

"What are you doing?" she said, putting a finger in the center of his chest.

"Helping, if I can," he stammered.

"If you let on anything about me or my mission, I will kill you," she said as she stared him down hard. "I'm under strict orders that no one knows of our existence."

"So, there are more of you?" he asked.

"What do you think?" she rolled her eyes.

"Of course there are more of you," he reasoned.

She spun around, dropping to a knee and placing her thumb against the scanner pad on her trunk. The lock clicked open, and she slid the panel open to expose the tools of her new trade.

"Oh my god," Broderick gasped at the sight.

She pulled her black fatigues out, placing them on the bed next to her and then stood up, staring at the man as he ogled the case full of weapons.

"Turn around so I can change," she said with a twirl of her finger.

"Oh, ya, of course," he got flustered at the thought as he turned his back to her. "Who are you, special ops?" he asked again.

"Not your typical special ops, but you might say that" she said hesitatingly as she slipped out of her school uniform and then shrugged as if realizing it for the first time herself. She pulled her pants on and then her shirt, sliding the belt tight and clipping on the iPhone.

She began fastening the holsters for her silenced pistols around her waist and noticed he still had his back to her. "You can turn around."

He spun around slowly as his jaw dropped at the sight of her.

She carried two pistols with silencers, a few grenades and a sniper rifle jutting out over her left shoulder and ammo all over in pockets in every possible spot. She went through touching each piece with her hand and checking it off in her head before nodding to herself and heading back towards the door. Hesitating for a second, she crouched down and retrieved her school uniform from the floor and tucked it into her backpack and swung it on her back.

"What do you want from me?" he asked timidly.

"What can you offer?" she raised an eyebrow.

"I know this campus better than anyone else. All the tunnels, hidden passageways, anything that is here, I know about." His face brightened as he realized his worth.

"Can you handle a weapon?" she asked, pulling another pistol from her trunk.

"Airborne," he nodded, catching the gun as she tossed it to him and then handed him four more clips.

"Keep your head down and watch my back, can you handle that?" she asked.

"Sure can," he grinned.

"Let's go," she nodded.

"Where to?" he asked.

"A place I can observe the terrorists and have a clean shot at the man with the trigger to the bomb," she said as she strode out the door into the hall.

"A bomb, you never mentioned a bomb." He grabbed her by the arm and spun her around.

"You do realize this just began moments ago," she sighed. "When was I supposed to brief you?"

"True," he agreed with a nod and shrugged.

"You will just have to go on the fly. Where would be a place to hide a bomb that would destroy the entire campus?" she asked.

"The tunnels under the dining hall," he told her. "If the bomb were strong enough, it would cause the entire campus to implode and fall into itself, killing everyone above like a giant fault in an earthquake."

"Ok, first take me to a spot so we can see what the terrorists are up to, and then we can look for the bomb," she decided.

"Alright, this way." He pointed and they raced down the corridor to the stairwell and back to the tunnels.

Broderick raced down the tunnels as Cali stayed right with him, scanning from side to side, memorizing the tunnels as she went, making note of each twist, turn and passageway leading away from the tunnel they were on.

They stopped at a spiral staircase in the center of the passage as Broderick caught his breath. Cali waited patiently for a moment and then stepped onto the first tread of the staircase and stared upward.

"Where does this lead?" She motioned with her head.

"Straight up through the walls of the dining hall and into a mezzanine above the hall where the duct work and mechanical equipment are," he said looking up at her. "The top has a hatch that enters a mechanical room with some areas we might be able to access that looks down on the hall."

Cali nodded and began to climb. Spinning around and around, she had to twist her shoulders a bit to avoid catching the sniper rifle on the railing, but finally, she reached the trap door. The barrel of her rifle scraped the cover, so she slid the strap until it hung safely clear of the door.

Pushing her shoulder into the door, she lifted it open and carefully let it rest on the floor of the mechanical room she now entered. Stepping over the slight ridge, she turned and helped Broderick up.

He nodded his thanks and then motioned over to one side where a dim light filtered into the room.

They crept quietly over and peered through a louvered panel about as tall as they were and twice as wide. The louvers were a few inches apart and had mesh over them to prevent debris from being drawn through the openings.

From their birds-eye vantage point they could see the entire hall, the entrance to the kitchen on the right side, the hallway entrance at the far end. The restrooms lay directly beneath them.

Cali studied the dining hall as she scanned over and over again, from one side of the hall to the other. Men in black uniforms lined the walls, creating a nearly continuous line of black enclosing the students who sat at the tables silently, either staring at each other, or looking around horrified at their captors.

Cali felt Broderick turn towards her, so she looked over to him, questioningly.

"What do you think?" he asked.

"I was told that Mr. Burslie was involved in this, and he had some of your security men in it as well." She saw him tense up. "I didn't realize how many of them were involved though. There are at least twenty men in the room alone, and I'm guessing there are more securing the rest of the campus."

"The fellow on the far side by the kitchen entrance is Burslie," Broderick confirmed. "But this is only a small amount of my security force, and most of them were supplied in the last few weeks by the government's security contingent. There has to be at least a hundred men not accounted for."

"How many of those men do you feel you can completely trust?" she asked, turning back to peer at the man Broderick had identified as Burslie.

He thought silently for a moment. "Sixty men," he finally replied. "I can vouch for at least fifty men who would take no part in anything like this."

"That leaves us with a possible enemy force of sixty counting the men in the hall," Cali reasoned. "We need to see where those men are and discern if they are able to aid us in retaking the school."

"I think I know where most of them should be right now," he nodded. "Shift change and breaks would put a lot of them in the break room in one of the tunnels."

"Then we should check that out," she agreed.

Broderick began to turn away, but Cali stood staring out at the hall.

"What is it?" he asked, turning back.

"Take a look at Burslie," she said, handing him some binoculars she had tucked into a pocket. She focused her gaze on the man on the dining hall floor as her contacts allowed her vision to zoom in effortlessly.

Broderick took the binoculars and focused them. He gasped as he saw something strapped to the man's chest and arm. "Is that what I think it is?" he whispered.

"He is wearing a triggering devise on his belt that will allow him to detonate the bomb manually, but I expected as much. It is what I hadn't expected that is the concern. Follow the lines from the trigger as they slip under his clothing," she instructed.

Broderick went silent as he did as he was told. He gasped as his inspection exposed the added risk, she now showed him.

"What is that?" he asked.

"It is a biometric trigger," she explained. "If we kill him, the bomb will be triggered automatically. The lines lead to a heart sensor on his chest and a pulse monitor on his neck. I assume that if he were simply terminated, say with my sniper rifle, the stopping of his heart and pulse would trigger the bomb."

"So how do we neutralize him?" Broderick wondered.

"I don't know yet," she sighed. "Let's go find your men." She turned and disappeared down the staircase.

Broderick looked at Mr. Burslie a moment longer, then pulled his gaze away and heading down the stairs after Cali.

Cali waited patiently at the bottom of the staircase for Broderick to reach her and then followed him as he headed to the break rooms where his men should be.

After a while of moving through the tunnels they reached a large wooden door positioned in the middle of the passageway. Broderick touched a code into a keypad lock, pulled the door open, and walked inside.

The horrific scene of blood and bodies everywhere met their stares of shock. The remnants of a brutal gun fight filled the room as bullet holes riddled the walls, tables, and most everything else. Men in black uniforms lay strewn across the floor, on tables, against walls, lying on overturned furniture. Numerous victims sustained multiple wounds, including what appeared to be a fatal shot to the head.

Broderick rushed to one officer, kneeling to feel for a pulse, but then dropped to the floor, fighting to keep his composure.

Cali touched the man on the shoulder with a comforting hand as he turned his face up to hers, eyes welling with tears as he forced himself to stay in control.

"He was my brother-in-law," he said about the man next to him. "Are they all dead?"

Cali changed her vision to heat imaging, showing no one in the room with ambient body temperatures except for herself and Broderick.

"It appears that way," she said, the sympathy heavy in her voice. "I'm sorry."

"I think this is most of my guys who have been with me long enough to trust," his voice waivered.

Cali did a quick count and there were close to sixty men lying dead in this one room. She closed her eyes, trying to pull herself together. Where was Josh? Was he still on campus, and if so, was he ok?

Chapter 34

Voices echoed down the hall as the terrorists Josh expected to come investigate the noise he made arrived. He stood and steadied himself behind the door and waited.

"What the hell?" A man's voice reached him from the other room. "Next door."

Shuffling footfalls told Josh that at least four men gathered outside his door, and one took hold of the lock and released the latch.

Josh drew all of his muscles into a taunt position, knowing that he needed to do this perfectly in order to survive. He focused and waited.

The door swung inward, racing to slam Josh into the wall, but he leapt up into the corner, bracing his hands and feet against the adjoining walls and scampering to rest his back against the ceiling.

The echo of the metal door slamming against the stone wall satisfied the men entering the room that no one hid behind the door, and they turned their attention to checking behind the bomb. As the front man on either side stepped behind the bomb and out of sight of the other two standing by the doorway, Josh dropped down from his roost and struck.

The maneuver played smoothly in his head as he released his pressure on the walls and he landed on top of the nearest man, grasping his head and twisting it before his feet touched the ground. Releasing his grip on the first man as he slumped to the floor, Josh leveled a kick that struck the second man in the neck as he turned to identify the movement coming from his side.

Josh's foot crushed the man's windpipe, and he dropped to his knees wheezing his final gasps of air.

The sounds of bodies hitting the floor brought the other two men from behind the bomb, their guns raised and firing as Josh vanished through the doorway.

They raced out after him to find the tunnel empty.

Josh sprinted into the adjacent room, pressed his thumb against the sensor and the false back of the trunk clicked open. He reached in and drew out his silenced pistol and took out the men entering the room one after the other with a clean kill shot to their head. As the men slumped to the floor, Josh gathered his supplies and quickly stripped down to slip on his black fatigues and fasten on his weaponry before hurrying out of the room and into the tunnels.

Josh traveled along the tunnels, surprised by how close to the surface he was when he found a spiral staircase that led to a small outbuilding on campus. He peered through the lone window in the small structure as a pair of uniformed officers passed close by. How long had he been locked up? Had Burslie put his plans in motion yet?

He didn't need to wait long, as a message came across his iPhone from Grayson. "Terrorists have contacted authorities. Plot in motion." The signal indicator flickered on his device and then went out. Josh tried several things to reconnect, but he stayed cut off from the outside world. He touched the screen to identify connectivity issue, and two words flashed in capital letters, "SIGNAL JAMMED."

He needed to find Cali and coordinate their next move. He tapped the screen and pressed the locator button, hoping that the terrorist wouldn't be jamming signals on the campus itself since they would need to communicate and coordinate their movements somehow.

He waited an anxious moment and then a red dot blinked on his screen. He touched the identify target button, and Cali's name popped up. It showed her in the tunnels at the center of campus. Josh jumped onto the staircase, sliding down the steps quickly, running through the tunnels in an instant, closing the gap between him and Cali.

He rounded a bend colliding with a group of guards walking in the opposite direction. His momentum carried him through the group of four guards, sprawling them upon the ground behind him as he tumbled to the hard floor, rolling the best he could, allowing him to come to his feet.

He turned hesitantly as he wasn't sure if they were loyal guards or terrorists. The clarification came quickly as they jumped to their feet, drawing their pistols. Josh took three long strides to the nearest passage leading from the one the main passage, using his pistols to shoot out the lights in the corridor, sending the tunnel into blackness. He raced deeper into the tunnel until darkness concealed him. His eyes changed into night vision, and he watched as the men moved cautiously along the passage, hugging the walls, and feeling out their every step.

Josh dropped the first man with a shot to the head and aimed at the second when out of the corner of his eye, he saw another man pull out something and point it in his direction. He wasn't overly concerned as the man couldn't see him, but then the realization as the identity of the object struck him, but this realization came too late as the light came on, sending an explosion of pain through his head.

The flashlight caught Josh in the night vision mode and the excruciating pain incapacitated him momentarily, but even as he fought the pain, he turned, racing down the passage blindly, in an attempt to escape the men. Bullets ricocheted off the tunnel walls as he wove from side to side, disoriented by the sudden light.

Running as quickly as he could, he slid his free hand along the wall until he lost contact with the wall and turned into the next passage. Reaching his pistol around the corner back into the tunnel, he fired a few shots to slow his attackers down and give him a chance to clear his head.

He shook his head and pulled his other pistol, holstering the one in his right hand. His eyes now returned to normal, and his disorientation waned, as he prepared for the men to come for him. He crouched and waited for the assault that never came. He slid to the edge and peered carefully down the tunnel, but there were no signs of the men except for the one who lay dead in a dark mass on the floor of the black passageway.

Looking to his right, he saw a spiral staircase leading upward and he moved over to it, aiming his pistol up the rungs to be certain it wasn't occupied. Putting his pistol away, he quietly climbed the stairs. They seemed unusually long, but he continued until he found himself poking his head through an open hatch into a mechanical room with motors and air handlers.

He moved over to light streaming through large louvered panels, taking his sniper rifle off and setting it against the panel as he leaned closer to peer through the slats.

The dining hall, lined with uniformed guards as the students sat quietly in the center of the hall, lay below him. He scanned the hall for Cali and gave a sigh of relief when he couldn't locate her. Cindy sat subdued with her friends; the normal confidence drained out of her. Students from every age group who Josh hadn't seen before filled the hall with around two hundred fifty students surrounded by twenty guards.

He went to turn away but froze when his eyes fell upon Burslie. He wore blue jeans, tennis shoes, and a white T-shirt, but it wasn't his attire that drew Josh's attention. An object Josh immediately identified as a triggering device attached to Burslie's belt drew his gaze, but even that wasn't so daunting. But the wires visibly running under the man's shirt to connect to what appeared to be a sensor on his chest and neck sent a chill down Josh's spine.

Josh read about this, not since becoming a special op, but in his normal life. Normal, Josh laughed, gone forever.

Burslie wore what some called a life trigger. As long as the person hooked up to the trigger lived, the bomb could only be triggered manually, but if the man died, the bomb would detonate.

Josh looked over at the sniper rifle longingly. How he wished he could take out Burslie and the other terrorists that easily. He knew he could eliminate most of them with ease, before they knew what hit them, and if he had Cali, or Sydney, or Tal, they could have ended this quickly. But with that switch, Burslie needed to be subdued, or else the bomb would be unleashed.

Chapter 35

Cali and Broderick gathered themselves from the devastating scene of the Chatterly security force's massacre and headed back towards the dining hall in hopes of discovering the location of the bomb and possibly diffusing it.

As they moved cautiously along, they heard gun fire from the passage ahead and approached the conflict slowly. They slid up to a darkened opening as the sound of the gun fight echoed from the tunnel.

Cali slipped past the opening to lean against the far side as Broderick brought up his pistol to the ready and leaned against the wall next to the opening on his side.

Footfalls warned them just before three men burst into the tunnel. Broderick leveled his gun at the men. "Freeze," he ordered, they spun in unison on him, weapons raised.

Cali killed all three with efficient head shots from her silenced pistol as Broderick stood staring in shock. Cali pulled the clip from her gun and placed a fresh clip in its place, looking back at the man stoically.

"What?" she asked.

"Nothing," he shook his head looking down the darkened tunnel. "Let's check back in with the dining hall."

Cali nodded her agreement and then began to shake. A little at first, but then her entire body shook as she stared down at the dead men lying at her feet. Tears ran down her face as she felt the impact of her first kill hit her like running headlong into a brick wall.

She dropped to her knees as Broderick knelt down beside her, leaning in close to look at her face.

"First time, huh? He questioned.

She nodded as she took in a ragged breath between her sobs.

"How could I do such a thing so automatically and without feeling?"

"I don't know. It could be your training. The intensity at which someone readies for a mission often desensitizes them from the horrors they may encounter during that mission."

Cali nodded as she lifted her eyes from the floor to meet his. "Did this happen to you?"

"Ranger, remember? Spent my time preparing for the very worst in every situation and learning how to put the emotion out of it and do what needed to be done. That is the only way you will stay sane in all of this."

Cali stared hard at him, uncertain that what he spoke of happened in his past as he recalled it with such intensity that it felt like the here and now.

"We need to find that bomb," Cali said wiping her tears from her cheeks getting to her feet. "Or else people much more innocent than these men will die."

They carefully moved down the dark passageway coming across the body of a man Cali knelt to check his vitals. She changed her vision to night vision and looked him over. A single shot to the head. She frowned in thought.

They reached the spiral staircase and Cali led the way up. As her head cleared the hatch, she spotted a figure against the louvered wall, pulling her pistol instinctively as she rose out of the stairwell.

****

Josh scanned the hall when he heard someone coming up the stairs. He ducked and rolled back towards the opening hatch, drawing his pistol as he rolled. He came to his feet, his pistol right in the face of familiar green eyes.

****

Cali's pistol pointed right at Josh's face when Broderick came up behind her, the click of his gun in her ear as he drew down on Josh. Cali reached behind her, pushing down Broderick's arms as she lowered her weapon.

Josh brought his pistol down and took Cali into a warm embrace.

She hugged him back, burying her head in his shoulder.

"You decided to let him in on this?" Josh asked her with a jerk of his head toward Broderick.

"I didn't have much of a choice and he has been some help," she told him.

"Hey, I'm right here," Broderick complained.

"Yeah, sorry," Josh said extending a hand, but not letting go of Cali with his other arm. "Dmitri," Josh told him, deciding to keep his cover for now. "We're here to help eliminate the threat here."

"Wish you could have done so before they took hostages," Broderick said.

"We all do," Cali interrupted, pushing away from Josh.

"What do we know?" Josh asked her.

"We know that you can use all the help you can get All-American," Tal appeared before them in the mechanical room as he switched his camouflage suit off.

"Tal," Cali exclaimed, jumping into his arms, and giving him a big hug.

"Where's Sydney?" Josh asked looking around.

Sydney appeared in front of him, embracing him affectionately.

"You don't think Grayson would have sent him in alone, did you?" she motioned at Tal as she grinned up at Josh.

"When did you guys get in?" Josh asked smiling widely.

"We were in the dean's office when the dean made his announcement," Sydney explained.

"How did you make your suits do that?" Cali asked, looking Tal up and down.

"It's a new application that Grayson programmed into our iPhones before we came in. He said your suits could do it too as long as we gave you the application when we got in here," Tal explained.

"That is awesome," Josh grinned as he moved over to Tal. Extending his hand to the boy, Tal took it in his and shook it back. "Glad to see you," Josh beamed.

"I know you are, but we can get into that later," Tal said with a smirk, and then turned to the man standing with his mouth hanging open, staring at them. "Who's the dude?"

"Mr. Broderick, these are our friends," Cali introduced, "Tal and Sydney. The deal you and I made about our existence extends to them as well, ok?"

"No problem," Broderick said dumbfounded.

"So, what have you two found out?" Sydney asked, turning her attention back to Josh and Cali.

"Mr. Burslie is behind the terrorist plan, at least from the inside," Josh explained.

"Burslie? That's impossible," Broderick scoffed.

"I think Burslie is actually Sarcassi Natolei, an international terrorist who had some sort of plastic surgery to look like Burslie," Josh continued, looking at Broderick irritated.

"How many men does he have and what kind of support can we count on from the rest of the security detail who isn't on their side?" Tal questioned.

"We think they have between twenty and forty men, counting those on the inside of the buildings and those patrolling the grounds," Cali told them. "As far as any help from the other security officers," she paused looking sympathetically at Broderick for a moment and then back at the others, "we found them killed in the tunnel break room."

"All of them?" Sydney gasped.

Cali nodded.

"That leaves the four of us," Tal sighed.

"Five," Broderick interjected. "I don't know anything about you four or if I can really trust you, but if you're with Cali, you can count on me as well."

"There is something else," Josh added, drawing their attention to him. "I found a bomb in a tunnel below us. It's a combination of a dry power and a liquid that mixes once a trigger is tripped."

"That must be how they got it onto campus without anyone seeing it," Cali surmised.

"They brought it in one load at a time," Sydney agreed.

"Where is the trigger?" Tal asked.

"Natolei has it down there," Josh motioned with his head to the slatted opening leading to the dining hall.

Tal strode over to the louvers with the others close behind, taking a look down into the dining hall where the students and teachers now sat, hostages to terrorists.

"That's the one, with the white shirt and dark slacks," Josh pointed out. "Notice the switch on his belt."

A heavy pause filled the room as the only sound came from the hum of the motors around them.

"Son of a bitch has a bio switch on," Tal spat. "I was going to suggest we all just take them out and be done with it, but with that switch..."

"We have to find a way to render him unconscious without allowing him the time to press the trigger," Josh finished.

Tal spun away from the opening, pacing back towards the stairs. "What about disabling the bomb, since you know where it is."

"I thought of that, but I don't have that knowledge unless the rest of you do?" Josh pointed out.

"Just flip on your iPhone and download the information from Grayson," Tal said confidently as he pulled the device from his belt. He tapped the screen several times before looking dumbfounded at Josh.

"They're blocking any outgoing or incoming signals. Unless we know how to do it ourselves, we won't be able to diffuse it." Josh tossed his hands up in disgust as he finished.

"So here we are, deadly weapons of anti-terrorism, useless on our first mission?" Sydney grimaced.

"This is your first mission?" Broderick exclaimed.

"Settle down, we'll figure this out, just give us a second," Cali said placing her hand on his chest to hold him back from the others.

"We need to get someone close enough to take Natolei down," Josh thought out loud.

"Why not you, All-American, they already know you go to this school," Tal said sarcastically.

"I can't; I think Natolei is onto me, he has been interested in my trunk since they scanned it when I came into his dorms. They ransacked my room and the only way I found the bomb was by tracking my stolen trunk and accidentally getting locked in a room with it."

"I can do it," Cali said softly, causing everyone to turn to her.

"No, I can do it," Josh spoke up as he began taking his weapons off.

"That's just stupid," Cali said shaking her head. "They don't know Tal or Sydney, but the students and teachers know me. It won't seem out of the ordinary for me to be in there with them."

"How about me?" Broderick injected.

"They would kill you like the rest of the real officers," Cali told him, fear filling her eyes.

"She's right," Josh said stepping between them. "You wouldn't have a chance."

"Neither would you," Cali told him.

Josh turned to her, his eyes awash with pain at the thought of putting her in harm's way.

"I'm as much a part of this team as you are," she assured him. "I can take care of myself."

"Let her do it, Josh," Sydney put a hand on Josh's shoulder from behind. "It's our best chance to get close to Natolei."

"Ok, that's settled," Tal sighed irritated with the emotional display. "What do the rest of us do?"

"You take out as many terrorists as you can without them knowing," Cali said as she pulled her dark suit off and pulled her backpack off to retrieve her school uniform. She motioned for everyone to turn around and quickly changed back into her undercover persona. "Remember, no prisoners, no witnesses."

As she said the words, she spun quickly to Broderick as terror flashed across his face.

"Accept you, since you swore secrecy," she added.

The look on his face relaxed, but only slightly as he looked to Tal, Sydney, and Josh nervously.

"I can show you the tunnels and maybe we should take another look at that bomb," Josh changed the subject.

The others nodded.

"How about getting that download before Cali leaves," Josh suggested.

Sydney moved over to first link with Josh's iPhone and then Cali's to download the camouflage program for their suits.

Cali finished straightening her uniform and slipping her iPhone into the pocket of her skirt but then took it out again. "Well, I guess I'm set," she sighed.

"Broderick can keep an eye on you from here, and we will clean up the stragglers in the tunnels first and then move up to the main buildings," Josh instructed.

"Do you know how to use one of these?" Cali asked handing her iPhone to Broderick.

"Not really," he looked sheepishly back at her.

"Here, I'll type in the words, 'she's ready' and all you have to do is hit this send button," she typed the words in as she spoke and pointed to the send command on the screen. "I get as close to Natolei as I can and then give you a twirl of my hair like this," she twirled her hair with a finger. "You hit the send button, and I will wait for them to make the first shot, taking down the guards closest to Natolei before I take him out."

They all nodded their understanding of the plan and moved over to the stairs, leaving Broderick standing there, staring after them.

Tal gave Cali a pat on the back and went down the stairs.

Sydney gave Cali a hug and raced after Tal.

Josh moved in front of Cali as she watched Sydney spiral down the stairs. She looked up and his worried expression made her sigh.

"Don't worry, we can do this," she whispered in his ear as she pulled him to her.

"I know, but you can't blame a guy for worrying," he whispered back.

"It's nice to know it matters," she said, kissing him on the cheek and heading down the stairs.

Josh turned back to Broderick for a moment. "Just hang tight here and let us know when she's ready. Let us do what we were made for," Josh said before slipping down the stairs, closing the hatch after him.

Broderick stared after the four teens, "made for?"

Chapter 36

By the time Josh reached the bottom of the stairs, Tal and Sydney waited impatiently with Cali already gone.

"Let's do this," Tal said with a bit of excitement as he touched his iPhone, blending into the surroundings almost completely.

Josh chuckled as his suit blinked out of sight and then Sydney joined them. They changed their vision to infrared to be sure they could keep track of each other and began to sweep the tunnels for terrorists.

Josh headed back towards the bomb, and it wasn't long before they encountered a group of five officers, dressed in their black uniforms, weapons drawn, looking for anything suspicious.

The first man took three shots to the head before the rest of the men were put down quickly in the same fashion. They dragged the bodies into a storage room off to one side and closed the door quietly.

"We need to have a plan, so we don't all shoot the same guy again." Josh told them.

"I will take the first guy on the right, then Sydney, you take the first guy to his left and Tal will take the first one behind the others." Josh saw the blue, red, and green heads created by the infrared vision giving a nod and they continued down the hall.

They moved along silently, eliminating another group of three and then a larger group of six, before they reached the room containing the bomb.

Staying concealed in their suits, they looked the bomb over and over again, until the bitter truth became evident. They didn't have the knowledge to disarm the weapon.

"Let's move up to the main building where the dining hall is and try to take out as many terrorists before Cali is in place." Josh suggested.

Tal and Sydney agreed, and they headed up the staircase to the main floor. A buzz came from their iPhones as they looked to see the signal that Cali was in place. Nodding their understanding to move ahead with the plan, they turned the corner in the staircase and moved up to the main floor. What they found, none of them were prepared for.

****

Cali took her time, preparing her story as to how she remained uncaptured for so long. Once she began the climb to the dining hall level of the main building, she calmly walked towards the doors, only to be surrounded by four heavily armed men in black security uniforms.

"Where have you been?" one of the men asked, shoving the barrel of his rifle into her face.

"I didn't feel well so I was sleeping in my room," she said frightened, not needing to act as the barrel hovered between her eyes.

"Get in there," the man said, pulling his gun back and pushing her towards the closed doors of the dining hall.

Another man opened the door and parted the men lining the inside of the dining hall to let her in. The men closed ranks tightly, once more as she walked into the hall.

Stephanie came running to her, taking her by the hand and pulling her back to the table and the other students. They sat down as the others crowded in close to her as Stephanie whispered.

"Where have you been, we've been worried sick about you?" she told Cali.

"I fell asleep in our room. What's going on?" Cali asked, feigning ignorance.

"We've been taken hostage by terrorists," Stephanie told her.

"But why," Cali asked?

"They want the president to release the prisoners from Gitmo," Cindy interjected from one side of the table. "He won't ever do that," she added, crossing her arms.

"Let's hope he does," said a red head girl with tears streaming down her freckled face.

"He won't," Cindy repeated sternly. "We don't give in to demands from terrorists."

The girls at the table began to cry quietly, not wanting to draw the attention of the men surrounding them.

Cali looked around, trying to get a layout of everyone's position and note those who played a part in this. To one side, a table of teachers sat, worried looks spread across their faces. She noticed the kitchen staff, sitting with Grace at another table, all accounted for.

She scanned the room for Natolei, finding him talking to a man in the security detail, black uniform, waving his arms dramatically. The man and Natolei looked down at something in the man's hand and then both men turned and looked at the table where Cali sat, the man then pointed directly at Cali and the blood ran from her face as her eyes met the man's cold eyes.

****

Josh, Tal, and Sydney thought they would walk right up into the main building from the tunnels without detection the same way they skimmed through the tunnels. Instead, they found nearly twenty men in security uniforms, sandbags lining the stairwell entrance to the hallway, a large caliber machinegun on legs pointing down at them as they turned the corner of the stairs.

Josh spotted it first, diving back, taking Tal and Sydney in an arm, and diving back down the stairs just as the gun opened fire on them, the bullets penetrated deep into the concrete, leaving large divots in the wall, and raining debris down on them as they tumble down a flight of stairs.

Tal grabbed his ankle, groaning loudly as Josh and Sydney got to their feet and took an arm, dragging the boy back into the tunnels. They went far enough to get around a corner on a branch passage and turned off the camouflage setting on their suits.

Sydney bent down, inspecting Tal's leg.

"It's sprained pretty bad," she told them.

"I could have told you that," Tal grimaced.

"What do we do now?" Sydney asked.

"They knew we were coming," Josh said as he fought to catch his breath.

"Maybe they suspected someone would be coming and that is what we walked into," Tal gritted his teeth.

"Why would they have infrared imaging on us? They wouldn't have known about our camouflage suits." Josh said, as his eyes shot wide with realization.

"The only way they would know is if they caught Cali and made her tell them," Sydney gasped.

"Or Broderick sold us out," they all said, spinning to each other in shock.

****

Cali's heart stopped when her eyes met Broderick's. He stood calmly telling Natolei her mission to neutralize him and their end game.

Weapons drew down on her immediately as they surrounded her table, the other girls cowering with their heads against the surface of the table. Cali looked right at Broderick, not losing eye contact as she placed her hands on her head and stood. She then lay down on the ground putting her hands behind her back as directed as the rifles still pointed at her.

A man came behind her, she heard him, but she didn't see him as she kept staring at Broderick, and he at her. The man slipped a zip tie onto her wrists and pulled it tight. They then lifted her by each elbow and roughly pulled her before the man she came to subdue.

Sarcassi Natolei stood, smiling widely as Cali knelt before him, with Broderick standing by his side, Cali's iPhone in his hands.

"Mr. Broderick has told me of your plans and that of your conspirators," Natolei gloated. "My men have already taken the precaution to use infrared eye gear to see them coming from the tunnels and you should be the only member of your pitiful team left alive in a moment."

He nodded to Broderick who touched the send button on the iPhone just as she had instructed. Broderick looked back at her, a smirk on his face, but also a hint of regret flashed across his face for a split second.

As if on cue, machine gun fire came from the corridor outside the dining hall. The students screamed with fear as the noise echoed through the building.

When the echoes finally quieted, Cali stared blankly at the two men before her. Broderick showed no emotion, but Natolei brightened gleefully.

"You see, little girl," Natolei taunted, "Your little friends did not stand a chance, just as *you* never stood a chance."

Cali's sadness turned to rage as she imagined her friend's lifeless bodies, lying bloody in the stairwell. Diving forward, she broke the strap on her wrists effortlessly as she lunged on top of the surprised Natolei.

Cali quickly struck the man in the temple, knocking him unconscious as they tumbled over backwards. She rolled over him and then recovered quickly to take hold of him under his armpits and drag him towards the kitchen. She pulled Natolei's pistol from his belt and hit the first guard to move between the eyes before she slammed the door shut and twisted the deadbolt.

****

Tal made his way as quickly as he could back up into the mechanical room, only half expecting to find Broderick there. Josh and Sydney went to take up positions after they took out the machine gunner in the stairwell.

Tal slipped the sniper rifle off his shoulder and uncovered his scope as he looked down on the dining hall. A gunshot brought his attention to Cali, dragging Natolei into the kitchen and slamming the door shut.

The guards ran to the door of the kitchen as more flooded into the dining hall from the surrounding hallway.

Tal watched as the men conversed frantically with the man he was been looking for, Broderick. Broderick stood in the center of their argument, but didn't speak or react to their outbursts. He merely stood there as the men argued around him.

Tal scanned the room and as far as he could tell, the hostages remained unharmed. The bomb hadn't gone off yet, so he assumed that Cali now controlled an unconscious Natolei. He tapped out a message on his iPhone and sent it. He put the scope to his eye, centering the cross hairs on Broderick's forehead and waited.

****

Josh and Sydney prepared to make their move on the machine gun turret set up at the top of the stairwell when a single shot rang out, sending men scurrying from the sand bagged machine gun.

Looking to each other, they shrugged and advanced quickly, finding only two distracted men with the machine gun, looking more down the hallway at the dining hall than at the stairwell.

Josh shot the one to his right, in the head, and Sydney did the same to the other. They moved silently into the defensive position and Josh disabled the weapon.

They went around to a side entrance of the dining hall and a message came across their iPhone. "Cali has Natolei and is held up in the kitchen."

Hope sprang across their faces as Josh motioned for her to follow him, not waiting as he hurried off to a door further away from the main entrance. Six men watched the door, weapons at the ready, their concentration on the door so high, that they didn't see the camouflaged Josh and Sydney slip up behind them.

A soft click as Josh and Sydney placed a fresh clip into their pistols became the last sound the men heard before they went down in lifeless heaps. Turning off their camouflaged suits they stepped over the dead men to the door and Sydney gave it a soft tap in a patterned knock.

The lock clicked and the door opened slightly as the end of a pistol jutted through. The door then flew open as Cali pulled Sydney inside with Josh following close behind.

Cali held Sydney in a tight hug for a long moment and then released her to give Josh a big embrace. She paused, realizing they were missing one. She looked at them, sorrow filling her eyes along with the tears welling up in the corners.

"He's fine," Sydney explained as Cali let out a relieved sigh, "Just a sprained ankle."

"When I heard the gunshots and Natolei told me they were waiting for you with infrared gear, I thought I lost you. Do you know that Broderick is in on it and sold us out?" The hate swelled up in her as she spoke.

"Where's Natolei?" Josh asked.

"Over here, sleeping like a baby," Cali smiled proudly as she led them to the corner where she propped the man up in a seated position.

"Did you remove the bio switch?" Sydney asked.

"I wasn't sure how I could do that without setting off the bomb," Cali admitted.

"I know how," Josh said, the girls turning to him in surprise.

"How?" Cali questioned.

"I hook the bio switch to me," he shrugged.

"Won't the other terrorist want to kill you to detonate the bomb then?" Sydney stated the obvious.

"They want to kill us anyway," Josh pointed out. "At least this way, the hostages might stand a chance."

"Let's do it," Cali nodded, kneeling down to Natolei and tearing his shirt open to expose the wires and sensors on his chest that led down to the switch on his belt.

"We have to be quick, not to interrupt the readings while we are doing it," Josh instructed.

The girls nodded as Cali took hold of the sensor on Natolei's neck feeling his pulse and Sydney took hold of the one on the man's chest monitoring his heartbeat.

"On three," Josh said pulling his shirt off over his head.

Cali and Sydney's eyebrows shot up reflexively as they took in Josh's bare chest.

"Concentrate," Josh scolded. "On three," he repeated.

The girls nodded.

"One, two, three," Josh said each number in a slow rhythmic pattern and on three; the girls yanked the sensors off of Natolei and placed them onto Josh's body.

What they hadn't realized was that the sensors contained sets of needles ensuring firm contact into the skin. Natolei had taken time to easily insert the needles, a half inch long, into the right position. Cali and Sydney had no such luxury and plunged the needles painfully into Josh's neck and chest.

Josh cried out in pain as the blood ran down his neck and his chest.

Cali and Sydney both had the insight to keep pressure on the sensors to curb the flow of blood and held them there until the bleeding subsided.

The three sat in silence, Josh panting over the exertion at controlling the level of pain that raged through him unexpectedly as the sensors were placed. The girls letting their nerves settle down over the trauma they caused Josh.

"Now that we have the bomb threat covered, what do we do about the hostages?" Sydney brought them back to the reality of their situation.

A buzz on the iPhones brought all of their attention to the screen of Josh's device. "Lining up hostages for execution." The words flashed.

Josh came to his feet, pulling the manual trigger for the bomb off Natolei's belt and walked over to the door with Cali and Sydney close behind.

They opened the door enough to see that the terrorists lined up all the females in the room along one wall and positioned a row of armed men twenty feet from them, their weapons at the ready.

"Good, we have your attention," Broderick shouted as he looked at the door. "Here is your choice. Return Natolei or these innocent ladies will die. You have two minutes before we start shooting."

Josh let the door close quietly and looked to Cali and Sydney. "What do we do?" Josh lifted an eyebrow and shrugged.

"If we give them what they want, everyone in there and in the surrounding area of the school will be dead," Cali reasoned.

"But we can't just let those women die out there," Sydney said desperately.

Josh sat for a minute, and then pulled his iPhone out once more, flicking through the different applications on the screen. His furrowed brow turned into a look of excitement as he spun back to the door.

"Alright," he shouted. "He'll be coming out."

The girls looked at him in shock.

"You can't be serious," Cali shouted.

"After all we have been through to get to this point," Sydney cried.

"Tell Tal not to kill Natolei," he pointed at Sydney.

She hesitated for a moment, staring uncertainly at him.

"Please, just trust me on this. This is the only way," he pleaded.

Sydney nodded and turned away as she tapped out a message to Tal.

Cali moved over to Josh as he knelt down and slipped his shirt back on carefully attaching all the wires into the iPhone. He looked up at her as she stood staring down at him.

"I hope you know what you're doing," she told him.

"Do you trust me?" he asked, hopefully, for the right answer.

"You know I do," she sighed, coming over to give him a kiss.

Chapter 37

Tal couldn't believe the message when Sydney sent it to him. "Don't shoot Natolei," it told him. He hoped All-American wasn't going to screw this up.

Tal placed his eye upon the scope as he focused it on the kitchen door that now swung open slowly. Natolei stepped out of the door with his hands held high above his head. Sydney and Cali stepped out behind him, but no Josh.

Typical, Tal thought, Josh probably looked for a position to get a clean shot on Natolei himself and didn't want Tal to take him out. All-American wanted the glory.

Tal focused in on Natolei's head, his finger sliding lightly against the trigger.

****

Cali and Sydney walked out behind Natolei, his hands held high as he moved into the dining hall. The men readying the firing squad in front of the women all turned and gathered around Broderick as Natolei and the two girls approached.

Cali and Sydney held their empty hands out to their sides, two pistols tucked neatly in the back of their pants within quick reach.

Natolei let his arms down as he reached Broderick who then stepped forward to embrace him.

****

At that point Natolei flickered, only slightly so that no one saw, no one that is, except a sniper with his scope trained in on the terrorist's head.

Tal saw the flicker and knew at that moment what he needed to do. As Natolei's eyes looked up to his hiding place, Tal's finger squeezed the trigger.

Broderick's head exploded still in Josh's arms, the disguise holding a split second longer than the man's life as the teens burst into motion.

"Down, get down," Cali and Sydney shouted.

The room filled with hostages lurched for the floor, covering their heads as gunshots rang out and the soft sounds of silenced pistols contrasted the rifles.

Tal fired shot after shot, never pausing more than a split second between targets.

Cali and Sydney dove across the floor taking out uniformed terrorists one after the other as they slid on their backs on the polished surface.

Josh with his pistols blazing took man after man down until the other three were cleaning up the lone stragglers or the ones rushing in from the hallway. He turned, calmly walking back into the kitchen to where Sarcassi Natolei lay tied and gagged in his underwear. Josh calmly stripped off the man's clothes he had borrowed for the charade. He placed them neatly in a pile on a counter and stared at the terrorist for a moment.

Reaching down he pulled the gage from his mouth. A smile erupted as he glared up at the boy.

"You really think you can stop our movement to bring down your wicked nation?" Natolei spat as he shouted at him. "Now I will be just one more voice crying for justice against the oppressor, another combatant at Guantanamo Bay."

Josh looked emotionlessly at the man as he ranted on the floor.

"You know what I'm going to scream the loudest about? You and your band of twisted teens who feel that they can go around killing anyone they choose. You will be exposed for the killers that you are to the world, and you will have no place to hide."

"Why did you have to kill her?" Josh asked so softly that it was almost indiscernible.

"What?" Natolei asked.

"Why did you have to kill Ms. Cutlage?" Josh asked.

"We noticed her watching Abdalann and felt she was a threat. She was with you? The boys had a really good time with her before they started to question her. She screamed like she was enjoying it." Natolei gave Josh a wicked smile.

"Wrong answer," Josh said, pulling his pistol and unloading a slug into the man's head between the eyes. He holstered the weapon and walked calmly out the back door.

Grayson met him there with members of the bomb team who notified him the bomb had been neutralized and removed the bio-detonator from him.

Grayson stepped into the kitchen and then came out with the rest of the team in tow.

"What happened to Natolei? He has a bullet hole in his forehead and is still in restraints?" Grayson questioned as the other's eyes fell on Josh.

"For Ms. Swanson," Josh said flatly without looking at any of them.

Grayson nodded.

The Northern Lights Special Ops members gathered any trace of their belongings and quietly left the campus amidst the chaos that followed when the authorities came in to clean up. When the main terrorists were eliminated, the rest surrendered peacefully.

After Homeland Security met with all the students and teachers, the local police released a statement to the press. Local law enforcement was called into an active shooter situation and had come in and neutralized a hostage situation. There was no mention of a bomb, terrorists, or any foreign involvement. Teacher and student casualties were addressed along with some of the deaths of the internal security force on campus.

Cali said her goodbyes to Stephanie and the other girls, telling them she was going back to India, and they could email her.

Josh ran into Trevor as he left and they wished each other well, Trevor certain that Josh headed back to run some sort of Russian crime ring.

Josh stepped up to the limousine sent for him by Grayson when Cindy appeared at his side. She looked at him curiously as if looking at him for the first time.

"I will miss you Dmitri," she whispered in his ear as she hugged him. "But daddy has promised me he will find out where you are," she purred in his ear, "No matter who you really are."

Josh tried to pull away as she said this, but she held him tightly, only letting him go enough to kiss him passionately for the longest time. When she did pull away, she gave him a wink and strode away, looking back over her shoulder she raised an eyebrow and said, "We'll be seeing you, you can count on that."

Josh watched her leave, dumbfounded at how much she knew or thought she knew. He stepped into the car, and it sped away to the private air strip where they landed days before.

Grayson met him as he stepped out of the limo.

Shaking Josh's hand, Grayson congratulated him. "Nice job Josh. The team said you were a good leader in there."

"The team?" Josh questioned.

"Even Tal," Grayson's eye twinkled. "Said he was amazed you thought to impersonate Natolei all by yourself."

Josh laughed. "He would say that."

"We do have a problem," Grayson cut to the chase.

"Cindy?" Josh asked.

"The Director is already searching for your identity," Grayson sighed, "Seems you made quite an impression on the young lady."

"It's my animal magnetism I guess," Josh shrugged.

"Get on board," he said with a nod to the airplane, "the others are waiting." He turned and boarded the plane, leaving Josh standing on the runway.

He stood there watching the sun set against the trees on the far side of the runway. He had entered a life-threatening situation with three other members of his team and ...

He stopped, remembering that was at Chatterly with five other members of his team and one was not returning to White Water, MN. Ms. Swanson had been there for him and his friends from the start and now they were supposed to move on without her. Reaching into his pocket, he pulled a locket out and opened it, exposing a much younger Ms. Swanson, smiling back at him. She slipped it into his hand as she lay dying in his arms. He would keep it until he knew what she would have wanted him to do with it.

Pushing the locket back into his pants, he strode up the stairs into the plane as his teammates gave him a loud cheer of welcome.

****

They were back at school the next morning, not given any slack by Grayson, but ordered to be there.

Their parents welcomed them home, all realizing that they couldn't know where they went or what they did.

Kevin noticed something about Josh right off and asked him if he was ok.

"Yeah, fine. Just want to try and get back to somewhat of a normal life," he said flatly.

That afternoon at lunch, Josh, Cali, and Sydney sat at their usual table when Mack and the other football players sauntered up.

"You been gone a while," Mack told him. "You going to hang with the misfits instead of the cool kids, California?"

"I would say that I am hanging with the cool kids," Josh replied, not looking up from his lunch.

"You little asshole," Mack started to come at Josh, but he never got within striking distance of him as Tal stood, holding the boy by the collar, feet dangling off the ground helplessly.

When the others tried to go to their teammate's aid, they found Cali and Sydney blocking their approach. The look in the girls' eyes left no doubt they were serious.

Josh stood slowly, wiping his hands on a napkin and then dropping it onto his tray. He walked casually over in front of Tal, still holding Mack in the air. When he reached the dangling boy, he tilted his head up at him, moving closer so their eyes met, and Josh whispered softly to him.

The boy's eyes shot wide, and he nodded, fear streaming through every orifice in his body.

Josh gave a nod to Tal who set the boy down, his feet churning to get away even before they touched the ground. He raced away, looking back at the four of them only once, and hurrying down the hall, the rest of his group trying to catch up and find out what Josh had said to him.

Josh and Tal bent over laughing uproariously as they sat down, the two girls looking curiously at them.

"What did you say?" Sydney asked, breaking into a chuckle.

Josh started laughing harder and Tal wiped tears from his eyes as he turned to her.

"He told him that if he didn't leave us alone, Josh would let everyone know how he liked to dress up in his sister's dresses and stand in front of the mirror."

"How did you know that?" Cali laughed.

"A good operative does his recon." Josh chuckled as the others roared.

****

That evening, they laid Ms. Swanson to rest in a plot next to Josh's mother, in the local cemetery. All the parents attended as well as Tal, Josh, Cali, Sydney, and Mr. Grayson.

They opened the casket one last time, on Josh's request, and he moved close to place the locket across her folded hands. He closed the lid softly and they listened to taps being played as the casket lowered into the ground.

Everyone cried, except for Josh and Grayson. The two stared at the grave blankly, emotionless and stoic.

"She knew the risk," Grayson said softly as he stood next to Josh.

"She might have, but that doesn't make the loss any less painful," Josh answered.

"She believed in you, all of you," Grayson said looking at his four teenage operatives. "She knew that you could do incredible things."

Josh nodded as he turned away from the others, taking a few steps, and then turning back.

"Just point me in the direct of the next bastards," Josh said, gritting his teeth.

"You need to take some time and speak with some counselors before we send you four out again. It was a pretty traumatic mission," Grayson informed them.

The other teens nodded their agreement.

"Just let us get at those son-of-a-bitches, and soon," Josh spat, and walked off as Kevin hurried after him.

Cali, Tal, and Sydney stared at his back with concern and then hurried to catch up, walking by his side, Kevin still following.

Cali took his hand, Tal placed an arm around his shoulders, and Sydney placed her arm around Tal's waist.

They were a team and connected like no other team that had come before them. They were the Domestic Anti-Terrorist Unit; code name Northern Lights and their job had just begun.

The End.